Praise for *Samuel Taylor's Last Night*

"[T]he book's ultimate accomplishment is, in fact, the masterful integration of the drama and overall performance of writing, on one side, and, on the other, the tragedies, comedies, and other theatricalities hardly absent from Samuel Taylor's life."
—LOS ANGELES REVIEW OF BOOKS

"When the dust settles . . . what emerges is a convincing portrait of a man filled with moral conviction whose career has stranded him at the bottom of the ladder."
—THE NEW YORK TIMES

"[T]his novel's whirling blocks of prose suggest faces glimpsed from behind a podium, or the landscape outside a spinning car, or the fast-moving crises of our time."
—INSIDE HIGHER ED

"Part novel, part mémoire, part inventory of everything thought and seen in the heterogeneous landscape of the daily life of 'just another poor bastard who thinks his life is worth a permanent entry in the archive,' *Samuel Taylor's Last Night* lists and leans, careens and lurches, swerves and accelerates through a range of rhetorical shifts of gear as its narrator-protagonist turns his psychic pockets inside out and throws all the small-change detritus and wide-ranging vibrant currency of his mind into full view."
—JOHANNA DRUCKER, author of *Downdrift* and *Graphesis*

VIA Folios 129

Samuel Taylor's
Hollywood Adventure

Samuel Taylor's
Hollywood Adventure

Joe Amato

BORDIGHERA PRESS

Library of Congress Control Number: 2017961924

Printed in the United States.

Published by
BORDIGHERA PRESS
John D. Calandra Italian American Institute
25 West 43rd Street, 17th Floor
New York, NY 10036

VIA FOLIOS 129
ISBN 978-1-59954-118-1

with & for Kass

Character is plot, plot is character.
ATTRIBUTED TO F. SCOTT FITZGERALD

CONTENTS

PLAN B
Pretense as Prologue

*

This is when I pretend to be him reading.
This is when I pretend to be her reading.
This is when I pretend to be you reading.
This is when I pretend to have readers, this is when I pretend
someone is paying attention, this is when I pretend a secret liberty
and a private exchange and a public privilege.

This is when I pretend there are still things you can do with words
that you can't do with any other medium.
This is when I pretend to know what those things are.
This is when I pretend you can do these things without letting words
have their say.
This is when I pretend words will have their say, even up there, in the
cloud.

This is when I pretend I'm a novelist.
This is when I pretend to have a plot.
This is when I pretend to be entertaining.
This is when I pretend not to let my language get in the way of my
story.

2

This is when I pretend I don't wish that we didn't have to call
everything that looks like a book, a book.
This is when I pretend there's room at the table for everyone.
This is when I pretend I'd rather talk about brains, and heart, and
courage.

This is when I pretend that loyalty is important too, and that this
   view will probably do better in translation.

This is when I pretend I'm a man.
This is when I pretend I'm a white man.
This is when I pretend I'm a black man.
This is when I pretend I'm a black & white man.

This is when I pretend I'm a woman of color.
This is when I pretend I'm in transition.
This is when I pretend I'm not gay.
This is when I pretend I'm me and that my identity is beside the
   point.

3

This is when I pretend we're more alike than different.
This is when I pretend to care about what you think.
This is when I pretend writing is therapy.
This is when I pretend to suffer.

This is when I pretend to have done my research.
This is when I pretend to be comprehensive.
This is when I pretend to be a scholar.
This is when I pretend to be a littérateur.

This is when I pretend I'm interested in knowing about every
   little thing.
This is when I pretend I'm interested in knowing about every big
   thing.
This is when I pretend I'm interested in hearing about your kids or
   your grandparents.
This is when I pretend there's nothing more interesting than
   literature.

4

This is when I pretend to hate dumb people.
This is when I pretend to hate ignorant people.

This is when I pretend to hate *smart* as an adjective.
This is when I pretend to hate provocateurs.

This is when I pretend to like music and musicians.
This is when I pretend to like art and artists and all things artisanal.
This is when I pretend to like doctors and lawyers and engineers and
     publishers and editors and cops and robbers and heroes and slaves
     and, I don't know, Thorstein Veblen.
This is when I pretend to like formulaic writing.

This is when I pretend to like the Beatles more than the Stones.
This is when I pretend to like the Stones more than the Beatles.
This is when I pretend "Stones" and "Beatles" are not stand-ins for,
     what, raw and cooked?
This is when I pretend to split the difference and call it even.

5

This is when I pretend any work of art might not, at some moment in
     time, be deemed great by those who know something about art. Or
     work.
This is when I pretend there are great works of art that will never not
     be deemed great by those who know something about art. Or work.
This is when I pretend such distinctions are beside the point, and I'm
     not working.
This is when I pretend the failure to make such distinctions
     diminishes us, and I'm working.

This is when I pretend to believe in evolution.
This is when I pretend to believe in vaccination.
This is when I pretend to believe only in what is empirically verifiable.
This is when I pretend to believe in god and, I don't know, Thorstein
     Veblen.

This is when I pretend not to intervene.
This is when I pretend to elect those who will not intervene.
This is when I pretend to elect those who will intervene.
This is when I pretend to intervene.

6

This is when I pretend I'm not part of some bloody machine.
This is when I pretend everyone is not part of some bloody machine.
This is when I pretend some hands are bloodier than others.
This is when I pretend not to have innocent blood on my hands.

This is when I pretend those we elect will not have innocent blood on
    their hands.
This is when I pretend those we elect can by sheer force of will stop
    the shedding of innocent blood.
This is when I pretend to be outraged by the failure of those we elect
    to regulate the bloody machine some think of as *empire*, others
    global capitalism, still others *a shining city upon a hill.*
This is when I pretend to have all the answers.

This is when I pretend the bloody machine is not one way of looking
    at progress.
This is when I pretend the bloody machine is not worthy of some
    respect.
This is when I pretend those who run for office are motivated only by
    self-interest.
This is when I pretend to have a finite number of options. I mean
    optics. No, options.

7

This is when I pretend were I to kill someone, I wouldn't get religion
    right quick.
This is when I pretend were I religious, I wouldn't kill someone.
This is when I pretend there's no such thing as evil as a, pardon me,
    real abstraction.
This is when I pretend nothing's sacred.

This is when I pretend to be paranoid.
This is when I pretend my paranoia is justified.
This is when I pretend my paranoia justifies a certain lack of
    discrimination, as between a Thermidor, say, and a Humidor.

This is when I pretend my certain lack of discrimination permits me
   to forgo the commonweal.

This is when I pretend public corporations are the problem.
This is when I pretend private companies are the problem.
This is when I pretend government is the problem.
This is when I pretend to wish upon a star.

8

This is when I pretend my credo has become "Demand More, Expect
   Less."
This is when I pretend to date myself and so implore you not to
   dox me, or if you do, to do so with all the spite in the world, you
   bloodsucking retread darknet muthafuck. And don't get me started
   on alt-right transgressions, because this is when I pretend not to be
   that kind of transgressor. Or trespasser. Or whatever.
This is when I pretend my brand has become "From Poverty to the
   NYTBR in 59 Years Flat."
This is when I pretend to have no tat, no piercings, no distinguishing
   marks of any kind aside from a few odd scars and wrinkles *& when
   you wish upon a star / it twinkles.*

This is when I pretend a coarse language does not portend a coarse
   public sphere.
This is when I pretend to be civic-minded today does not portend a
   coarse language.
This is when I pretend we need accountability.
This is when I pretend we are accountable only to ourselves and,
   maybe, Thorstein Veblen?

This is when I pretend to like feminists.
This is when I pretend to like fabulists.
This is when I pretend to like mycologists.
This is when I pretend to like mereologists. I mean meteorologists.
   No, mereologists.

9

This is when I pretend to hate pedophiles.
This is when I pretend to hate rapists.
This is when I pretend to hate escapists.
This is when I pretend to hate the innocent.

This is when I pretend to like the filthy rich.
This is when I pretend to like the poor, the homeless, the
   downtrodden.
This is when I pretend to like the other.
This is when I pretend to like myself.

This is when I pretend I can live without a weather forecast.
This is when I pretend I can live without a blender.
This is when I pretend I can live alone and friendless, just me and my
   entheogens.
This is when I pretend I can live with someone.

10

This is when I pretend two women are talking about something other
   than a man.
This is when I pretend two men are talking about their emotional
   well-being.
This is when I pretend two philosophers are talking about something
   other than philosophy.
This is when I pretend a woman and a man are talking about a man
   and a woman.

This is when I pretend to avoid scumble.
This is when I pretend to wallow in sfumato.
This is when I pretend to prohibit appropriation.
This is when I pretend to relish technique, and flavor, and funk,
   and would that you could see the smile plastered on my mug at the
   moment.
This is when I pretend to like children.
This is when I pretend to hate cats and dogs.

This is when I pretend to like dogs and cats.
This is when I pretend to hate social media.

11

This is when I pretend writing can be fun, nun!
This is when I pretend writing can be a misery.
This is when I pretend writing can be labor.
This is when I pretend writing can be work, and no I don't feel sorry
  for myself.

This is when I pretend to like Italians and Jews.
This is when I pretend to hate Mexicans and Native Americans.
This is when I pretend to like Arabs and Asians.
This is when I pretend to hate all races and ethnicities and tribes and
  collectives.

This is when I pretend to know English.
This is when I pretend to know Spanish.
This is when I pretend to know Finnish.
This is when Yiddish I pretend to know.

12

This is when I pretend to speak French.
This is when I pretend to speak Mandarin.
This is when I pretend to speak the vernacular.
This is when I pretend to speak truth to power.

This is when I pretend to be noisy. I mean nosy. No, noisy.
This is when I pretend to like words.
This is when I pretend to be discreet.
This is when I pretend to like silence.

This is when I pretend to be concerned about guns.
This is when I pretend to be concerned about hijabs. I mean jobs. No,
  hjiabs.

This is when I pretend to be concerned about those who pretend to
   be concerned about the First Amendment.
This is when I pretend to be concerned about adolescent fantasies of
   control and freedom.

13

This is when I pretend to like my job.
This is when I pretend to have money.
This is when I pretend I can retire.
This is when I pretend I never want to retire.

This is when I pretend to be at the mercy of forces beyond my ken.
This is when I pretend to have a say.
This is when I pretend to speak of universals.
This is when I pretend to be trapped in particulars.

This is when I pretend to like Camaros.
This is when I pretend to like horses.
This is when I pretend to like walking.
This is when I pretend I can't walk.

14

This is when pretend I'm able-bodied.
This is when I pretend I'm empathetic.
This is when I pretend I'm athletic.
This is when I pretend I have no arms.

This is when I pretend to appreciate nature.
This is when I pretend to appreciate cities.
This is when I pretend to appreciate environmentalists.
This is when I pretend to appreciate citizens, especially prisoners.

This is when I pretend to hate students.
This is when I pretend to hate teachers.
This is when I pretend to hate higher education.
This is when I pretend to hate a living wage.

15

This is when I pretend to like labor unions.
This is when I pretend to like big business.
This is when I pretend to like everything Lower East Side.
This is when I pretend to like the village of Liverpool, NY.

This is when I pretend to hate everyone and everything I like.
This is when I pretend to hate everyone and everything I pretend to like.
This is when I pretend to hate everyone and everything I don't pretend to like.
This is when I pretend to like everyone and everything I pretend I don't like.

This is when I pretend *how* not *who*.
This is when I pretend *what* not *why*.
This is when I pretend *when* not *where*.
This is when I pretend tomorrow and tomorrow and tomorrow.

16

This is when I pretend no man is an island.
This is when I pretend to love.
This is when I pretend not to love.
This is when I pretend there is no such thing as love.

This is when I pretend to have faith.
This is when I pretend to suspend my disbelief.
This is when I pretend or did I mean to *upend* my disbelief?
This is when I pretend to be dancing circles around myself.

This is when I pretend to be cynical, Mom.
This is when I pretend to be chill, dude.
This is when I pretend to be just, sonny.
This is when I pretend to be blue, honey.

17

This is when I pretend to be cute.
This is when I pretend to be sincere.
This is when I pretend to be invincible.
This is when I pretend to be cruel.

This is when I pretend to have rhythm.
This is when I pretend to address the mysteries.
This is when I pretend to have been caught with my pants down.
This is when I pretend to be dangerous.

This is when I pretend to be classic.
This is when I pretend to be hip.
This is when I pretend to be ill.
This is when I pretend to be off my rocker.

18

This is when I pretend to have needs, like water.
This is when I pretend we have needs, like water.
This is when I pretend our needs change, but not water.
This is when I pretend someone wants to profit from our needs, like
    water, by developing algorithms and employing sensors and the like
    to ascertain our daily terrestrial comings and goings.

This is when I pretend I can update and upgrade for the rest of my life.
This is when I pretend I can subscribe to everything I need.
This is when I pretend I can encrypt every waking fucking moment.
This is when I pretend I am not a human being, I am the elephant in
    the creative writing classroom.

This is when I pretend I'm into gaming.
This is when I pretend I'm into yodeling.
This is when I pretend I'm into snorkeling.
This is when I pretend to try your patience.

19

This is when I pretend I haven't read Zuboff.

This is when I pretend I've read Piketty.

This is when I pretend I haven't read Krugman, or Weber, or Durkheim, or Tarde, or Whitehead, or Deleuze, or Hofstadter, or, repeat after me, Thorstein Veblen.

This is when I pretend to understand Hegel. I mean Adorno. No, Hegel. No, Chuck Berry.

This is when I pretend to go back in time.

This is when I pretend to go forward in time.

This is when I pretend to be stuck in time.

This is when I pretend to be on time.

This is when I pretend to be on the take.

This is when I pretend to be writing for fame and fortune.

This is when I pretend to have a career.

This is when I pretend to have a calling.

20

This is when I pretend this is my most accomplished book.

This is when I pretend this is my most important book.

This is when I pretend this is my most moving book.

This is when I pretend this is my worst book.

This is when I pretend this is *All the King's Men*.

This is when I pretend this is *From Here to Eternity*.

This is when I pretend this is *Invisible Man*.

This is when I pretend this is *Samuel Taylor's Hollywood Adventure*.

This is when I pretend to be LOWERCASE.

This is when I pretend to be uppercase.

This is when I pretend to be a stylist of the *surtout, pas trop de zele* school.

This is when I pretend to be a hairstylist.

21

This is when I pretend to be a buck-toothed saint.
This is when I pretend to be a freckle-faced sinner.
This is when I pretend to be a dirty-blond terrorist.
This is when I pretend to be a reluctant and picaresque protagonist.

This is when I pretend it's hell.
This is when I pretend it's heaven.
This is when I pretend it's somewhere in between.
This is when I pretend I can tell the difference.

This is when I pretend you dig deep enough you'll hit rock bottom.
This is when I pretend up up and away.
This is when I pretend don't know much about history.
This is when I pretend come what may.

22

This is when I pretend you know what I'm saying.
This is when I pretend you don't know what I'm saying.
This is when I pretend you don't like what I'm saying.
This is when I pretend what I'm saying is what I'm not saying.

This is when I pretend the writer is alive.
This is when I pretend the earth is dying.
This is when I pretend Elvis has left the building.
This is when I pretend I'm dying.

This is when I pretend nobody knows you when you're down and out.
This is when I pretend I haven't used that line before.
This is when I pretend it's nothing to write home about.
This is when I pretend to fuck a duck.

23

This is when I pretend people are animals too.
This is when I pretend animals are people too.
This is when I pretend I needn't apologize for my appetites.

This is when I pretend to be pure of heart and unenamored of your cool semiautomatic.

This is when I pretend nobody knows anything.
This is when I pretend everybody knows something.
This is when I pretend somebody knows everything.
This is when I pretend nobody knows anybody.

This is when I pretend to be acting.
This is when I pretend to be performing.
This is when I pretend to be aspiring.
This is when I pretend not to be perspiring.

24

This is when I pretend the art must be evaluated independently of the artist.
This is when I pretend the artist must be evaluated independently of the art.
This is when I pretend it depends what we mean by *evaluation*.
This is when I pretend to resolve these issues for once and for all.

This is when I pretend the novel isn't a form of exegesis in which the exegete is attempting to tease out a truth in the textual folds of an imagined history.
This is when I pretend I wouldn't want to be younger, wouldn't want to bask in the glow of late sixties and early seventies rock, wouldn't want to lament the loss of a lyricism addressing social loss, wouldn't want to luxuriate in the heady days of the early Web, wouldn't want to indulge in a social imaginary of my own making, wouldn't want to write while forgetting I was writing.
This is when I pretend I wouldn't want to be older when I was younger.
This is when I pretend I wouldn't want to be taller, a better guitar player, more up on reality hacks, easier going, less lumpen, less acerbic, less anxious, less postromantic, less debauched, less smitten with psephology, more grounded, more coherent, more devoted,

more secure, more responsible, more responsive, more and less
cosmopolitan, better-dressed, better, stronger, faster, gentler, freer,
kinder, wiser, oversexed, in possession of a more robust genotype,
more en plein air, more sprezzatura, more of a *Menschenkammer*, less
fond of pretending to imagine

> wild celestial rides
> on a liberated circus elephant
> far above this traumatized land sea and
> air
> where the signpost up ahead reads

> *this train*
> *sometimes I wonder why*
> *nothing's impossible I*
> *once I built a railroad*
> *it's very clear*
> *somewhere over the*
> *it's very clear*
> *you may have heard of*
> *it was a teenage wedding*
> *I know every engineer on every*
> *cry, cry, cry*
> *you've got to hide your*
> *gimme gimme*
> *the beat goes*
> *did you ever have to*
> *get up off of that*
> *you know that it would*
> *I guess the Lord must*
> *war*
> *people*
> *mother, mother*
> *funny day*
> *if you want me to*
> *ain't but one way*

have you been a
there's talk on the street
listening to the Mu
like a jungle
fight the
ain't it funny how
we don't make it
mission accomplished

gotta get down to it

Reality's dark dream, he wrote

mission
accomplished
and in fine print at the bottom

"We've been monitoring your transmissions
and you're beginning to get on our nerves
especially those of you with too many clubs knives guns
    bombs
money and shit you don't need."

and off in the distance we can hear laughter
yeah, even in space
and it's a creature comprised of every living thing on Earth
and then some, like some inked
Rat Fink that dripped from Monté's pen
before Big Daddy Roth laid claim to the creation
and it's on a broomstick, of course
and it's adjusting its New York Yankees cap
of course
and in compliance with the Intergalactic Game Engine
    Rulebook it's
flipping us off

and me and Dumbo we
topple back down to this traumatized land sea and
air
the two of us seeing fit to return the favor in kind we
flip off the planet's inhabitants
that would be all of us, truly
some having earned it more than others
but all of us
having put ourselves in this precarious position together . . .

This is when I pretend I could go on like this forever, without a seat
   belt or parachute or escape clause.
This is when I pretend you could go on like this forever.
This is when I pretend I'm not pretending.
This is when I pretend.

This.

This is how you pitch a sequel

You say that, dramatically, the whole thing turns on a misperception. A misapprehension. A misunderstanding. A simple mistake. Or maybe wishful thinking. Or the inadequacies of our interfaces. Or even retcon.

You say the whole thing turned on a simple mistake.

She'd texted him, you see. Nora. He'd done her a solid, he'd gone out of his way, he'd gone above and beyond to help her with her book. It was something they did for each other, a simple act of kindness and camaraderie, the place where their souls met, because a writer's soul is in her words, even if to him what he did for her was a simple favor, one she'd returned in kind many times prior.

You say he helped her with her book, you say their writing was the place where their souls met, because a writer's soul is in her words.

And toward the end, even as her health was failing, even as she seemed to be falling away from him, he loved her madly.

You say he loved her madly. But you say she seemed hesitant, uncertain, and he couldn't be sure what to make of her uncertainty, whether this meant she no longer loved him.

You say he wasn't sure if she loved him, and you say this was perhaps because she wasn't sure if she loved him, souls met or unmet.

You say nonetheless he received a text from her on his tiny iPhone screen—this was back when iPhone screens were still tiny—and he read

"I love you"

You say he read "I love you" on his tiny iPhone screen. You say how much joy this brought him. You say how he was overcome with joy, and overcome with relief.

You say he was overcome with joy.

He was overcome with joy because he knew that whatever else, this life could be miraculous in what it gives and forgives. And he knew that this life had given him what he'd most wanted—her love. And he knew that to be given as much required that he be forgiven his shortcomings. Forgiven by her, Nora. And he knew that his love for this woman had not been misplaced.

You say that this was everything to him. You say it was all the light he'd ever wanted, and all the light he needed to go on.

You say this.

Then you say but there's a catch.

When he saw—he of Lasik'd eyes—when he saw

"I love you"

what he was really seeing was

"I owe you"

See? you say. You say this for emphasis' sake.

And it wasn't until months later, after Nora was gone, that he'd happened to scroll back through their texts together, this time with his reading glasses on. He smiled occasionally as he scrolled through, until he scrolled across

"I owe you"

At which point his heart skipped a beat.

You say this—you say his heart skipped a beat. Because it did—it actually skipped a beat.

And then you tell the rest of your story about Samuel Taylor, and your listeners will henceforth know something crucial about his story that will color everything they've heard, and everything they're going to hear.

You say this—that this will color everything they hear.

Yes, you say—when Samuel Taylor had introduced his wife to the doctoral student with whom he'd bonded during his tenure travails, he hadn't realized that Nora, even as her health was failing, even knowing that she and Samuel Taylor had been through hell together, was deeply conflicted about their marriage. And you say that when the two made it their mission to show the student the doctoral ropes, Nora had been secretly dismayed to witness her husband's fondness for this young woman.

Yes, you say—when Nora died, and when the young woman rushed to Samuel Taylor's side to help him through the ordeal, what stopped him from falling fully and carnally into the young woman's arms was the knowledge that Nora had loved him unequivocally to the end. And you say that a few years later, after the young woman landed a job as an assistant professor of English with a specialty in medieval studies; and after her parents were killed in a car accident; and after she'd lobbied on behalf of Samuel Taylor for a tenure-track opening on her campus, in her department; and after he failed to land the position: you say that this young woman, Kass, had always had designs on Samuel Taylor.

You say these things, then you begin anew.

EPISODE 1

". . . and thence we came forth to see again the stars." [1]

Legend has it that John Wayne had large hands. And everyone knows what Carleton Young says to Ranse Stoddard about legends. But did John Wayne really have abnormally large hands? He was a pretty big guy, after all.

It was difficult to tell from watching the films. It was difficult from watching the films to ascertain onscreen fact operating through the scrim of onscreen fiction. Watching Wayne in *Red River*, for instance, the film that made an actor out of a star, at least in John Ford's eyes, Samuel Taylor tried focusing on Wayne's hands. But it was difficult to tell. And difficult to tell even during the handshake scene at the pub with Victor McLaglen toward the beginning of *The Quiet Man*. Handshakes were important to Ford, and to Wayne, and to Maureen O'Hara, who in *an interview* years later *recounted that* the three had *made a handshake agreement in 1944 to do the film* together, according to the IMDb trivia page that Samuel Taylor was fading in and out of. But could you trust IMDb?

Not always.

Fade-ins and fade-outs notwithstanding, this was anything but idle speculation. Samuel Taylor was preoccupied with the Duke's gun-handy hands one hazy summer afternoon when his Hippocrene had dried up and the tiny green he frequented when feeling blue was a long drive through traffic. To put it another way, his spirits could use a pick-me-up but the

---

1   Dante Alighieri, *Inferno: The Divine Comedy*, Volume 1, trans. John D. Sinclair (New York: Oxford UP, 1961). For further reading, friends, see Chip Astrome, *The Heights and Weights of Stars* (New York: McGraw-Hill, 1972).

only spirits in his apartment resided in an empty bottle of walnut liqueur his brother had brought back with him from Dubrovnik, and which he sniffed now and then for reasons mysterious even to him; and, now that the "heavy marine layer"—as local forecasters called it—had lifted, it was too hot to make believe he enjoyed playing miniature golf. It was in this restless state of mind and body that Wayne's hands spoke with unexpected pertinence to a newly-hatched idea that had marketplace legs. Or so he'd gotten it into his restless head. The idea had acquired a patina of workaday urgency when he'd heard that morning from their agent, Sylvia, to the effect that Kass and his latest treatment was dead in the water, that the producer with whom they'd been in negotiations was offering to renew only as a free option what Sylvia believed to be their best spec script, and that the only meeting on the horizon was with his Hidden Hills dentist to replace a discolored crown on one of his cuspids. Development hell, hell—with few exceptions there *was* no development. DVD had, thanks to streaming, gone the way of VHS, and everyone and his uncle and his aunt and his cousins were aspiring screenwriters, resulting in a glut of projects with no one to finance them and curiouser and curiouser intermediaries cropping up pedaling ever more dwindling entrée for a not inconsiderable fee. And in the midst of this anamorphic frenzy, novice writers were being cautioned by agents and managers, up to their keisters in reading material, to the effect that an errant slug line could sink a project.

All Samuel Taylor could think about was John Ford famously tearing pages out of scripts while in the middle of filming. To be stuck toiling away at the Tinkertoy stage of filmmaking, redrafting letters of transit on a ship of fools—what kind of writing life was that?

Kass was back east, despite Samuel Taylor's pleading, teaching the summer session to boost their cash flow. And so here he was in LA all by his lonesome, and at fifty-six no less, plying his screenwriting trade on behalf of himself and Kass in an entertainment town that bore little resemblance to the way he'd imagined it as a child, which childlike imagination could never for that matter have imagined the extent to which Hollywood glamour of yore had served to closet its above-the-line gay or promiscuously heterosexual denizens, among whom even the most ostensibly über-masculine or feminine or allegedly upstanding often suffered under the repressive yoke of studio politics, never mind the tsk-tsking of Hollywood's older teetotaling residents, while they conducted their boozy backyard orgies. He was never much taken by tawdry backstories anyway, whether having to do with the stars' sexual exploits, or abusive relationships, or violent episodes. For him it was what was onscreen that mattered, but he realized too that the flesh and blood bodies that brought us such delights were anything but flickering quanta of light, and that the casting couch had carried over into the assaultive present.

Today much, if not all, was out in the open, but the financial mood was grimly mercenary and the career desperation had been plasticked over, even while publicists had become expert at hyping red-carpet make believe to yield a 14 or better adults 18-49 rating, which was still an achievement for televised bread and circuses circa 2016. Like everything else in US culture, and for all the talk of TV's second golden age and biblical box office returns and cross-media marketability, things were a mess in filmland, and one need hardly be a *laudator temporis acti* to view the steadily declining Oscar audience as a sign that cinema's glory days were past.

To be sure, there had been improvements. The new Hollywood, with it's new one-off studio arrangements, might think twice before casting white actors to play brown characters, or casting Italian Americans—whose whiteness, after all, was as recent as the Second World War—to play Latinos. And vice versa. Yes, Hollywood was mercifully more diverse, not least because film production had long since gone global, what with Bollywood and Nollywood. And if Wang Jianlin had anything to say about it, and he did, a seismic shift in production services was underway. OK, women were getting more lead roles, or so it seemed, even if their pay scale still wasn't where it should be. And if onscreen age remained stubbornly younger than offscreen years, it was hardly as young as it was when William Holden tried valiantly to carry the lead in *Picnic*. Indeed none other than Meryl Streep had observed that acting had, generally speaking, gotten better.

Anyway, from the standpoint of those whose raison d'être was to see their words rendered as moving images, and who didn't have an uncle named Steve, and who were too old school to beg for money via Kickstarter, and who longed for the days of packed movie houses, well: things were a mess.

For Samuel Taylor's present purposes, though—and even in an era where Peter Dinklage could be cast, or so it appeared, without undue emphasis on his stature—short was still, by and large, tall. And anyway, *Down these culturally dissolute and reflexively allegorical streets an aging déraciné man must go*, as he'd quip to his aging déraciné friends, all of whom had, like him, elected to relocate to La La Land and had, like him, experienced something of the émigré's sense of dislocation.

Like his worst plots, his scripted plight was, shall we say, filmdom formulaic: implicit in his every creative whim, regardless of how wildly insouciant, was his tacit commitment to a purely notional mass entertainment product with a purely notional mass entertainment budget. Too often what this amounted to, allegorically speaking, was the worst words in the best order. He knew he might very well be but the hapless agent of a sprawling conglomerate that would ultimately give financial imprimatur, or not, to his creations—to his agency, such as it was. Money had a say in ontological divinations after all, he thought—if it didn't make him sweat, like Marc 5' 10" Lawrence, its absence surely did—or maybe he was simply wallowing in some relational flux, unable to reckon with his impending anonymity? Maybe all of this was beyond his ken, as his very being was but the improbable arrangement of matter and energy arising in conjunction with some unknown quanta of meaning?

Or maybe he was just a hack, he thought, catching himself using *quanta* twice in five paragraphs.

He had the order of things to blame for his lapses and excesses, at any rate, and surely not himself. Right? Or was the point rather that no man is an island, hence that we all share responsibility for our altering fortunes and misfortunes, whether individual or collective? Here in the land of Twentieth Century Fox and what Didion had called "the Fox sky," which hovered over the ranch where Fox had filmed so many westerns, was it possible our fates were ineluctably intertwined, that we were bound to one another simply by virtue of having respired under the same sheltering welkin? Or was the atmosphere itself little more than another matte shot to sustain the illusion of brother- and sisterhood?

He knew in any case that most up-and-coming millennial whoopers viewed him as superannuated, youngsters who would hardly bother to look up the word, though it did help that Kass was only thirty-five. It helped, yes. Though here he was greeted with the annoying realization that if things worked out between them, their difference in age all but guaranteed that she become the grieving widow, as he had been the grieving widower. Perhaps she too would fall in love again.

Kass and he had been a thing for a year now, but exactly what kind of thing, in long-term terms, had remained decidedly unclear. They jetted off to see each other when they could, and they collaborated online, but the romance was for the time being the long-distance affair of two writers: libido stalled by time and space, intellect eroticized by a shared interest in all things différanced. When they decided initially to hook up—they rendezvoused in Aspen almost three years to the day after Nora's death—he'd been down on his luck for nearly a year. He'd achieved some success as a showrunner for a new cable series with a self-named if cosmetically enhanced protagonist, based loosely on his own experiences, but midway through the second season he'd run into problems with the other producers, a situation he'd seen fit to satirize in his spare time, scribbling elements of a faux teleplay while preparing a writing portfolio, which he thought of as *disjecti membra*, for Plan B.

Plan B amounted to a part-time faculty position—the euphemism these days for non-tenure-line jobs was *contingent faculty*, which managed to sound both a tad more dignified and considerably more dicey than *adjunct faculty*, albeit the latter moniker was now applied to those part-timers who comprised a large portion of the contingent—teaching creative writing at UC-Riverside, where his drinking buddy Horace, a full prof in the English department there, had assured him he could provide some inside leverage. Not that Plan B appealed to him, exactly—and Plan B for a writer-academic was in effect Plan C anyway—but he had managed to overcome the perpetual state of dudgeon regarding all things scholastic to which he'd succumbed in the wake of his prior academic sojourn.

In truth the portfolio, like the faux teleplay, was turning out to be another exercise in self-indulgence, a quasi-therapeutic mixed bag, a hodgepodge of refreshingly unconstrained proportions, or some hybridized something or other that, in the woke aftermath of his TV work, pleased him to no end. His uneven sampling of inventive snuff exhibited, he hoped, more than passing resemblance to serious writing, provided one could look past the obvious lack of formal discipline. Which, as he knew, could be said of his oeuvre, which after all would always pay homage to the Dadaist strain in twentieth-century letters while revealing the lapses—of aesthetic judgment, as some would have it—inherent in pondering imponderables. He liked to have fun as a writer, and he imagined his readers as liking to have fun too. And he liked to think about things that troubled his thinking. The last time he'd received any critical attention as a literary artist had been five years prior, while still a garden-variety academic, venturing into the sci-fi genre with tongue planted firmly in cheek—and not. And like his work itself, the responses had been mixed.

Mixed. But then why not toss the sci-fi item into the portfolio? And why not create a novel structure for Plan B that would at least salvage...

But if such ratiocination sounded even to him like a rationalization of his own shortcomings, he knew better than to capitulate to those public and private appetites busy infusing the market with less of more, and an awful lot of less. Moreover, to the extent that, among more staid writers anyway, to excuse one's excuses signaled the anticipation of a certain lack of readerly comprehension, or worse, an unwillingness to comprehend—and on what grounds, went the complaint, should readers be treated to such authorial condescension, when the problem could very well be the writing?—excuses once articulated weren't unlike instruction manuals. And provided such articulated excuses accurately represented the complexities of assembly, why complain about instruction manuals?

After a protracted legal battle with the other writers, in any case, he'd managed to walk away with three hundred grand—word on the street was *only three hundred grand*—and their accountant had advised that he put two-thirds of that money where it couldn't be touched, for retirement. He checked around and learned that most of his academic friends had already accumulated a half a mil or more, and the consensus was that one had to have *at least seven-fifty* to live reasonably well in the third act of one's life. So the accountant's advice seemed a no-brainer, however cash-strapped it left him, and he socked away two-hundred grand in a 401(k) and Roth IRA.

This meant that he and Kass were living essentially off of her paycheck and his remaining hundred grand in savings, which savings—given his $2500 monthly rent and the cost of schmoozing in this town, ingratiating oneself with the landed entertainment gentry being the default mode of social intercourse—were drying up faster than the San Joaquin aquifer.

And this was why the scheme kept nagging at him and he'd kept nagging his friends: how many people would pay to buy a book about such stuff? A coffee-table book. Large high-res color photos, glossy pages. Short bio, followed by the vital stats. E.g., Marc 5' 10" Lawrence. Maybe even indexed from shortest to tallest? Weight would be more difficult— Gable reportedly dropped 35 lbs. to star in *The Misfits*, to which some attributed his heart attack shortly after filming was completed—but allowing that best guesses were a little like legends, maybe they could become a little like facts.

Sure, you could look it up. But wouldn't it be handy to have the skinny on all of your favorite celebs in one convenient little print package? Wouldn't it? And for those so inclined, a Kindle edition?

Kass found the idea "nutty."

Him, he could already feel the Pacific tide tiding him over. If *Underwater Dogs* could make a splash, as one wag had remarked, the public's infatuation with celebrity culture might just send *The Heights and Weights of Stars* into the stratosphere.

*

According to IMDb, Brad Pitt was 5' 11" tall. So as far as he was concerned—because it was all relative anyway, right, even if relative was itself relative?—Brad Pitt was 5' 11" tall. And Alan Ladd was 5' 6¼" tall. And Clark Gable was 6' 1" tall, same as Heath Ledger.

He burped sweet and sour, the strong espresso and brown sugar cinnamon Pop-Tart he'd gobbled down for breakfast coming up a bit. Then he sniffed the walnut liqueur.

John Wayne, he was 6' 4" tall. He always had a hunch he'd have liked Wayne the man, despite his wretched politics, and happening across Wayne's dying words while checking his height, Samuel Taylor felt vindicated in his hunch. He was certain Victor McLaglen, 6' 3" tall, liked Wayne. Ditto frequent costar Ward 6' 2" Bond. Ditto frequent costars Bruce 6' 1½" Cabot, Harry 6' Carey and Paul 6' Fix. (Was Fix really a six-footer?) Ditto James Arness, who, at 6' 7" tall, really did seem to dwarf Wayne in the four films they did together, especially *Big Jim McLain*. So either John Wayne was shorter than 6' 4", or James Arness was taller than 6' 7", or both. But as far as he was concerned, John Wayne was 6' 4" tall, three inches taller than Robert Mitchum, whom Wayne had seemed happy to let steal just about every scene in *El Dorado*. And at 6' 4" or very damn close to it, that made him an inch shorter than Henry Brandon, who played Ethan Edwards's blue-eyed, English-speaking, nemesis double, Scar, in Samuel Taylor's favorite Western, *The Searchers*.

Fess Parker, who was in *Island in the Sky* with both Wayne and Arness, was 6' 5½" tall, smack dab in the middle of both, the same height as The Rifleman, and ½" taller than Rock Hudson. He thought about

Parker, and about Davy Crockett—or was it Daniel Boone?—or was it both?—and about that bottle of wine he'd tried the week prior from the Fess Parker Winery. Quite good. Good for Parker. And he seemed to recall that Parker had led a long life. He could look it up of course. Sometimes things work out. Sometimes wine ages well. Sometimes books sell. Sometimes treatments too. But this latter was getting rarer and rarer, like a good Sauvignon Blanc for under twenty bucks.

Samuel Taylor was himself 5' 9½" tall. That ½" was something of a point of pride, if not a sign of vanity, in that it put him precisely ½" above the national average for men of his age. But when he stood next to someone 6' 7" tall, he felt a wee bit inadequate. Imagine what Alan Ladd must have felt like standing next to James Arness. Based on IMDb data, there was at least 12¾" between them—over a foot. Did Alan Ladd ever stand next to James Arness, or did he avoid him at all costs?

Cagney wouldn't have. He liked being cast against bigger men—he knew it made him look tougher, and he was pretty tough anyway, even though he reads that famous line, "I ain't so tough," as if he lived it. According to IMDb, he was 5' 6½" tall, or a quarter inch taller than Alan Ladd, and 4½" shorter than his hard-drinking pal and costar in nine films, Pat O'Brien. Edward G. Robinson was a half an inch taller than Cagney, who was the same height as George Raft. And Bogey was an inch taller than Edward G, how about that?

De Niro? 5' 9½". Maybe this was why De Niro was a favorite. Ditto "The Great One," same height, and the same height as Stallone. Dustin Hoffman? 5' 5¾". Every ¼" counted in this biz, especially for little big men. And for The King, the one who could sing, at 5' 11¾". But if IMDb was right, this would mean that a certain famous casting director's notes he'd seen on Hoffman, putting him at 5' 6½", were clearly based on incorrect data. And who furnished this data?

Johnny Weismuller at 6' 3", his onscreen mate Maureen O'Sullivan 5' 3", his onscreen son Johnny Sheffield, fully grown, 5' 11½". And his offscreen son, Johnny Weismuller Jr., height unknown. Ditto Freddie

Bartholomew, though Wiki indicated that he sprouted up to nearly 6' in his teens.

Charlie Chaplin, 5' 5"—same as Buster Keaton—and Paulette Goddard, 5' 4," one of a dozen Mahler-sized half pints in Samuel Taylor's growing list gonna get us every time, as Randy 6' Newman joked: surely one of the shortest married couples in Hollywood, and they enjoyed marital bliss for a short time too, only six years. But was Chaplin's height with or without his tramp hat? And was Goddard's height with her hair up, or down? Rosalind Russell, 5' 8", positively dwarfs her in *The Women*, as she dwarfs Joan Crawford, 5' 3", and Norma Shearer, The First Lady of MGM, at 5' 1".

Wait. Was Norma Shearer really that short, and shorter than Paulette Goddard? And was it mere coincidence that Crawford's rival, Bette Davis, also clocked in at 5' 3"?

Debbie Reynolds, 5' 2"—taller than Norma Shearer? Reynolds was in one film with John Wayne, *How the West Was One*, also starring James Stewart, 6' 3", an inch shorter than Wayne and the same height as Coop.

And today's John Wayne, Clint Eastwood, exactly as tall as Wayne. More coincidence?

Maybe these heights weren't relative after all. Maybe the stars' agents and managers and studios had lobbied more and less successfully to add inches to inseams. Maybe Ladd was being stretched by two inches, but Wayne was being stretched only by an inch. In which case maybe Eastwood had been stretched by an inch.

Too many maybes.

And what about his oo-la-lah girls, among whom were Ingrid 5' 9" Bergman—an inch and a half taller than Bogey—and Sophia 5' 8½" Loren? Were they really this tall, Loren as tall as Peter Sellers? Was Maureen O'Hara really 5' 8"? And was Myrna 5' 5" Loy really a full 7" shorter than William Powell, and were Powell and Leonardo DiCaprio really the same height? Was Laurel a full 5" shorter than Hardy? Was Bud 5' 8" Abbott only 3" taller than Lou Costello? Was Anne 5' 6" Bancroft really an inch taller than Mel Brooks and the same height as Jack LaLanne and Peter Falk? And was Olivia de Havilland, at 5' 4", really one inch taller than her sister, Joan Fontaine, aka "Dragon Lady"? Remarkably, both of them were still alive into their nineties, separated by an ocean and a continent and longstanding hard feelings, but perhaps they wouldn't have minded had someone inquired?

A lost opportunity. But it would certainly be nice if someone were to get to the bottom of all this. In fact *that* was a book, with the actual real-life measurements, he was sure would sell tens of thousands of copies. Maybe even a million copies.

A million copies. Imagine. Even in an era of hundred-million global bestsellers like Harry Potter, a million copies was still a lot.

And after all, what star-struck kid doesn't want to know how tall the current heartthrobs *really* are? In lieu of which, reasoned Samuel Taylor, why *not* print the legend? What harm could it do?

*

Driving past the old MGM lot, which he would only wincingly refer to as Sony Pictures Studios, the sun blazing and the sole relief from the heat a slight onshore breeze, he couldn't for the life of him understand how his latest treatment had failed to gain any traction. "Haven't you learned anything from our discussions?" Sylvia had berated him. "If you were a known quantity, we might be able to do something with this," she'd continued. "But you need something simple, something that can be described in a ten-word logline. And besides, Jarmusch already did something with this idea in that ridiculous vampire film of his."

*

CHECK MATE

Samantha Feng has just graduated from MIT with a PhD in mathematics and a specialty in quantum cryptography—at the age of

22. Several recruiters from the CIA appear on campus, eager to hire someone with such credentials, and are assured by the chair of the math department that Feng is "the best he's ever seen." According to the CIA's dossier on Feng, she has no living relatives, and apparently this makes her that much more attractive to them. Feng meets with the recruiters, who offer her a solid position at Langley, but Feng indicates that she needs a vacation before settling into the job. They agree to give her two months to herself, and Feng packs up and drives south to a place she visited once as a child, Hatteras Village, at the southernmost tip of the Outer Banks. This was the last time she and her parents were together, and we learn they were both killed in a plane crash shortly after. When she arrives in town, she heads over to a local restaurant for dinner, and recognizes her server, Jane, a little girl she'd befriended so many years ago, easily identifiable by the scar on her cheek. The two become fast friends, and as Samantha's days grow long relaxing in the sun and surf, she befriends a number of locals, who live largely via a barter economy—laundry in return for dolphinfish filets, for instance—and this is how Samantha meets Derek Brand at the docks. A mate on the Albatross, a legendary fishing fleet, he cleans mahi-mahi faster and finer than anyone. The two become involved, and on off days, he and Samantha enjoy leisurely trips on the bay, digging for clams the old-fashioned way, with their toes. But gradually Samantha becomes aware that Derek seems to turn up with eerie consistency at her daily haunts, and with lame excuses as to why he's not out on the water working. Occasionally he presses her to be specific about the cryptology she's been working on, and she finally favors him with a lecture about how two particles, once entangled, behave in complementary ways even if they're a universe apart, and how we can't know which particle will behave which way until we actually look at them. This phenomenon can in turn be used as the basis for sending encoded messages, which can be decoded a universe away. It's all very cerebral, but Derek offers a romantic metaphor: two ships that pass in the night might be thus entangled, and might forever find themselves mysteriously linked across the seven seas. Romance ensues. But we discover the inevitable: Derek is working for the CIA, and has been sent to the Outer Banks to keep an eye on Samantha because Samantha's parents were suspected by the CIA of having been Chinese spies. With the arrival of another player, a femme fatale named Maddy (short for Madeline),

Samantha's vacation starts to resemble a cat and mouse game, and she must use all of her wits to figure out whether her parents were indeed spies and how to protect herself and Jane from the machinations of Derek and Maddy.

*

Could he say it in ten words? Well no, not quite. The problem Samuel Taylor faced was less Barton Fink than Joe Gillis: not how to sell a script about Joe Schmoe that Joe Schmoe would never pay to see, but how to sell a script for grown-ups to which the youth audience of Shanghai would flock in droves. Or to put it another way, how to sell a script for grown-ups to financiers in Dubai. Or to put it another way, how to sell a script for grown-ups. Or to put it another way, how to sell a script. He had zero intention of Kickstarting his way into Stacey Snider's office. He had zero illusions about a Twitter campaign gone viral. What he wanted, what he was insisting on, was that old-time Tinsel Town attention. And what he was willing to do for it was what was still, in his view, a fair trade: make good shit.

And in holding stubbornly to his make-good-shit convictions, Samuel Taylor was perfectly aware that there would be some dramatic irony in store for readers of his excuse-laden prose, such as he imagined them. And ironically, he was never keen on dramatic irony.

*

Joanne Woodward, 5' 4", Paul Newman, 5' 9½". Maybe this was why Newman too was a favorite. And the Sundance Kid an inch taller, at 5' 10½". They should have starred in at least one more film together—make it a triptych, for godsakes. They did the outdoors, they did the indoors, and just by being in two films together where their characters had at times to be actors—where they had to act like they were acting—they'd done the self-reflexive bit. They should have made a film set in contemporary times, but for two aging leads, contemporary times from the late seventies forward had perhaps less use than earlier eras, the audience demographic already plummeting in response to the summer blockbuster phenom.

Samuel Taylor found himself thinking about changing audience demographics, which led him to thinking about Ray Harryhausen. At one point earlier that morning, while munching on his Bavarian cream, he'd stood in front of the signed black & white photo hanging on his sponge-textured mauve-colored living room wall that his poet-friend, Laura, had been kind enough to gift him, a picture of Harryhausen working on the Ymir from *20 Million Miles to Earth*. The great animator's career seemed at least obliquely relevant to his own herky-jerky situation, though it might simply have been the four cups of unadorned burr-ground espresso. Harryhausen's finest and self-professed favorite hour came at the beginning of the sixties, with *Jason and the Argonauts*, a well-produced film with passable acting, saturated color, a great Bernard Herrmann score (as with *The 7th Voyage of Sinbad* five years prior), all scores by Herrmann admittedly being great, and most important, a convincing synthesis of his celebrated stop-motion effects and live action. In 1963, Samuel Taylor surmised, adult audiences who'd pay to see *Sunday in New York* might be able to enjoy the fantasy-adventure that *Jason* proffered, touches of hokum notwithstanding. A decade later, very near the end of the sixties—which end Samuel Taylor would date unapologetically at 8 August 1974—Harryhausen persisted with *The Golden Voyage of Sinbad*, and no adult audience willing to sit through *The Exorcist* would likely view this latest effort, despite a fine if slightly anachronistic score by Miklós Rósza and with John Wayne's son in the lead, as any but a diversion for the kiddies.

*

BIG DATA

Thirtysomething Julius Fermat, an only child and one-time Stanford whiz kid, has launched a firm specializing in screenplay evaluation to determine beforehand whether a film will be successful. Only problem is that so far his statistical chops have identified as promising several scripts that have gone on to be box office flops, bringing his business to the brink of bankruptcy. Desperate, Julius hires sight unseen a highly recommended and newly minted data analyst from Caltech, twentysomething Alex Song. Alex turns out to be a woman, and proves every bit Julius's analytical equal. Julius and Alex are gradually drawn to each other despite Julius's haplessly logical approach to relationships. It's not long before they score a minor success by correctly predicting the popularity of an indie feature, but they learn to their dismay that the contract they've signed leaves them with negligible profit. When an old grad school chum presents Julius with an offbeat romcom script to see if it has commercial potential, Julius runs the numbers and concludes that it has limited box office appeal. But when Alex reads the script, she sees merit in it, and the quarrel that ensues as Alex tries to show Julius the value of the human heart in understanding the popular appeal of love stories threatens to upend their budding romance, even as the firm flirts with financial ruin. (It's a happy ending of course. Over the final credits we see celeb after celeb on the Red Carpet lauding Fermat & Song, a firm that boasts attention to hearts AND minds.)

*

Patrick Wayne, 6' 1". Did he take after his father, hand-wise?

*

Sylvia's response to *Big Data*, the first synopsis Samuel Taylor had submitted to her, was an education in three words—"Too inside-Hollywood." Never mind what you *thought* you knew about the industry. One had to set aside all of those beloved behind-the-screen theatrics that yesteryear had dubbed Films about Films, films that Samuel Taylor too had regarded as such a salutary, and cherished, staple of the medium. These were mere exceptions to prove an anti-auteur rule that today's MFA students would doubtless struggle against in pursuing their cinematic dreams: the entertainment business was a business venture, and always had been, and businesses were predisposed against airing their dirty laundry, and always would be. In addition to the formal language of film, there was a corporate language that even would-be screenwriters would do well to learn if they hoped ever to see that letter of intent to distribute. And Samuel Taylor knew first-hand that the more these scribes absorbed that language, the more likely it was that their screenwriting efforts would falter at the altar of the almighty commodity.

Art and commerce? No. Art *as* commerce? Not quite. Commerce as art? Close. As Samuel Taylor saw it, this was Spielberg's distinctive gift and hard-won gambit: to recuperate the studio film to make it account—as an instrument of social expression and through sheer visual verve—for the popular filmic culture it had helped to shape. Sometimes the result was more art than commerce, sometimes not. But audiences could always be seduced by the variously familial trappings on hand without always registering that the projection and project before them was a matter of entertaining commerce (pun intended). And there was an art to exploiting artifice to such ends. Which is why the arrival on the scene of the actual survivors that Schindler helped to save was an essential concluding act in that bright star of Spielberg's cinematic universe, their arrival signifying his line in the sand between handheld 35 mm representation and reality. And which is why, when paired on that one occasion with a touch of Kubrick's more austere sensibility, the middle-aged prodigy presented us with the inescapably human limitations of his own animatronic toyshop.

Had he read all that someplace? Brave of Spielberg in any case, thought Samuel Taylor. And it seemed perfectly apropos that the director owned Rockwell's *The Connoisseur*. No, that wasn't Hitchcock with his back to us, standing before the AbEx painting, as Spielberg had once fancied aloud—that was Spielberg himself.

*

Audiences had grown up, had been growing up right along, and for the most part, like the country's better-nourished youth, the stars post-1960 *seemed* to have been growing incrementally taller than their Golden Age peers. Their stats? Ben 5' 7" Stiller, Tom 5' 7" Cruise, Bruce 5' 7½" Lee, Ice 5' 8" Cube, Sean 5' 8" Penn, Mark 5' 8" Ruffalo, Joaquin 5' 8" Phoenix, Mark 5' 8" Wahlberg, Jackie 5' 8½" Chan, Antonio 5' 8½" Banderas, Robert 5' 8½" Downey Jr., Don 5' 8½" Cheadle, Casey 5' 9" Affleck, Tom 5' 9" Hardy, Michael 5' 9" Rooker, James 5' 9¼" Caan, Robert 5' 9½" Duvall, Philip Seymour 5' 9½" Hoffman, Woody 5' 9½" Harrelson. Colin 5' 10" Farrell, Ray 5' 10" Winstone, Cuba 5' 10" Gooding Jr., Kevin 5' 10" Bacon, Kevin 5' 10" Spacey, Johnny 5' 10" Depp, Matt 5' 10" Damon, Josh 5' 10½" Brolin, Sean 5' 10½" Bean,Burt 5' 11" Reynolds, Kurt 5' 11" Russell, Eric 5' 11" Stoltz, George 5' 11½" Clooney, Jake 5' 11" Gyllenhaal, Viggo 5' 11" Mortensen, Javier 5' 11¼" Bardem, Russell 5' 11½" Crowe, Adam 5' 11½" Beach, Vin 5' 11¾" Diesel, Nick 6' Nolte, Christopher 6' Walken, Tom 6' Hanks, Matthew 6' McConaughey, Edward 6' Norton, Christian

6' Bale, Nicolas 6' Cage, Michael 6' Parks, Aaron 6' Eckhart, Ryan 6' 0½" Gosling, Terrence 6' 0½" Howard, Kevin 6' 1" Costner, Keanu 6' 1" Reeves, Harrison 6' 1" Ford, Jeff 6' 1" Bridges, Bradley 6' 1" Cooper, Colin 6' 1½" Firth, Hugh 6' 2" Jackman, Ryan 6' 2" Reynolds, Will 6' 2" Smith, Morgan 6' 2" Freeman, Gene 6' 2" Hackman, James 6' 2" Coburn, Sean 6' 2" Connery—Roger 6' 1" Moore, George 6' 2" Lazenby, Timothy 6' 2" Dalton, Pierce 6' 2" Brosnan, Daniel 5' 10" Craig—Brian 6' 2" Dennehy, Jim 6' 2" Carrey, Clive 6' 2" Owen, Daniel 6' 2" Day-Lewis, Forest 6' 2" Whitaker, Benicio 6' 2" Del Toro, Samuel L. 6' 2½" Jackson, Ben 6' 4" Affleck, Liam 6' 4" Neeson, Tim 6' 5" Robbins. Maybe Mel 5' 9¾" Gibson, the same height as Jack Nicholson according to IMDb, was roughly average stature? But the Celeb Heights site had both Nicholson and Gibson at 5' 9½", as did the Astrotheme site. Did ¼" make a difference, or not? What the hell.

And just how in the hell tall *was* George "Spanky" McFarland circa, let's say, 1935?

Should he be using a different metric, viz., meters? And what about Celebrity Heights? Were they the straight dope? They had Cagney at 5' 5", a full 1½" shorter than his IMDb listing, and Alan Ladd at 1" *taller*, in part based on Virginia 5' 5" Mayo's assertion that Ladd was taller than her—she claimed her height was 5' 5½"—and that Cagney and Edward G. were both shorter. And Celebrity Heights had Gable, for instance, at 6' 0½", a full half an inch shorter than his height at IMDb, even though he himself claimed to be 6' 2".

These discrepancies seemed to cry out for expert sleuthing, and Samuel Taylor's anxiety mounted in the face of Celebrity Heights and other size-savvy sites that were threatening to steal his thunder by combing the archives for testimony, hearsay, whatnot. But none of these sites had managed the editorial feat of a coffee-table volume. And this was looking more and more like an editorial challenge, a question of selecting the right mix of stars, if not always the brightest lights. How to decide who was in, and who was out?

The current crop of women looked to be sprouting even more than the men, but here again it was difficult to say whether the numbers argued for actual gains: Salma 5' 2" Hayek, Thandie 5' 3" Newton, Natalie 5' 3" Portman, Renée 5' 3" Zellweger, Scarlet 5' 3" Johansson, Julianne 5' 4" Moore, Keira 5' 4" Knightley, Amy 5' 4" Adams, Jennifer 5" 4½" Lopez, Naomi 5' 4½" Watts, Viola 5' 5" Davis, Kristen 5' 5" Stewart, Zhang 5' 5" Ziyi, Halle 5' 5½" Berry, Alicia 5' 5½" Vikander, Emma 5' 6" Stone, Penélope 5' 6" Cruz, Angelina 5' 6½" Jolie, Zoe 5' 6½" Saldana, Kate 5' 6½" Winslet, Rosario 5' 7" Dawson, Ashley 5' 7" Judd, Emily 5' 7" Blunt, Meg 5' 8" Ryan, Anne 5' 8" Hathaway, Cate 5' 8½" Blanchett, Gwyneth 5' 9" Paltrow, Jennifer 5' 8" Garner, Julia 5' 8" Roberts, Jennifer 5' 9" Lawrence, Katherine 5' 9" Heigl, Maggie 5' 9" Gyllenhaal, Charlize 5' 9½" Theron, Queen 5' 10" Latifah, Minnie 5' 10" Driver, Uma 5' 11" Thurman, Geena 6' Davis.

Davis, Thurman, Driver, Latifah, Theron, Gyllenhaal, Heigl, Lawrence, Roberts, Garner, Paltrow, Blanchett, Hathaway, Ryan, Blunt, Judd, Dawson, Winslet, Saldana, Jolie, Cruz, Stone, Vikander, Berry, Zhang, Stewart, Davis, Watts, Lopez, Adams, Knightley, Moore, Johansson, Zellweger, Portman, Newton, Hayek. But in this case he had a thing for Blanchett. And for Lucy 5' 3" Liu. And for Halle 5' 5½" Berry, and Scarlet, and…but in thinking about it, was Jude 6' Law's or Nicole 5' 11" Kidman's ass really the more pleasing to the eye in what, in his more mordant moments, he took to be a chief draw of *Cold Mountain*?

As for the women, he ventured that Sandra 5' 7½" Bullock was the average, at least among this crop of latter-day actresses, making the women a little more than two inches on average shorter than the men. He expected twice that, as he knew that Holly 5' 2" Hunter wasn't always looking up at her female costars, but the only way to find out for certain was to crunch the numbers, the *actual* numbers. In any case the glamour pusses, a number of whom could act, would feature prominently in *The Heights and Weights of Stars*—Greta 5' 7½" Garbo, Merle 5' 2" Oberon, Carole 5' 2" Lombard, Susan 5' 2" Lucci, Gina 5' 2¼" Lollobrigida, Hedy 5' 7" Lamar, Ava 5' 6" Gardner, Diane 5'

7" Cilento, Eleanor 5' 6" Parker, Elizabeth 5' 2" Taylor, Cicely 5' 3½" Tyson, Jean 5' 4" Simmons, Ursula 5' 5" Andress, Katharine 5' 5½" Ross, Audrey 5' 7" Hepburn, Jane 5' 8" Fonda, 5' 8½" Cher, Faye 5' 7" Dunaway, and Susan 5' 7" Sarandon, along with male glamour pusses like Warren 6' 2" (as his character reports in *The Parallax View*) Beatty and John 6' 2" Travolta; as would the UK thespian set, a number of whom were lookers—Edna May 5' 7" Oliver, Laurence 5' 10" Olivier, Peter 5' 9" Finch, John 5' 11" Gielgud, Vanessa 5' 11" Redgrave, Richard 5' 9½" Burton, Albert 5' 9" Finney, Paul 6' Scofield, Peter 6' 2" O'Toole, Vivien 5' 3½" Leigh, Anthony 5' 8½" Hopkins, Alan 5' 9" Bates, Tom 5' 8" Courtenay, Michael 5' 10½" York, Oliver 5' 11" Reed, Kenneth 5' 9½" Branagh, and Jeremy 6' 2" Irons.

And he mustn't forget those other Fondas, 6' 1½" Henry and 6' 2½" Peter. Natalie 5' flat Wood. Lee 5' 7" Remick. Emma 5' 8" Thompson. Richard 5' 7" Jaeckel. Edward James 5' 8½" Olmos. Montagu 6' 2" Love. Harold 5' 10" Sakata. Lilyan (height unknown) Tashman. Lila (height unknown) Kedrova. Robert 6' Stack. Ron 6' 1" Perlman. Powers 6' 2" Boothe. Stephen 6' 2" Tobolowsky. Dick 5' 11" Powell. James 5' 11" Gammon. Vincent 5' 8½" Gardenia. John 6' 1" Huston, Angelica 5' 10" Huston, Danny 6' 2" Huston. The faces multiplied, the names cascaded: Mary 5' 5" Astor, 5' 4" Mako, Ann 5' 5½" Sheridan, Sidney 6' 2½" Poitier, Frances 5' 5" McDormand, Carroll 5' 5" Baker, Meryl 5' 6" Streep, Isabelle 5' 3" Huppert, Tilda 5' 11" Swinton, Katharine 5' 7½" Hepburn, Spencer 5' 9" Tracy, Fredric 5' 10" March, Claude 5' 6½" Rains, Errol 6' 2" Flynn, Alan 6' 2" Hale, Alan 6' 2" Hale Jr., J.K. 5' 10 ¾" Simmons, Ian 5' 6" Holm, Janet 5' 5½" Leigh, Donald 5' 6" Pleasance, Julie 5' 7" Andrews, Christopher 5' 10½" Plummer, Donald 6' 4" Sutherland, James 5' 11" Donald, Paul 6' 2½" Sorvino, Timothy 5' 8" Spall, Owen 5' 10½" Wilson, Idris 6' 2¾" Elba, Fanny 5' 6" Brice, Barbra 5' 5" Streisand, Sissy 5' 3" Spacek, Andrew 6' Keir, Ellen 5' 6" Barkin, George 5' 7" Burns, Dana 5' 10" Andrews, Lawrence 6' Harvey, Tom 6' 1½" Tyler, Joan 5' 2" Rivers, Walter 6' Cronkite, Mike 6' Wallace, Barbara 5' 5" Walters.

Were Cronkite and Wallace and Walters stars though or simply TV celebs? They all had stars on the Walk of Fame.

Good enough—even if, to judge by the homeless and addicts encamped atop the carved granite, the Walk of Fame was fast becoming a walk of shame. Shame on us, Donald J. 6' 2" Trump.

And what about Giulietta 5' 2" Masina, Rani 5' 3" Mukerji, Jean-Paul 5' 9¼" Belmondo, Anna 5' 7" Karina, Brigitte 5' 7" Bardot, Jeanne 5' 3" Moreau, Marcello 5' 9¼" Mastroianni, Max 6' 4" von Sydow, Toshirô 5' 9" Mifune?

And what of those familiar if, for most viewers, nameless faces that showed up onscreen time and again and without which our favorite films would doubtless lose something vital? Una 5' 2" O'Connor, Charles (height unknown) Lane, Ming 6' the Merciless, John 5' 7" Qualen, Victor 5' 7" Moore, Charles 5' 6" Winninger, Henry 5' 4½" Travers, Charlie 5' 7 ½" Grapewin, Arthur 6' Hunnicutt, Royal 6' 2" Dano, Mary 5' 10" Wickes, Eve 5' 9½" Arden.

Of course he always liked Arden. Who else?

Wendy 5' 7" Hiller. Barbara 5' 5" Hershey. Paul 5' 9" Muni. Al 5' 8" Jolson. Eddie 5' 8" Cantor. David 6' Niven. David 6' 2½" Thewlis. Bruce 6' 1" Campbell. Sydney 6' Pollack. Wilford 5' 8" Brimley. Strother 5' 7" Martin. Lee 6' 2" Van Cleef. Joseph 6' Wiseman. Stephen 5' 8" Root. Espera (height unknown) DeCorti. Helen 5' 4" Mirren. Bette 5' 1" Midler. Maria 5' 1½" Ouspenskaya. Sheree 5' 4½" North. Marion 5' 5" Davies. Jeanne 5' 7" Tripplehorn. Jeanne 5' 4" Crain. Drew 5' 4" Barrymore. Cameron 5' 8½" Diaz. Rose 5' 4" McGowan. Ralph 5' 11" Fiennes. Edward 5' 9" Woodward. John 5' 9" Hurt. Russell 6' 1" Means. William 6' 2" Hurt. Gary 6' Busey. Buster 6' 1" Crabbe. Gary 5' 8½" Oldman. Lillian 5' 5½" Gish. Mary 5' 0½" Pickford. Helen 5' Hayes. Kenneth 5' 11" Tobey. Tobey 5' 8" Maguire. Luis 5' 7½" Guzmán. Mickey 5' 11" Rourke. Rene 5' 8" Russo. Goldie 5' 6" Hawn. Kerry 5' 4" Washington. Rudolph 5' 8" Valentino. Yul 5' 8" Brynner. Téa 5' 8" Leoni. Helen 5' 7" Hunt. Patricia 5' 8½" Neal. Fairbanks Sr. 5' 7" and Jr. 6' 0½". Melissa 5' 4" Leo. Ciarán 6' Hinds. Paul 6' 3" Robeson. Liev 6' 3" Schreiber. Michael 6' 3½" Rennie. Peter 5' 5"

Lorre. Edmund 5' 5" Gwenn. William 5' 7" Daniels. Marilyn 5' 5½"
Monroe. Kirk 5' 9" Douglas. Michael 5' 10" Douglas. James 6' 0½"
Gandolfini. Jeff 6' 0½" Corey. Steve 5' 7" Van Zandt. Monty 5' 10"
Woolley. Melvyn 6' 1½" Douglas. Deborah 5' 6" Kerr. Karl 6' 1½"
Malden. Rod 5' 10" Steiger. Lee J. 5' 11" Cobb. Hattie 5' 2" McDaniel.
James 6' 2" Garner. Willem 5' 10" Dafoe. Marcel 5' 6" Dalio. William
5' 11" Holden. Herbert 6' Marshall. William 6' 5" Marshall. Sterling 6'
5" Hayden. Pedro 6' Armendáriz. Jane 6' Lynch. Anthony 6 1" Quinn.
Robert 6' 4" Ryan. Jack 6' 4" Palance. Elisha 5' 5" Cook Jr. Forest 6'
4" Tucker. Mike 6' 4¾" Mazurki. Clint 6' 6" Walker. Fred 6' 1" Clark.
Fred 6' 6" Thompson. James 6' 6½" Cromwell. Richard 6' 1" Boone.
Eva Marie 5' 4" Saint. Tippi 5' 4" Hedren. Tony 5' 9" Curtis. Kevin 5'
9" Smith. Maggie 5' 5" Smith. David 5' 11½" Strathairn. Cliff 6' 0½"
Curtis. Thomas (height unknown) Gomez. Jamie Lee 5' 7" Curtis. Katy
5' 6½" Jurado. Grace 5' 6½" Kelly. David Patrick 5' 6" Kelly. John 5'
7" Garfield. Anthony 5' 10" Zerbe. Ricardo 6' Montalbán. Eddie 5'
11" Albert. Jimmy 5' 7" Durante. James 5' 8" Whitmore. Robert 5'
8" Conrad. Robert 5' 8½" Vaughn. Robert 6' 1" Vaughn. Ernest 5' 9"
Borgnine. Lee 6' 2" Marvin. Gilbert 5' 10" Roland. Benson 5' 9" Fong.
Ed 5' 9" Harris. Warner 5' 11" Oland. Danny 5' 11" Kaye. Sidney 6'
Toler. Walter 6' Slezak. George 6' 3½" Sanders. Harry 6' 2" Belafonte.
Diane 5' 5" Wiest. Woody 5' 5" Allen. Diane 5' 6½" Keaton. Michael
5' 9" Keaton. Julianna 5' 6" Margulies. Christine 5' 8½" Baranski. Gary
6' Cole. Alec 5' 10" Guinness. James 5' 7" McAvoy. Pam 5' 8" Greer.
Greer 5' 6" Garson. Bruce 6' Willis. Jack 5' 10½" Warden. Tom 6' 1"
Wilkinson. Bob 6' 2" Gunton. Treat 5' 10" Williams. Ray 5' 11" Teal.
Nicol 6' 3" Williamson. Jim 6' 2" Brown. Arnold 6' 2" Schwarzenegger.
Ruby 5' 2¼" Dee. Ossie 6' 2" Davis. Chief Dan (height unknown)
George. Oprah 5' 6½" Winfrey. Julie 5' 3" Christie. Charlotte 5' 6½"
Rampling. Richard 6' 1" Harris. Tommy Lee 6' Jones. James Earl 6' 1½"
Jones. Jennifer 5' 6½" Jones. Toni 5' 8" Collette. Lisa 5' 8" Kudrow.
Denzel 6' 1" Washington. Fred 6' 3" MacMurray. Charlton 6' 3" Heston.
Amitabh 6' 1" Bachchan. Martin 6' 1" Milner. Hal 6' 1" Holbrook.
Alan 6' 2" Alda. Bill 6' 2" Murray. Richard 5' 10" Pryor. Billy 5' 7"
Crystal. Yaphet 6' 4" Kotto. Gene 5' 10½" Wilder. Pam 5' 8" Grier.
William H. 5' 8" Macy. Richard 6' 1" Jenkins. Annette 5' 8" Bening.

James 5' 8" Dean. Burt 5' 8" Young. Dennis 5' 9" Hopper. Dennis 6' Farina. Stan 5' 11" Lee. Montgomery 5' 10" Clift. Martin 5' 7" Sheen. Martin 5' 7" Balsam. Martin 6' 2" Landau. Ned 5' 7" Beatty. Brad 5' 9" Dourif. Alan 5' 10" Cumming. Whoopi 5' 6" Goldberg. Al 5' 7" Pacino. Chiwetel 5' 10" Ejiofor. Omar 5' 11" Sharif. Andy 6' Griffith. Andy 5' 10" Garcia. Lana 5' 3" Turner. Kathleen 5' 8" Turner. Jodie 5' 3" Foster. Ben 5' 9" Foster. Claire 5' 3" Trevor. Ann- 5' 3½" Margret. Michael J. 5' 4½" Fox. Patrick 5' 10" Stewart. Norman 5' 5" Lloyd. Lloyd 5' 10½" Nolan. Christopher 6' 1" Lloyd. Lloyd 5' 11¾" Bridges. Beau 5' 10" Bridges. Ian 5' 11" McKellen. Malcolm 5' 8½" McDowell. Mary 5' 8" Steenburgen. 5' 6" Veronica Cartwright. Tom 6' Skerritt. Marcel (height unknown) Marceau. Haruo (height unknown) Nakajima. Claude 6' 1" Akins. Andy 5' 8" Serkis. George 6' 1" Reeves. Steve 6' 1" Reeves. Christopher 6' 4" Reeve. John 6' 1" Dall. Zachary 6' Scott. Ronald 5' 10" Colman. Butterfly 5' 1" McQueen. Tom 5' 11" Berenger. John 6' Malkovich. Gary 5' 9" Sinise. Klaus 5' 8" Kinski. Nastassja 5' 6½" Kinski. Dale (height unknown) Dye. Robert 6' 1" Montgomery. John C. 6' 2" McGinley. Jon 6' 2" Hamm. Bill 6' Paxton. Michael 6' Biehn. Vincent 6' 4" Price. Jan-Michael 5' 10½" Vincent. William 5' 7½" Conrad. Conrad 6' 2½" Veidt. Hans 6' 2" Conreid. John 5' 7" Leguizamo. Danny 6' 2½" Aiello. Danny 4' 10" DeVito.

DeVito an inch shorter than Thomas De Quincey, 4" taller than Alexander Pope? The names of far too many men, far too many white men, far too many dead white men?

Mae 5' West. Jean 5' 1½" Harlow. Melanie 5' 9¼" Griffith. Doris 5' 7" Day. Wesley 5' 10" Snipes. Rosie 5' 1½" Perez. Ben 5' 8" Kingsley. Jamie 5' 9" Foxx. Bryan 5' 10½" Cranston. Ricardo 6' Montalban. Keith 6' 2" David. Jon 6' 2½" Voight. David 5' 11" Keith. Robert 5' 8" Keith. Brian 6' 0½" Keith. Larry 5' 11" David. Ving 6' Rhames. John 6' Carradine. David 6' Carradine. Keith 6' 1" Carradine. Robert 5' 11½" Carradine. Alec 6' Baldwin. Anthony 6' 2" Perkins. Melina 5' 6½" Mecouri. Charles 5' 8" Laughton. Tyrone 5' 11" Power. Peter 5' 11½" Ustinov. Jane 5' 6" Darwell. Fay 5' 3" Wray. Elsa 5' 4" Lanchester. Sharon 5' 8½" Stone. Paul 5' 8½" Giamatti. George 5' 10" Zucco. Lionel

5' 10½" Atwill. Walter 6' Brennan. Liv 5' 8" Ullmann. Sigourney 5' 11½" Weaver. Shirley 5' 2" Temple (full-grown). Kay 5' 5½" Thompson. Setsuko 5' 4¼" Hara. Basil 6' 1½" Rathbone. Nigel 6' Bruce. Woody 6' 4" Strode. Charles 5' 10" McGraw. Ali 5' 8" MacGraw. Walter 6' 2½" Matthau. Jack 5' 9" Lemmon. Stanley 5' 8" Tucci. Alan 6' 0¾" Rickman. Steve 5' 9" Carrell. Rod 5' 10" Taylor. Will 6' 3" Ferrell. Amy 5' 7" Schumer. James 5' 11" Franco. Jeff 6' 4½" Goldblum. Rachel 5' 4" McAdams. Barbara 5' 5" Stanwyck. Barbara 5' 3¾" Eden. Joel 6' 2½" McCrae. Randolph 6' 2½" Scott. George C. 6' Scott. Roy 5' 9" Scheider. Robert 5' 10" Shaw. Richard 5' 5" Dreyfus. Danny 6' 4" Glover. Karen 5' 7½" Black. Shelley 5' 4" Winters. Barbara 5' 7" Shelley. Angela 5' 8" Lansbury. Richard 6' 1" Chamberlain. Thomas 5' 10" Mitchell. Radha 5 5¾" Mitchell. Edmund 5' 9" O'Brien. Warren 5' 11¼" Oates. Jason 5' 10" Statham. Louis 6' C.K. Roddy 5' 9" McDowall. Anne 5' 3¾" Baxter. Thelma 5' 1" Ritter. Lucille 5' 6½" Ball. Dwayne "The Rock" 6' 4" Johnson. Hulk 6' 4" Hogan. Mr. 5' 10½" T. Ben 6' 2" Johnson. Delroy 6' 4" Lindo. Alan 5' 9½" Arkin. Don 5' 11" Johnson. Franchot 5' 10" Tone. Winona 5' 3½" Ryder. Harry Dean 5' 8" Stanton. Dudley 5' 2½" Moore. Carey 5' 7" Mulligan. Red 5' 6" Buttons. Don 5' 6½" Knotts. 5' 7½" Groucho 5' 6" Chico 5' 5½" Harpo 5' 8" Zeppo. John 5' 8" Belushi. Chevy 6' 4" Chase. Steve 6' Martin. Jeffrey 5' 11" Wright. Teresa 5' 3" Wright. Stephen 6' Boyd. C. Aubrey 6' 2" Smith. Sam 6' 2" Elliott. John 6' 2" Goodman. Steve 5' 9" Buscemi. Christian 5' 8½" Slater. Adam 6' 2½" Driver. Adam 6' 2" West. Jean 5' 3" Arthur. Arthur 5' 10" Kennedy. Marlene 5' 4½" Dietrich. Burgess 5' 5½" Meredith. Kim 5' 6" Novak. Wes 5' 10" Studi. Thomas 5' 10¾" Sadoski. Zöe 5' 1" Kravitz. Burl 6' Ives. Chris 5' 10" Cooper. Charles 6' 1" Bickford. Raquel 5' 6" Welch. 5' 4" Roseanne. Matthew 5' 8" Broderick. John 6' 4" Lithgow. Keenan 5' 10" Wynn. Chuck 5' 10" Norris. Jet 5' 6¼" Li. Carl 6' 1" Weathers. Adolph 5' 10½" Menjou. S.Z. "Cuddles" (height unknown) Sakall. Louis 6' 2½" Gossett Jr. Mary Tyler 5' 7" Moore. Edward 5' 7" Asner. Agnes 5' 4" Moorehead. Tallulah 5' 2½" Bankhead. Michelle 5' 7½" Pfeiffer. Ed 5' 7½" Sullivan. Johnny 5' 10½" Carson. Merv 5' 9" Griffin. Dick 5' 6½" Cavett. Jack (height unknown) Paar. Jon 5' 7" Stewart. Bill 5' 8" Maher. Sam 5' 8" Rockwell. Anna 5' 2" Kendrick. Leo 5' 6" Gorcey, parents Bernard 4' 10" Gorcey and Josephine

4' 11" Condon. Huntz 5' 10" Hall. Rip 5' 10" Torn. Geraldine 5' 8" Page. Amy (height unknown) Wright. Jonathan 6' Pryce. Lindsay 5' 9½" Wagner. Timothy 5' 11" Bottoms. Linda 5' 6" Hamilton. Louis 5' 6" Armstrong. Diana 5' 8½" Rigg. Telly 5' 11" Savalas. Sam 6' 2" Shepard. Jessica 5' 8" Lange. Gal 5' 10" Gadot. Harry 5' 6" Morgan. Ray 6' 1" Milland. George 6' 2" Brent. Dan 5' 11" Duryea. Ryan 6' 1" O'Neal. Tatum 5' 7" O'Neal. Mia 5' 4¼" Farrow. Michelle 5' 4" Yeoh. Sam 6' 1" Waterston. Richard 5' 10" Gere. Cloris 5' 5½" Leachman. Carlos 6' Keith. Peter 6' 3" Coyote. Mads 6' Mikkelsen. Melinda 5' 8" Dillon. Sessue 5' 7½" Hayakawa. Sam 5' 7½" Jaffe. Maribel 5' 5½" Verdú.

He had a thing for Verdú. And Elsa Lanchester. And did he mention Lucy 5' 3" Liu?

5' 10½" John 5' 11" Paul 5' 9¾" George & 5' 6" Ringo. And for comparison's sake, 5' 10" Jagger and 5' 8½" Richards. And 5' 9½" Kirk 5' 10½" Bones 6' Spock. 5' 11" Karloff and 6' 1" Lugosi. 5' 7" Man of a Thousand Faces and 6' 2" Lon Jr. 6' 5" Lee and 5' 11½" Cushing. 5' 10½" Scarecrow, 5' 9" Tin Man, 5' 9" Cowardly Lion, 5' 8" Wizard, 5' Wicked Witch of the West, 5' 2½" Glinda the Good Witch of the North. Ol' 5' 7" Blue Eyes. Dean 5' 11" Martin. Sammy 5' 5" Davis Jr. Peter 6' Lawford. Victor 6' 2" Mature. Henry 6' 2" Silva. Jerry 5' 10½" Lewis.

And what to do about the heights and weights given onscreen, as in boxing films? One of the more curious examples was that close-up of Robert Forster's service file in his debut, *Reflections in a Golden Eye*, in which he's listed as 5' 10" and 154 lbs. IMDb had him at 5' 9½". He *was* another favorite, so . . .

Muhammad 6' 3" Ali.

Was any of this real? Or was it, like everything else, more or less real? Reel life, that old pun, turned plaintive. Numbers as culture, more or less, numbers as biology, more or less. Numbers as language. And then what?

*

As this one-time growing growth industry began to see its box office receipts shrink thanks at first to TV and then to the rise of digitally interconnected media with flat screens the size of *Guernica* or, for the constitutionally myopic, a watch face, film execs looked to ever more immersive effects to lure patrons back into largely vacated theaters. With the notable exception of enormously successful stage plays later turned into films, and the work of directors like Woody 5' 5" Allen and Lars 5' 7" von Trier and John 6' 4" Sayles, mainstream narrative film was moving decidedly away from literature-based content and theatrical stagings and toward its Méliès trompe l'oeil origins, even as documentaries were enjoying a resurgence that spoke to that other originating locus, Lumière actualities. And while the latter drew a predominantly adult audience, the former lured the middle-aged, children in tow, into the precincts of young adult fantasy, which in fact paralleled adult migration to YA lit. It was all rapidly becoming old news, Samuel Taylor realized, not least because much of the new news—climate change, say, or extinction, or the regularly-scheduled denial and recently-dubbed *fusion paranoia* accompanying such emerging realities—was too frightening to contemplate or televise for more than, oh, a half an hour a month, plus the irregular Facebook update. 3D was back, D-BOX was in, holographic projection was in the works, and VR was making immersive headway, along with *Rocky Horror*-style dousings and *Sound of Music*-style sing-alongs. Yeah, innovation was disruptive all right. Maybe, someday, a new kind of theatrical happening, streamed live and archived for the ages, would bring us back full circle to adult drama and epic, but that version, or vision, of posterity would hardly constitute cinema. In the meantime, today's awe-inspiring special effect would surely become tomorrow's shrug, Samuel Taylor reasoned, and as Disney at his impresario best understood, what would stand the test of time—fifty years hence, say—would be the particular pairing of form with content. What was provocative would become silly, what was unsettling, offensive, what was sublime, precious.

Right, precious?

Until, that is, and as VR augured, human cognition would be put at the wondrous mercy of a wrap-around freakout, a moving image imaged—or imagined?—by spooky intermediations of hardware, software, firmware, wetware, malware, greyware, adware, spyware. But that line of thinking was the once-and-future future, and anyone with a game console had the crystal ball-prowess to speculate in this regard. In any case CGI had reached the point at which its visual seductions were sufficiently potent to wow boomers like Samuel Taylor who were looking for any excuse to relive their younger, daydream-riven years, a nice counterpoint to their obsession with vintage clothing, vintage furniture, vintage guitars, and vintage coffee pots. Him, he went hot and cold on such chroma-keyed productions. On a warm summer evening he might enjoy spotting a hobbit or two, but most nights he'd just as soon catch a glimpse of the large raccoon that would occasionally forage in the moonlight under the orange tree out back, a more sustainable fiction.

*

He swung a right onto Pacific Ave, absent-mindedly jogging right and left again onto Main, a bit surprised to find himself driving past the sun-bleached, nondescript production office that had this very morning communicated, via his agent, the disappointing news. That such a tiny half-acre of Google Earth should be the source of his anxiety left him feeling oddly redeemed. Another left and right again, and he rejoined Pacific, following north until it turned into Neilson. He cranked up his air-conditioning.

*

TEN SLEEP

It's late September, early morning. Dylan Welles, a fit woman in her early thirties, is on the 20th floor of a Manhattan skyscraper under construction, overseeing the process with principal architect Geoffrey, who's sweet on her. Suddenly a crane support gives, causing a steelworker to slip and fall onto the edge of a scaffold. To the surprise of everyone, including Geoffrey, Dylan bolts into action, grabbing a rope, tying herself off, and gingerly but nimbly walking across the scaffold to loop a jury-rigged rescue harness around the steelworker, lifting the man to safety with the help of the other men. As everyone applauds, Dylan's cell receives a text from her brother, Blake: "10 Sleep, back Monday @ 4," with a link to a map of the region. Cut to Blake packing his climbing gear in Boulder, CO, three framed photos atop his dresser: Blake on Everest with his father and Yeshe, his father's Sherpa friend; Blake climbing with his father and sister; Blake with his climbing partner and coworker-engineer, Rad. An oddly shaped rock sits on the dresser alongside the photos. Rad's SUV pulls up next to Blake's apartment, and Blake joins three other climbers: Bobbie, a Native American climatologist; AJ, a veterinarian and Bobbie's lesbian lover; and Angel, an Iraq war vet. The five zoom off to Ten Sleep, Wyoming, where four more friends have already set up camp: Zeb, a carpenter; Maggie, his partner, a visual artist and newbie climber; Tia, who works in a music shop; and F-Hole, a musician (real name Francis), who has a thing for Tina, and who's brought along his dog, Grody. The plan is to head for Cloud Peak first thing in the morning, where Blake wants to climb the east face. Two nights later, Dylan is in her apartment in the middle of an advanced yoga pose when her cell rings. "Dylan, we've got a problem." "Conrad—what's happened?" The following morning finds Yeshe, hanging on a harness and rigging lights at a large indoor sports arena. His cell goes off, and he answers midair. The next thing we know he's sitting next to Dylan on a jet, headed to Colorado, where Blake has gone missing. Dylan and Yeshe stop first at Blake's apartment. Dylan notices the odd looking rock and takes it with her as they leave. When they arrive at Ten Sleep they meet with the search and rescue people—no Blake, and a massive storm is moving in. We learn that Dylan stopped climbing years prior, when her father was killed in a climb in Tibet with Yeshe. She's lost faith, and in particular, faith in the spiritual renewal she once experienced from climbing. But like her father and Yeshe, she still believes that the mountains haven't been put there for our recreational purposes—that climbers are supposed to measure themselves against the mountains, and not expect the mountains to conform to their abilities. This puts her at odds with Rad, who in her view has always been too competitive and not mindful of his surroundings. At the same time, Rad correctly observes that Dylan has herself sold out to the corporate-urban boom. Dylan leads a search and rescue party, with the climbers battling the elements to reach Cloud Peak, and discovering bodies buried in the rapidly receding Cloud Peak Glacier. As climbing conditions grow increasingly treacherous, it becomes clear that something supernatural is afoot. Bobbie's and Angel's deaths bring the revelation that the rock on Blake's dresser, which was given to Blake by Rad as a good luck charm, is a rock fragment that Rad had stolen from the Bighorn Medicine Wheel to the north. The denouement involves Rad redeeming himself by returning the rock to the Medicine

Wheel, and being consumed by spirits in the process. When Dylan and Yeshe make it back to Ten Sleep, they find Blake alive and well, as if nothing had happened, and Dylan regains her sense of spiritual centeredness in the wild.

*

Sylvia: "Too costly and too complicated." And here he was, hoping to avail himself of that classic climbing tale with its built-in uphill-downhill, rising-falling narrative. He figured that tossing in a supernatural element would make for some great reversals, perhaps even a veiled social allegory thenceforth to be dubbed the Anthropo-Scene–

Oh please. And Indian Country would have a field day with this one.

There was a lesson here too, he thought, for Georg (height unknown) Lukács, whose penchant for social realism now seemed to him, lo these many years since his grad school days—Samuel Taylor hit the brakes hard as a

RUMPLESTILTSKIN MOTHERFUCKER!

darted out in front of him from the curb—not a little unrealistic. No particular representational mode should hold sway if art were to be granted license to be art, and no such mode *would* hold sway in light of such successes as George 5' 6" Lucas's 1977 game changer, with notes lifted from the far more austere 5' 11½" Kurosawa and 5' 8½" Kubrick. Which film had furnished once and future viewers with a four-decade-long-and-counting cultural trope for our dire yet durable political-economic landscape.

Him, he preferred *American Graffiti*, but what the hell, Lucas had twice—no, thrice hit a cultural nerve. No mean feat. So Samuel Taylor tried, on this distressingly bright day, to look on the bright side. Then he caught a glimpse of a large billboard advertising Scientology—"Know yourself. Know life." *All men by nature desire to know*, he thought. By what quirky entanglement Aristotle and Obi-Wan had both flitted into view was anyone's guess, but the palm trees he'd been passing suddenly struck him as utterly incongruous, even sinister, in that everyday 5' 7" Hitchcock kind of way. And then he recalled his friend Barry texting him from the Biennale about his namesake, or one of them, Samuel A. Taylor.

What *is* this place, anyhow? He knew only one species was indigenous, but he couldn't identify which one. And he preferred the non-native liquidambars anyway.

For no reason at all he found himself thinking about his final fiction workshop, in which "elven" had appeared in two separate pieces, accompanied in one case by "dwarven," both pieces responded to favorably by eight students, two of whom had remarked as to how "relatable" the pieces were. If going west was not a far, far better thing, it was at least a far, far more enlivening thing. And not because he disliked his students, so many of whom had given him good reason to take Aristotle at his metaphysical word. But these were kids who had been bludgeoned into institutional submission by hard economic times after lives lived, in some cases, spending summers from dusk to dawn detassling pesticide- and herbicide-soaked corn. Some had even been crop-dusted, albeit accidentally, à la Cary 6' 1½" Grant in *North by Northwest*.

They had him on Twitter being chased by an Amazon drone, Samuel Taylor muttered to himself. Then he wondered what he could possibly write that would appeal to an audience hip to such one-offs, trifles, nonessentials. And let's face it: even Cary Grant knew he wasn't Cary Grant. That kind of insight was strictly premillennial.

Even the kids who weren't part of Agee's great unwashed had it pretty tough, the Chicago burbs coughing up their own dead-ended dreams, and many students in his classes, the first in their families to attend college, were working over twenty hours a week. Under the circumstances, it wasn't difficult to understand the appeal of escapist lit, the draw of that occult dimension that seemed of late to permeate the social imaginary, seeping out of every engagement with FB or Reddit or Pinterest or Snapchat or whatthefuckever game interface. What was discouraging was the inability of most of these kids to separate the literary or even ideational wheat from the chaff.

Kids, sure. Of course such sober pedagogical considerations had never stopped him from fantasizing about his more attractive female *kids*, and for all he knew his *kids* fantasized about him. A student body comprised student *bodies*, finally. Early in his career, as a young-ish single prof, he'd slept with any number of students, including on several occasions the odd student enrolled in his class. However frowned upon by the administration, to act on the erotic charge that often underwrites student-teacher differences in disciplinary knowledge and institutional rank seemed at the time a natural enough matter. As the years passed, such "matters" became a matter of what he regarded, despite his progressive convictions, as draconian institutional interdiction. On the one hand, he believed, students—at least those 21 and older—must be permitted, as adults, the full compass of adult activity; on the other, they must be protected from predators, or as some would have it, campus rape culture. Not an especially wieldy stance. And campus rape culture, which in his experience would be better termed frat rape culture, was hardly limited to campuses, or to frats, and sex with students, which had in his case developed into short-term romances, had always been, to his way of thinking and whatever the differences in age and rank, fully consensual, never mind that in two instances the romance had ended poorly and resulted in sexual harassment allegations.

Well. He'd been something of a dog and he knew it. And he knew too there was a very real problem with sexual violence and sexual harassment, and *something* had to be done about it.

As he became part of the greying professoriate, the aforementioned erotic charge, while not altogether absent, cast him in a more paternal if not parental light. He still had his masturbatory fantasies, and for all he knew his students still had theirs. (This latter thought in fact aided and abetted *his* fantasies.) But he had been a devoted husband, and student fantasies, while he was married, had been relegated to just that. It was only after Nora died that his fantasies—or more precisely, *acting* on his fantasies—had started to strike him as somehow untoward. He found he really didn't mind playing the paternal and even parental role, given that he was now older than most of his students' parents. And though he wasn't entirely decrepit, he took little pleasure in any case in imagining himself cast as some paternal object of desire in an yet another Electra drama.

There was a far less genteel way to express all of this, rooted in Samuel Taylor's far less genteel past, where *poontang* was as likely to elicit a mischievous smile from a female as a male intimate. But in the academic circles in which he grew accustomed to moving later in life, such language was verboten, and verboten or not likely to be misheard by novitiates as *poutine* or possibly *putain* or in rare and insufferably scholastic cases *Pétain*.

And then too there was Kass, from whom the word would elicit a mischievous smile.

No point in denying it: Samuel Taylor's move to LA had, all told, served as a tonic, whatever the stresses and strains associated with the only place where, as Kael had quipped, you could die of encouragement, and he'd long since stopped fretting over his dangerous liaisons. Of course every now and then a starlet serving him coffee at his favorite breakfast joint, pearly whites gleaming as she did her best to make an impression knowing full well that he knew people, as it were, in central casting, triggered something in him, but under the circumstances he couldn't say for sure what exactly it was. He'd left behind the neoliberal precarity of academe only to confront the libidinal hilarity of late-middle age.

And then too there was Kass, from whom the sentence prior would elicit a mischievous smile.

Red light. Full stop. Colorful Angelyne (height unknown) billboard dead ahead, alongside her neon Vette. She was three years his junior. He knew this because he'd once gotten into an argument about her aesthetic merits. The other party had been a fan. He wasn't a fan, he wasn't not a fan. But he couldn't help feeling then, as now, that whatever the aesthetic merits of Angelyne, it was small beer in the world in which he'd once imagined himself a known, if lesser-known, quantity, no matter how many laid eyes every day on Angelyne and her Vette, Chili Palmer included.

And perhaps because of this cheap shot at poor Angelyne, for a moment he felt even smaller than he had immediately after Sylvia's phone call, smaller even that Hume 5' 6" Cronyn near the end of *People Will Talk*, his dark night of the 5' 4" Scorsesean soul about to descend upon him right there in the driver's seat midday, in ur-la-la land, within sight of the mighty Pacific, site of Norman Maine's—James "George Clooney's height" Mason's—watery, self-inflicted demise. Fortunately the moment lasted for the mere fifteen seconds it took for the light to turn green.

Spike 5' 5" Lee. Roman 5' 5" Polanski. Kevin 5' 5" Pollak. Mickey Rooney, 5' 2". Andy Hardy was taller than The First Lady of MGM. Interesting. And a full foot shorter than Michael Caine, which contrast was played to the hilt in *Pulp*.

And Andy's sometime date, Judy Garland, the winner at 4' 11½"? Garland's husband Vincente Minnelli towered over her at 5' 9", daughter Liza stooped to kiss Mom at 5' 4".

But Garland was out of the running if "Cartoon Queen" June 4' 11" Foray had anything to say about it, or Dolly 4' 11" Parton. Though Peter Dinklage at 4' 5" suddenly didn't seem all that short. Billy Curtis was 4' 2", and the last surviving member of "The Lollipop Guild," Jerry Maren, reached a mere 3' 4" at the time of his casting, according to Wiki, though IMDb had him at 4' 3". Did he really grow another 11" after he was nineteen, or was this an error? An inquiring mind wanted to know.

At the other end of the spectrum, André the Giant at 7' even, the winner!

Check that: Shaquille 7' 1" O'Neal. Right?

And in the hoofer department, 5' 9" Astaire and, sans heels, 5' 4½" Rogers. Gene Kelly at 5' 7", Donald O'Connor 5' 7", Leslie Caron 5'

1½", Cyd Charisse 5' 7½", Ann Miller 5' 7", Eleanor Powell 5' 6½", Russ Tamblyn 5' 9", Mikhail Baryshnikov 5' 7, Gregory Hines 6', Bill Robinson (height unknown), The Nicholas Brothers (heights unknown), Sutton Foster 5' 9".

Akim 5' 5" Tamiroff. Brian 5' 8" Donlevy.

Donlevy. Now there was a character on- *and* offscreen. Samuel Taylor just couldn't get enough of Donlevy and Tamiroff together under 6' 0½" Sturges that one time, the year after they both appeared in *Union Pacific*. But why? What brought him back time and again to such celluloid heroes, or antiheroes? Whence his unabated pleasure? Was he viewing through his eyes alone or was he imagining that his 5' 8" father, gone for so many years now, had a fondness for such long-dead displays of unbridled masculinity? Did he harbor such fondness himself? Or was it just a good story with the right cast to pull it off, a cast that actually enjoyed working together under a director whose script would win the first Oscar for Writing Original Screenplay? He recalled that his 5' 4" mother, gone for so many years now, also enjoyed the film. And let's not forget William 5' 9½" Demarest.

Maybe this was why Demarest was a favorite. As for Mom and Dad, *may the force be with you.*

Whatever this place was, the stuff of server farms and cloudless clouds, like the very smoke and mirror artifacts that had been transmogrified into such stuff, seemed destined to saturate the air, dreamed up as if with ageless Angelenos in mind to hold snug against the receding shoreline. Were the region's tremors releasing paranormal vapors from some chthonic cache? Or were they instead emanating from some distant eastern horizon, crossing Mojave-qua-Sahara desert and High Sierra alike to circulate among the countless susceptible aspirants? Or perhaps they wafted in ineffably off the ocean, out of the cradle, endlessly rocking?

And what would the residents of South Central LA make of all this?

Was the ocean blue like the sky or was it green like the synthetic lawn lining the entranceway to the small bungalow in front of which he'd just parked his shiny new 16' 4 4/5" 6768 lb. Range Rover? And what kind of Amazon rankings might he reasonably expect?

EPISODE 2, SEASON 2

Season 1, all twelve episodes, had been released at once to allow for the then newly fashionable practice of bingeing. Everyone loved it, even acerbic Anthony Lane, who made acerbic mention of it as TV's revenge on *Network*.

But in the middle of writing season 2, episode 2, the episode itself about writing episode 2, concerns were raised by several of the writers that the Samuel Taylor protagonist had begun to go the way of Howard Beale. Upon reflection and while sipping a warm Sambuca *con la mosca* served to him by a twenty-two-year-old PR major with one of the cutest derrières he'd ever eyeballed—he had taken of late to appeasing certain of his more thin-skinned acquaintances in the hopes that they might smile favorably enough upon his work to encourage their teenagers to read it, hence the euphemism—Samuel Taylor felt this recent setback might have been a reflection of the writers' waning enthusiasm for their exhaustingly ambitious and infuriatingly reflexive lead.

So later the next morning, after the PR major left Samuel Taylor's apartment in a rush, late for her classes after having spent a few extra minutes, after some last-minute entreaties on her part, face down on his sofa with her skirt hitched up to her waist, her panties stuffed hastily into her purse—this certainly would pass both YA and *Shades of Grey* muster, he thought—Samuel Taylor suggested to the room that perhaps they should bring things to a blessed end, gradually fusing the darker threads of his narrative to treat viewers to one of those brooding denouements that could be read as both brooding and savagely ironic, which is to say, comic. They needed a body, and since his was the only body in sight, they didn't have many alternatives. Indeed, they appeared to have no alternatives at all. He, or his persona, must die. The problem though was that this was precisely Beale's fate, and while nobody in the room was averse to paying homage to Chayefsky, there was unanimous agreement that following a critic's public lead, especially a critic as excoriating as Lane, was positively verboten.

But they killed him off anyway and

and a voice as if from offstage…which in the heyday of postmodernism might have prompted its author to resort to screenplay format
. . . a voice (O.S.) as if from the future, or perhaps Rome ca. 40 BCE,
or perhaps John Facenda—no, it was a living voice, neither identifiably
male nor female—was heard to say,

"No."

And that changed everything, even the alleged entreaties by the PR
major who, face down on Samuel Taylor's sofa and—we neglected to
say—sucking hard on his thumb, with her panties stuffed hastily into
her purse, had grunted several times as he climaxed. Nat King Cole's
version of "(I Love You) For Sentimental Reasons" had been playing on
Samuel Taylor's iPad during this brief but graphic bit of sodomy, after
which, this by consensus, an extradiegetic score, cello only, would follow
the PR major to the door. (Exit on a diminished 7th in C, as expected.)

If we were to understand the voice, neither identifiably male nor
female, what gave offense, finally, was hardly the lack of affirmative
consent—the PR major's entreaties, of the "You're going to make me,
aren't you?" variety, having been strongly reminiscent of Madeleine (5'
8") Stowe's appeals in *The Two Jakes*; or the sardonic choice of soundtrack;
or the—depending on one's druthers—coarse "I don't fuck what I
don't eat" repartee. It wasn't the sex, or porn, or porn-sex—the explicit
sexism per se—that gave offense. It had more to do, evidently, with the
stultifyingly commonplace gendering of such sexual escapades by (in this
case a roomful of) male writers who were—here the tenor was nothing
short of adamantine—*the rapaciously white intellect masking its racism
and sexism behind the façade of unimpeachably male narration*. It was
the conceit that gave offense, in short (and as many a publisher would
later observe in rejecting the manuscript), a conceit that animated the
image, the scene, the situation, the concept. (Samuel Taylor could not
help but imagine how particularly inept and insipid the voice would
find multiple compositional alter-egos.) Things might appear especially
incendiary, both to more race-challenged viewers and to those aware
of that historical precedent whereby the appearance of a black figure
signals some illicit sexual transaction, were further specifics of the tryst

to see the light of public day, to wit: that Samuel Taylor was an older (for our present purposes) white man of, he would say, fair complexion and irredeemably straight hair, his family of European peasant stock not long off the boat, and that the PR major was (for our present purposes) a woman of mixed Filipino and African-American heritage and, as she liked to say, of pecan complexion, twists hanging off to one side, her US ancestry extending all the way back to the antebellum South. And such viewers would probably be that much more incensed to learn that, the night the PR major arrived, she and Samuel Taylor had stripped off each other's clothes and frantically maneuvered into the sideways 69 position, during which initial engagement she had inserted her middle finger into his anus to massage his prostate while conducting an irresistibly (to him of course) wet fellatio, one that included the stroking of his testicles with her tongue and which culminated in his first orgasm in a year, but not before she had herself climaxed as he rhythmically licked, nibbled, and then sucked the lowest extremity of her estimably distended clitoris.

Her name was Marty.

No—that's not right. Marty was a trans woman of color and a long-time acquaintance of Samuel Taylor's whom he'd met at the pharmacy of the local drugstore. The PR major was a white woman. And she was a returning student, in her early thirties, which put her at approximately two, not three, decades younger than Samuel Taylor. And they never had sex—to use an outworn language, they were just sweet on each other. <Insert meet cute> <Insert "turnt," somewhere, if book is published by 2020.—JA>

Or maybe she was a he—yes, that's it—in which case please to reconceive the anatomical mechanics, power dynamics, and probable impossibilities of the foregoing. Toss in the fact that California sunshine was involved, a realization prompted by spontaneous typographical flashback to an Esalen lecture he'd heard decades prior, albeit during that flashback, he was no longer a he, shaved her legs, etc.

Wait. That spontaneous typographical flashback was in reality merely a memory blip in the wake of an unfortunate encounter with BDSM-inspired deferral. Which is to say, in the way of reading a novel rife with BDSM overtures. The Esalen lecture was lifted from a paper by a former grad student, Luke something. He wondered what the fuck ever happened to Luke something...

And it must be resolutely observed, in any case, that it was Samuel Taylor who was wearing the panties. And that whenever he wore panties, he felt a twinge of phantom pain in the missing toe on his left foot, the little piggy that stayed home.

A man older than Samuel Taylor might be forgiven for thinking that if you're going to get screwed at your job, you might as well get screwed. A man younger than Samuel Taylor might be forgiven for thinking that such thoughts are unforgivable. Let's split the difference and admit that there are some holes [ahem] out of which it is difficult to dig oneself. *Dig?* This might be as *conceptual* as Samuel Taylor can get about race and sex and the rest.

Nonetheless one—she, he, they—felt obliged to observe that, notwithstanding the voice, Samuel Taylor was his own man. And notwithstanding the voice, the PR major, like Marty, was her own woman. Or man. Or maybe cis male? And notwithstanding the voice, authorial motivation would be sussed only by a complex reckoning, which would ultimately have to contend with Samuel Taylor's ludic if inflammatory antics, including his soft (sweet?) spot for Bavarian creams, and similar such grace notes. And notwithstanding the voice, why should *any* of this be deemed illicit? Unless someone was drunk...

Were you? Was he? Is he?

Am I?

Still, regarding that words, *antics*: perhaps it's time to strive for some emotional clarity. We seem to have lost the stimulus behind the perseveration. This is not, after all, a funhouse.

You're probably suffering. Not hungry—for hunger there are better narratives to redress the ancient need for bread, if narratives are to have anything to do with it—but suffering. Perhaps you're simply aging, and the effects of age have become more and more apparent in recent years. Perhaps you have a serious health issue, or someone close to you has, so serious as to provoke contemplation of death and its consequences for loved ones. Perhaps you've lost a loved one recently—a friend, a parent, a sibling, a spouse, or perhaps even a child. Perhaps you're in the midst of a break-up—a divorce or some less formal but equally painful split. Perhaps you're afflicted in ways that are difficult for others to understand—as a caretaker, for instance. Perhaps you're engaged in some profound moral quandary, one that has kept you awake nights. Perhaps the life you thought you would live is not the life you find yourself living, because your skills are, as they say now, fungible, or your wage has stagnated, or your house has been repossessed, or your kids ain't got no shoes, or because something inside you is broken as a result of abuse or hatred or discrimination or oppression or the struggle most of us are engaged in just to get ahead a little, just to let the world come at us for a change instead of having to chase after it, just to find some modicum of sanity or meaning or care, and you just can't take it anymore. Even if your losses are of the more quotidian variety, you may well be wondering how reading such accounts as the one offered herein will help to assuage same.

And the answer is that, with all due respect for your suffering, for all suffering, of all life forms, you are not reading scripture, this is not a self-help manual, and whatever solace you seek hereabouts will likely emerge solely from experiencing expressive possibility as a possible path to social intimacy, recognizing in some potentially alienating encounter, rendered in words, a glimmer of what it's meant for you, and means for you, to be alive in, and alive to, this earthly habitat. And in this transaction, nobody—*and that includes*, he speculated, *mon semblable*—can own anybody else's pain, trauma, or for that matter, joy.

Speaking of which, when did it stop being enough just to want to get laid? Depending on what one meant, or means, by "laid"? *I confess,* he confesses, *sometimes I wish I were Bond, James Bond—the one who put the hurt on Johnny Stomp.*

Oh Christ.

Come to think of it, Christ was flogged. It all seems, suddenly, and regardless of one's preferred toys, merely an invidious jumble of pronouns and verbs. As one scop had put it, "desire without an object of desire." Or as another scop put it, *Whatevs.*

Though it must be said that if literature can't help heal, what can? If the old masters were wrong about suffering—and it must be said that the old masters, afflatus notwithstanding, might not have been attuned sufficiently to the suffering of women—what hope is there for us, when whosoever wishes will search and archive and hold at arm's length our every mood, as if to bring home that each of us, big shot or no, is but the Dane's quintessence of dust?

Hi everyone! It's me, the author… Don't you think a free indirect bomb should go off right about now? Maybe fifteen seconds of Irwin Allen-rock-and-roll? Or half a cup of We Are Happy To Serve You? How about a few bars of Muzzy Marcellino? Are we trending? What about our assets? The national debt? Rabbits' feet? A critique of exploitation via self-exploitation? Damsel in distress? Is there an algorithm behind this?— and do you think the Kuleshov effect is relevant? (FWIW, I've used the literary equivalent of motion interpolation only sparingly, and cut for performance.) Is this how the author inveigles his way into the reader's heart? I bet you're wondering if I storyboarded this thing. PM me, AMA, or . . .

All of which is to say that, voice or no voice, season 2 was in big trouble. And that a YA readership, with or without trigger warnings, was probably out of the question.

FADE TO SEPIA

EPISODE 3

As they hiked together uphill over a particularly rough stretch of talus, he realized he was back at square one, and as the reality set in, those self-imposed constraints that had for some years served as a means of giving shape to his everyday practice began to seem not only arbitrary, but insufficiently motivated. His mind was changing, and as the two advanced gingerly and incrementally up the trail, he grew gradually more convinced that this change could have a profound effect on his sense of proportion, of relation, of beauty. There were some constraints from which no creature on Earth could hope to escape, he thought, no matter the mind's levity, to which fact their laboring bodies, casting their long morning shadows, bore ample witness. Was artifice really to be drawn from such a fundamentally different well?

His boot caught the tip of a stone and he stumbled forward, catching himself.

"Pay attention dummy."
"Right."

His moiling body, too full of its own gravitas: for a moment he fancied himself instead a free and mobile body, acted upon only by outside forces beyond his ken. A free body, acted upon by outside forces.

A free body. Over the prior few weeks a new project had punctuated his more contemplative moments, and it now began to punctuate his forward motion. His writing would come to him initially as a constellation of more and less articulable concerns, concerns that would need to be explored and shaped into some identifiable symbolic pattern, much as if he were assembling a jigsaw puzzle, though what he saw in his puzzles puzzled his readers. The new project was a nostalgia piece, embellished snippets from his past and plainly fictive fragments to be assembled into some splotchy mosaic. He was intent, as are most memoirists worth their salt, on finding his Boswell in himself, but at the same time he was drawn to self-cannibalizing in the belief it would yield, with the proper crucible, potentially novel departures from actual experience. And so he had settled on his nostalgic opening: *That cold winter evening, so long ago.* Puzzle, mosaic, text: he always required what he thought of as a way in, and this was to be his way in.

*

That cold winter evening, so long ago.

Moving upward still, this time each step calculated to catch an iceless patch of concrete. His breathing was measured as he climbed, the air too frigid to gulp down. His backpack hung from his right shoulder, and inside, his movements joggled a single textbook, a spiral-bound notebook, log and trig tables, a small slide rule he rarely used, two blue-ink Bics with well-chewed caps, an automatic pencil, a tube of spare leads, an eraser, and a green pack of Wrigley's Doublemint, iconic even then, with three sticks remaining.

As he reached the top of the stairs, he noticed that the moon was out, and full, or close to it. He had to be back at the bottom of the stairs in ninety minutes for his ride home. The stairs sat on the westernmost edge of the campus, which campus sat on a hill overlooking the city. Here the rise was particularly abrupt, hence the stairs. Archbold loomed to his south. He'd yet to set foot in it.

He hurried toward the auditorium, passing several huddled figures equally intent on their destinations. He didn't know quite what to expect. This would be his first major exam as a newly-minted college student. He'd gone to every lecture, held in a large auditorium that seated perhaps 250. The lecturer, a senior prof in the Physics Department, Professor G————, merely repeated what was printed in the textbook, and there was audible discontent among his peers at the end of every class session. For him the difficulty had proved to be not the mathematics, but the various applications of same, physics at this level nothing if not application. And one of the applications that had cropped up regularly had been sailing.

Vick Jr. had zero feel for sailing, having never himself sailed and having never been interested in sailing, never mind that sailing, to judge by the fact that he'd never met anyone who had sailed, was as exotic in his circles as study abroad. The only perennial reference to sailing in his home life had been Popeye—the Sailor—which cartoons he sometimes watched with his father, who himself had suffered notoriously from seasickness during *his* two shifts of seven-eight days abroad, to and from England during the war. Years later he'd find himself drifting away to Little River Band's "Cool Change"; he'd befriend a marine biologist who'd write a memoir about his *watery self*; and he'd marry someone as wedded to things aquatic as her father had been to the Navy, someone who'd teach him, at long last, how to be comfortable in the deep end, over his head.

For the present the only hope in sight had been the weekly recitation sections, where a brilliantly able graduate assistant, Dan Knight, had taken it upon himself to rectify the professor's shortcomings. Knight could break down an elementary concept like tension into its elemental molecular forces, which Vick Jr. could not at the time know would, years later, help clarify for him why tuning a shorter guitar string to a specific pitch requires a little less tension, and results in a slinkier feel, than tuning a longer string. Whereas, in contrast, the free body diagrams of Vick Jr.'s statics and dynamics course, for instance—another thorn in his side—always left him wanting to know more about how to reconcile external with internal forces and energies. Even assuming, say, the primacy of the conservation of momentum, there were assumptions at work as to what it meant to bracket certain physical actions and reactions, and in many of the classes that would comprise Vick Jr.'s course of study, from deformable bodies to thermodynamics, there would lurk a host of obscure axiomatic conditions dictating what was meant by a *system,* so defined, which conditions would take him years to fully grasp, and later, to forget. In the midst of which general confusion Knight's discerning intellect, combined with his sympathetic classroom presence, was such that everyone in Vick Jr.'s recitation section felt at least prepared to give it the old college try.

This would be the first of four such exams.

He found the assigned building and hastened inside. His glasses fogged immediately, and he stopped and took them off—his vision too poor to proceed without them—leaning against the wall and using the hanky in the back pocket of his jeans to wipe them off. It was primarily for this reason that he carried a hanky, and had been carrying a hanky for most of his life, and would continue to carry a hanky as a senior. Now, his young face gradually thawed, and he started off again, his glasses still fogging a bit. Turning a corner he entered a plush auditorium, with cushy seats and flip-up desktops. The room was already well populated by, he assumed, those students who lived on campus, all of whom knew well enough to leave at least one seat on either side of him or, in a half-dozen cases, her.

He spotted three empty chairs at the end of one row, and headed for the seat in the middle, guaranteeing him nobody to his left. He placed his backpack in the aisle seat and removed his coat, draping it over the seat. Then he picked up his backpack and placed his coat where his backpack had been, seating himself while opening the pack to withdraw the automatic pencil and eraser. He glanced shyly at the pretty-ish student two seats to his right, their eyes meeting for a moment before she looked away. He settled into his seat, looked around the room. Quiet prevailed—an anticipatory quiet. He tried not to tense up.

But let us be clear: he was tense. And there were good reasons for him to be tense. Here he was, after all, a townie-gownie-among-gownies on this nut-frosting night, seated among his would-be peers, so many of whom had headed north from one or another Big Apple borough to frolic away their undergrad years in their Upstate dorms, hence were in an important sense not his peers. Here he was in the midst of his first major college exam, itself having all the makings of a first salvo to ascertain if he could hold up under pressure, hence was indeed college material. And here he knew that Professor G———— of the Physics Department was a silly enough silver-spoon-up-his-ass twit to imagine that sailing, *sailing* for Christsakes, could furnish a habitus-neutral example to help elucidate, via testing, the subtle mysteries of applied math for all students, both have-saileds like Professor G———— and have-not-saileds like Vick Jr. Put simply, there was no telling what surprises lay in store. And whatever surprises lay in the store, this would be a test not simply of native smarts but of social being.

And let us be clear: *habitus* was not yet a part of Vick Jr.'s lexicon, which was itself yet another indication of Vick Jr.'s habitus. Such are the perils of writing about the past.

Several minutes passed before Knight and two other graduate assistants entered the room to administer the exam, each carrying an armful of blue books, mimeo'd test questions inserted in each. Professor G———— was nowhere in sight. It was 6:50 pm. Knight appeared to be in charge. The three took a seat at the front of the room and waited. At 6:55 pm, Knight and the two other grad assistants distributed the blue books.

"Please keep the exam materials face down. Do not start working until we tell you to."

Knight's delivery was firm but his tone was almost conciliatory. He knew that Professor G———— was a terrible instructor, and his students knew that he knew without him saying as much.

The pretty-ish student seated to Vick Jr.'s right passed copies to him, and he rose out of his seat to reach for them, mumbling a barely audible "thanks" as he did so. He passed his remaining copies to the grad assistant who was walking the aisle to collect extras.

The exam was to last one hour. It was now 6:58 pm. Several students rushed into the room late, making something of a racket as they located an open seat, the graduate assistants presenting each with blue books and test questions. Thirty seconds later an older, bearded, black male student wearing an Army fatigue jacket waltzed into the room at a leisurely pace. When a grad assistant presented the student with a copy of the test materials, Vick Jr. imagined that the transaction had been conducted with a certain level of deference, the assistant offering the materials to the student as if for inspection. Vick Jr. was put off by this, but then maybe the student's air of indifference meant simply that he knew what he was about, both as a student of physics and in the larger scheme of things. It was after all the fall of 1972. One minute before the top of the hour, Knight rose from his seat.

"Before we begin, please remember that you must show all your work. This is essential. *Show all your work.* If you require additional blue books, please just raise your hand and we'll get them to you as quickly as we can. I will record the time remaining on the chalkboard behind me in fifteen-minute intervals. Are there any questions?"

Silence.

"Very well then. You may begin."

The rustling of paper. Vick Jr. could almost hear his heart pounding.

*

Periodic splotches of Indian Paintbrush and a bright yellow flower neither recognized intensified the browns, greens, and greys. It was early summer, the trail still damp in spots, the dust minimal. The two hiked steadily for half an hour, the lodgepole pines thinning, before a clearing in the trees appeared above them and to their right.

"There it is."
"Yep. Maybe two more switchbacks?"
"More like six. Pace yourself."
"I just hope we don't run into another Boulder bobblehead."

"She wasn't that bad."

"Wasn't that bad? You meet a stranger on a trail and the first words out of her mouth are whether you want to sign a petition to get End of Life Options on the ballot? And not a hint of irony. Fuck that shit."

"Let's try to enjoy ourselves, shall we?"

They advanced, slowly, resting for several seconds at the end of each turn in the trail. Eight switchbacks later they reached the first of the false summits, pines giving way to outcroppings of juniper.

"Getting near the timberline, looks like."

"Yeah. Didn't you read the topos?"

"I rely on you for that, honey."

"And what if something happened to me?"

"I'm good in the clutch."

"Uh-huh."

They found a series of flat-faced rocks with a view of the lake below, not far from where they'd parked their car. They pulled off their packs, took out their water bottles and two peanut butter sandwiches, and made themselves comfortable.

"Is this the chunky?"

"Read the label on it. Does it say chunky?"

"Oh."

"'Godsakes. Do you want me to wipe your ass for you?"

"Only when I'm old and grey and full of sleep."

"Jerk."

It was 9:30 am and the sun was beginning to warm things up. They'd lost maybe six degrees with the elevation gain and stood to lose another nine anyway before they summited. It wasn't an especially difficult hike, but they were after all only hiking enthusiasts, not members of that hardcore crowd that rather annoyingly ran such trails on a weekly basis in running tights and without as much as a bottle of water on hand, eyes fixed sternly on their feet and inattentive to such niceties as what the pair would later learn was Old Man of the Mountain; and even more annoyingly, performing Downward-Facing Dog for thirty or forty seconds at the base of summits prior to their run back to the trailhead.

The summit would take at least an hour longer to reach than it had taken the pair to make it from the trailhead to the first false summit. The distances were nearly equal but the trail ahead was much steeper, rising nearly 3000 feet over two miles. No trees from here on out. No trees.

"I've been thinking."
"Stop the presses."
"Shut up honey."
"Sorry. Thinking about what?"
"How there are fewer and fewer places to hide."
"Hide from what?"
"The world."
"Too much with us, is it?"
"Getting to the point —"
"That was funny, c'mon."
"Getting to the point where nothing we do isn't tracked. Used to think cars at least were a sanctuary."
"For getting laid you mean?"
"I mean, you're listening to the radio, and some tune comes on, and you think you're having some private epiphany —"
"Aren't they all private?"
"Some epiphany, OK? And then you realize it's satellite radio, so anyone could track your signal."
"But your iPhone—the one in our pack, mine too—gives our location to anyone who cares to locate us. We're giving up privacy for security. It's an old story."
"Not so old when it's everything we do and we didn't ask for it—"
"Though we 'agreed' to all sorts of software and user stipulations the moment we turned our phones on."

"Did you read the fine print? Do you understand what you're signing, really? Does anybody?"

"True enough. So what's your point?"

"So we start to internalize. I mean, you used to be able to get into your car, roll up your windows, and scream your guts out without worrying about anyone hearing you."

"You still can."

"Yeah, but you might not because you start to realize that your car really isn't a safe space. It's a connected space, a mapped space, a monitored space —"

"I get it."

"Right. And after a while the awareness that this is the case becomes a sensibility. A way to think, behave. And so nobody screams in their cars anymore."

"A great loss to civilization, I'm sure."

"And you know, I think deep down inside, aging boomers realize this. I think that's why so many of us feel we were born too late. We're not some lost generation with our heads in the clouds."

"Do have a look around, dear."

"Smartass. Listen, I'm saying that even if a lot of us ended up finding pretty much what we were looking for, we realized that we gave up something important to get it, something we can't get back. Not our youth, I mean—everyone gives that up, if they're lucky. It's that we—we –

"Just say it."

"Well, we can't get back to the garden. The best we can manage is the pixeled desktop version. And I think this is why so many are so angered to learn that the government has been spying on us, and via that same ersatz mindscape. It's just one more betrayal in the nature of things, one more sign of our precarious hold on the analog world, the world we live in. Gradually the unreal accelerates past the real."

"Unreal? I'll tell you what's unreal. Here we are at, what, 10,000 feet on a beautiful day in early July, and suddenly I find I've been hiking with Edward Snowden. Hock me a chynick—you're ruining my Rocky Mountain high."

"I thought you were whiter than god, or John Denver. And y'know, Nora used to say the—sorry."

"It's OK sweetie."

A passenger jet flew over, its fluctuating rumble piercing the sky.

"Must be way up there."

"That's what I'm talking about—you can't get away from it. I bet they even see contrails in the Himalayas."

"I believe flights are routed around them, Mr. Buzzkill. Look—can we please leave the *lacrimae rerum* behind and enjoy the day?"

"I ain't exactly salting the earth with my tears, I'm just inquiring. Besides, this ain't exactly Mount Kailash."

"You know what I mean. Just this once sweetie?"

Something about the way Kass said "just this once" that caught Samuel Taylor's attention.

"Is something wrong?

"No—no, everything's fine."

"You sure? It's not b/c —"

"No. It's just that this is only our second time hiking together, the weather is better than the last time we were in Aspen, and I—I know Nora had a lot more hiking experience than I do, but—I just want this to be —"

"I understand honey. For the record, you're a great trail boss."

Samuel Taylor smiled, reaching out to hold one of Kass's hands in one of his as they sat quietly together. Then they finished their snack, took a last long look at the view, and resumed their ascent, Samuel Taylor trailing behind his new guide, both taking note of the cairns that began to appear at irregular intervals as the terrain became rockier and the trail harder to make out.

EPISODE 4, SEASON 2

(Which was henceforth to be the episode that Samuel Taylor, alone among his confrères, would refer to as *The Episode*. This was around the time he'd taken to describing himself privately as a "lapsed poet looking for a reason to believe in poetry again," or alternately, as a "storyteller trying to rekindle his belief in story." Poet or storyteller, he was wont at the time to hold forth to the effect that reality required "less augmentation, more illumination," his fanciful riffs cropping up irregularly in the midst of scenes, sometimes ending with a *pax vobiscum* centered at the bottom of the page, a curious flourish in that he was hardly a believer and certainly not Catholic. Worth noting too is that *The Episode* was the last episode with which Samuel Taylor would have any direct involvement. What follows is a partial transcript of the writers' collective imagination, tweaked in accordance with the doctrinal logic of the eternal Bavarian cream.)

*

If I am sad can I inspire joy? If I am in turmoil can I bring peace? If I am incomplete can I make whole? If I am poor can I offer wealth? If I am uncharitable can I elicit generosity? If I am unjust can I impart wisdom? If I am suffering can I help heal? If I am without faith can I provoke belief? If I am dying can I give life?

*

If you are savage should I be gentle? If you are undecided should I imagine resolution? If you are despondent should I counsel hope? If you are a stranger should I seek friendship? If your world is empty should I speak of beauty? If you are in love should I turn away?

*

If we had been popular would life have been easier? If we had been luckier would we have been happier? If we had traveled more would we have been worldier? If we had stayed together would we have grown apart?

*

What has been denied has been conceded. What has been harbored has been liberated. What has been relinquished has been attained. What has been destroyed has been rekindled.

*

They were the ones who thought it was more important to agree than to be on the same side. They were the ones who thought it was more important to be right than to be good. They were the ones who thought their penchant for doubt did not itself amount to certainty. They were the ones who thought without thinking that their bellies would be full.

*

There is a spirit. I name it spirit. There is a soul. I name it soul. There is a material world. I name it.

*

(Numbers shield us from conflict. Numbers make it all sound so serious. Can there be a good number? A good number of numbers? Is 10 a good number? No. Is 10 a good number of numbers? No. Is 10 at least a funny number, or number of numbers? No.

(Enough already with the numbers.)

*

*

*

If you are sad can I inspire joy? If I am dying should you give life? If we would be true. If we would be true.

pax vobiscum

EPISODE 5

Samuel Taylor was buzzed into the bungalow by a thirty-ish 5' 4"?
125 lb.? woman with numerous piercings who he always felt bore a
strong resemblance to Rosanna 5' 4½" Arquette in *Pulp Fiction*.

"Hey Shell. What's the word?"
"Franco goes in where the others have been."
"Oh shit."

Shelley ushered Samuel Taylor down a hallway and through a door
leading to the basement, brushing past a handmade plaque of wood-
burned maple that read

DAVY'S LOCKER ROOM
Abandon All Confirmation Bias
& noms-du-cinéma
Ye Who Enter Here

Every time he saw that sign all he could think of was Richard 6'
2" Roundtree emerging from that subway station. Would that he were
Richard 6' 2" Roundtree. If he grew his mustache back…

The two clunked down the steps together, Shelley leading the way, Joe
sensing in the descent, as he always did, an eerie echo of an earlier phase
of his life—*ancient history*, to his way of thinking, a tortured katabasis.
But in truth this was owing merely to the state of the basement area
itself, something of a cluttered, confining cross between a Purple Rain
recording studio—and on odd weekends it doubled as a high-end studio
for many of his friend Davy's musician acquaintances—and a sanctuary
for vagabond gamers. Gaming was not officially part of the business,

but 6' 1" 170 lb.? Cut and 5' 11" 200 lb.? Harper, the other two techs, were known in their idle moments to indulge their mutual passion for roguelike. The dimly-lit space boasted floor-to-ceiling stacks of every imaginable audio-visual-digital device, in every imaginable configuration, with cables rocketing out in all directions—underfoot, overhead, and in some cases suspended in the air via temporary measures linking point alpha to point omega via the shortest route possible—LEDs blinking, routers routing, and servers serving, the hum of white noise emanating throughout a sure sign that massive doses of electromagnetic radiation, mercifully of the non-ionizing variety but still—Joe sided in this case against what the science was saying—potentially hazardous, would saturate all occupants. It must have been some kind of hell to spend an eight-hour day thus entombed, but neither Davy nor his staff seemed to mind, Morlocks to a man, and woman.

Still, the space was not without its few amenities. A half bath had been plumbed in one corner of the basement, and in the corner opposite, a sink sat in the middle of a few feet of Formica countertop supporting a coffeemaker and microwave. Wedged into the cabinet space beneath protruded a small fridge. And in an unusual departure from geek custom, the basement also boasted a small, well-lit room, just visible from the entrance, reserved for printed matter. A solitary armchair sat in the middle, the walls lined with shelves, the shelves stuffed with a selection of Davy's favorite film and art books and trade magazines. Joe had spent random minutes during past visits reading the shelves, and plucking a volume or two to examine its contents. Of the books on film, most of the names on the spines were familiar to him: Bordwell, Bazin, Eisenstein, Cook, Godard, Monaco, de Lauretis, Kael, Clover, Kawin, Balázs, Metz, Truffaut. Titles that could pass for coffee-table books typically occupied his cursory attention: Bayer's *The Great Movies*; Everson's *The Bad Guys*; Blum's companion volumes, *A Pictorial History of the Silent Screen* and *A Pictorial History of the Talkies*; *The BFI Companion to the Western*; Hardy's *The Encyclopedia of Horror*; and Schickel's *The Stars*. Two shelves were jammed tight with books and journals featuring an array of art and music and cultural criticism by such luminaries as Arnheim, Wollheim, Steinberg, Gombrich, Goodman, Kramer, Schapiro, Berger, Greenberg,

Hughes, Elkins, Krauss, Danto, Sontag, Kracauer, Willis, Christgau, Ruskin, Schjeldahl, Winterson, Rosenberg, Jameson, Marcus, Taruskin, Focillon, Wölfflin, Baldwin, and Lippard. A shelf at the bottom was lined with a number of scripts, new and old, each held together with brass fasteners. However stuffed and stuffy, the room seemed an altogether livable space, surrounded by the wilds of technics and metrics. All that was missing to sustain the life of the mind and body was water. You had to walk to the far end of the basement to reach a water cooler.

"Have a seat, I'll go get him."

Joe spotted an old director's chair with "DIRECTOR" spelled out on its ragged canvas back, sat, and waited. Shell's opening salvo, lifted from John 5' 7" Cassavetes, had put him on his guard. War films were likely to be on today's agenda, as they had been for some time now. Joe liked war films well enough, but 5' 7"? 180 lb.? Davy had a habit of repeating himself. And you never knew whether he was going to talk to you or at you. He could establish connections and relations among anything and everything, which could have the effect, if you weren't listening carefully, of turning everything into anything. What this meant is that it could be a while before they'd get around to the reason for 150 lb. (as of this very morning) Joe's visit. But he didn't have to wait long before his stout friend emerged from some obscure gap between the mountains of equipment.

"I have a hankering for a film where Ol' Blue Eyes has a hankering for an Italian babe."

He was smiling and winking all at once. So 5' 7", thought Joe, has a hankering for 5' 5". It took him a few seconds to work it out. Talky action film, good cast. Near the beginning, Ol' Blue Eyes threatens to smash a bottle across the resilient mug of Charles 5' 8½" Bronson, El Brute, who's playing a Navajo code talker who doesn't like "gooks." Also starring Steve 5' 9½" McQueen, The King of Cool, and released a year after *The Blob*. McQueen was another favorite, ergo QED: yes, Joe had a thing for men his own height. Maybe it made him feel, in an upwardly mobile culture, just tall enough.

"You can stream it, I think. Illegal but safe."
"How's the weather out? Sunshine and Santa Claus?"
"It's getting hot."
"I hate this motherfucking chickenshit detail."

Otis 6' 2" Young with Nicholson and Randy 6' 4½" Quaid, Quaid's first film with Nicholson.

"Where do you think that expression comes from?"
"You mean *The Last Detail*?"
"No."
"Oh, you mean *Gypsy*."
"Not that either. 'Never send a boy to do a man's job.'"
"You lost me."
"Nicholson brought to mind Colonel Nicholson. I've been thinking about Hawkins's foot."
"Christ Davy, not Hawkins's foot again."
"But what about the boy-man adage?"
"Early twentieth century I would think."
"Barrymore's [5' 10"] finest hour."

Joe rolled his eyes. Davy had been like this ever since the advent of TCM, soaking up movie trivia since his teen years as if every tomorrow were the last syllable of recorded time. You just had to be patient, wait for him to come around. And Joe was more patient than most, pleased as he was that his friend had finally found his calling, and that his weekly subscription podcast, *Davy's Locker Room*, in which he unearthed odd bits of movie lore, had a following more than sufficient to cut living-wage paychecks to a staff of three. Davy took great pride in reminding everyone that even the late great Robert 6' 1" Osborne— well, one of Robert Osborne's representatives—had once contacted him in pursuit of a pertinent factoid. And Davy had a continuing hand in helping to digitize and to improve access to UCLA's massive Film &

Television Archive. He'd made his bones the hard way, countless hours spent watching and rewatching celluloid in every conceivable format, or ogling the pertinent hard copy library holdings out of which search engines drew their seemingly endless generations of information. Plus he had no fewer than 225 hours of college credits under his belt, mostly literature, art history, and of course film—but with no degree, because he cared not a fig about degrees. And he knew people.

Davy was a walking talking database who hadn't yet turned forty, but then too he was more than a database: from codex to DVD, he had a feel for nuances of word and image, sound and light, as these had been transmitted down through the ages, coupled with a knack for engaging with the new. This combination of insight and openness, as Joe had come to realize over the years, was exceedingly rare. But to the casual acquaintance Davy's critical acumen might go unnoticed, cloaked as it was by his curatorial preoccupation and, sure, his predilection for data mongering, to wit: how many BIG HEAD shots in *Notorious* (this was Hitchcock's preferred term for extreme close-ups, as Joe McElhaney had documented); average box office of films with "adventure" in the title; a list of all remakes boasting at least one actor from a prior remake. And so forth. While Davy was aware that, podcast aside, he'd never entirely escape the limbo of digital drudgery, he was a cineaste at heart. And this is why in fact his data could be so revealing, he and his coworkers having for instance confirmed beyond any reasonable doubt, and against the suspicions of many, that the use of religious terms like *faith, soul, salvation* and the rest appear with equal frequency in the dialogue of conventional Hollywood films regardless of era. Or that the number of scenes in which two or more actors were talking and at least one actor was smoking in films released between 1940 and 1970 was roughly ten percent of the total number of scenes in which two or more actors were talking.

Everyone these days had their film lore and fun facts, the arcana of film production gradually becoming fodder for your favorite pub's trivia contest or your once-in-a-lifetime TCM Classic Cruise once IMDb and Wiki and the rest had entered the [cough] picture. Everyone today knew that Robert Blake's reference to *The Treasure of the Sierra Madre*—a film he had a small role in as a child actor —in two scenes of *In Cold Blood* was mere coincidence and based on Truman Capote having reported that this was Perry Smith's favorite film. Everyone today could find films other than *American Sniper* in which the end credits were run sans sound. (For instance, *The China Syndrome*.) Everyone today had developed their niche of (let us be generous) expertise. Davy was fond of food scenes, and aside from the usual suspects, like Albert 5' 9" Finney's tavern meal in *Tom Jones* and *Babette's Feast* and *Big Night*, he liked to cite Bruce 6' Dern's breakfast scene with Barbara 5' 4½" Harris in *Family Plot* and Armendáriz smashing crabs in *We Were Strangers*. (Joe was fond of Kelly and Grant with burger and drumstick, respectively, in *To Catch a Thief*, and Belafonte and 5' 11" Mostel eating matzo brei together in *The Angel Levine*.) And everyone today had their favorite off-the-beaten-path performances, which in Davy's case included Evelyn 5' 4" Keyes's remarkable turn in *99 River Street*.

Discerning critical judgment was rarer if not exactly rare. Davy argued convincingly, for instance, that the sequence in *The Country Girl*, in which Bing 5' 7" Crosby (his travel buddy Hope at 5' 10") plays a has-been song and dance man, is one of the great musical moments in cinema, in that the crooner's remarkable and seemingly effortless audition performance is met in the film with derision by the producer of the show for which he's auditioning, forcing the viewer to consider what's at stake in performance as such. That Crosby lost the Oscar that year to Marlon 5' 9" Brando for the latter's breakthrough role as Terry Malloy in *On the Waterfront* always bugged Davy, but as he liked to say, if he could live with anyone winning it other than Crosby, it was Brando. And he saw at least a trace of Crosby's audition scene decades later in *Inside Llewyn Davis*, when Oscar 5' 8½" Isaac performs marvelously to a stone-faced F. Murray 5' 10" Abraham.

Many these days could render such appraisals, at any rate. And the esoteric reaches of film scholarship, which Joe felt had bordered at times on haruspicy but to which his friend Davy had always graciously deferred, had in any case uncovered striking formal and cultural resonances to explain movies both as art and as social and institutional artifact. Still, among the data tribes, who but Davy might have ventured, for instance, that the question regarding Joyce and his stream of consciousness technique that stymies pulp Western writer Holly Martins (Joseph 6' 2" Cotten) during his address to the literary society in *The Third Man* is not in fact screenwriter Greene's sly swipe, voiced from the ostensibly lofty but nonetheless corrupt heights of Viennese high culture, at the ugly American infatuated with cowboys and Indians. Yes, Greene disliked modernists such as Woolf and Forster for what he saw as the absence of religious conviction in their work, but he admired Joyce, especially his short stories. And Greene was surely aware that his script owed much to pulp noir. So as Davy saw it, the nod to Joyce served to align, however tenuously, Martins's peregrinations in postwar Vienna, his search for the truth behind his friend Harry Lime (Orson 6' 1½" Welles), with the Dublin wanderings of Joyce's *Ulysses* a quarter-century prior, and in particular, with Stephen Dedalus's quest for a symbolic father figure. Martins, a songbird as opposed to, say, an eagle, after all looks up to Lime, or used to. He regards him much as one might a more worldly, wiser confidant, and during their Ferris wheel tête-à-tête, Lime's brilliantly caustic mind gets the rhetorical better of his naive friend. Martins ultimately has to kill his toxic chum, who in a moment of self-recognition gives him permission to do so, whereas Stephen's sauntering with his surrogate father Leopold Bloom leaves him unrequited, their relationship unresolved. Neither Martins nor Dedalus obtains quite what he is after. A stretch perhaps, and Davy would hardly draw a parallel between Alida 5' 5" Valli and Molly Bloom, but an intriguing one.

And then of course there were the intertextual cinematic echoes, such as Walter 5' 10" Abel expressing to Gregory 6' 3" Peck toward the end of *Mirage*, while peering down through the open window of an office building, a misanthropic sentiment nearly identical to Lime's Ferris wheel spiel sixteen years earlier.

Though four months prior to the release of *The Third Man*, the film *Champion* includes a somewhat similar discussion between Kirk Douglas and Luis van Rooten, who remarks looking out his office window how "people look small down there." Luis van Rooten, born in Mexico City, also known for his remarkable little book of poems, *Mots d'Heures: Gousses, Rames: The D'Antin Manuscript*, a 1967 manuscript purporting to be the work of an unheralded French author, with critical gloss. When read aloud however with a marked French accent, the poems homophonically mimic English nursery rhymes. Which is what they are—English nursery rhymes translated homophonically into nonsense French, *Mots h'Heures: Gousses* yielding for instance "Mother Goose."

(He was 5' 3½".)

And thus went Davy's discourse. If *The African Queen* were distilled into data points, this in itself would hardly explain why assistant director Guy Hamilton's *Goldfinger* was the most iconic, if not the best, Bond film; nor would it explain why cowriter James Agee must have had a blast working with Huston on the script, given that both were hard drinkers like their protagonist Allnut, hence how it seemed somehow fitting that, or so went the story, only Bogey and Huston, who lubricated themselves with whiskey and whiskey alone while in Africa, failed to fall ill from the unfiltered water everyone else was unwittingly drinking, which illness seems to color, in a good way, Hepburn's performance in particular; and such data left unresolved the question of precisely what it was about Jack Cardiff's cinematography or Allan Gray's (Józef Żmigrod's) score that, in addition to the casting, brought this story of an odd couple, as they say, to life. Like everyone else these days, Davy knew the data points, if you will—Cary Grant whistling "Singin' in the Rain" while faking a shower in *North by Northwest*—but he also understood their significance—that bit of diegetic business an obvious wink to the art, not to say artifice, of cinema. Davy understood why it might be easy for novice film initiates to confuse Allen Garfield (from Newark, height unknown) with Val Avery (from Philadelphia, height unknown), Avery a much older man and a more hard-boiled heavy, but Garfield one pushy SOB onscreen too, and both with similar dialects. He saw cinematic ghosts not simply in the leads—Clooney as a somewhat less debonair Grant, as everyone had remarked—but in the character actors. Tom Hanks for Jimmy Stewart, OK. Canadian Michael 5' 9½" Ironside for Canadian

John 6' 1" Ireland, yeah. How about George 6' 4" Kennedy as a gruffer George 6' Tobias? Tom 5' 11" Sizemore for Aldo 6' 0½" Ray? Edward 6' 1" Burns for a far meaner Lawrence 6' 1" Tierney? Kim 5' 7" Basinger for—pace *L.A. Confidential*, not Veronica 4' 1½" Lake, but—Rita 5' 6" Hayworth? An aging Dabney 6' 1" Coleman for an always-already aged Clarence (height unknown) Kolb? Seth 5' 11" Rogen for Elliott 6' 3" Gould, definitely. Davy noticed odd similarities, such as how much Paul Lukas (born in Budapest in 1891) sounded like Bela Lugosi (born nine years prior in a part of Hungary that is now Romania, moved to Budapest in 1911). And wasn't Morgan Freeman the only actor working today whose onscreen gravitas might be a match for Spencer Tracy's?

Davy was aware too of the little miracles the old studio system could cough up courtesy of the remarkable talent they'd cultivated with their carrot-and-stick, money and contract stipulation maneuvers, films like *The Proud Rebel*, where Jerome Moross's score, never mind the leads, lends an air of dignity to Curtiz's oater, despite its echoes of *Shane*. Or an even smaller, more memorable, nearly forgotten film noir, *Woman on the Run*, where more intelligence seeps out in 77 minutes than in many of today's overworked tent-poles. Or *Yellow Sky*, where "Wild Bill" Wellman is given a good cast and the leeway to develop psychological shadings that would surface more fully just two years later in Mann's watershed *Winchester '73* and, several years after that, in Aldrich's *Vera Cruz*, a film Truffaut and Godard viewed as a landmark. (That Saul Bass had coordinated the advertising campaign for the latter surely hadn't hurt its reception.) By this time of course *noir*, inaugurated circa 1940 according to the party line, was in full swing.

But what about Ida 5' 4" Lupino's *Outrage*, which opened the fifties by addressing with insight and empathy the trauma associated with rape, an issue the studio system didn't quite know how to handle even as films as disparate as *Johnny Belinda* in 1948 and *A Streetcar Named Desire* in 1951 and *Man of the West* in 1958 and *Where the Boys Are* in 1960 and *Something Wild* in 1961 attempted to create a dramatic context for same, with mixed results. *All About Eve* was a better film than Lupino's, as was *The Asphalt Jungle*, as was *Sunset Boulevard*, all midcentury milestones.

But Lupino was pushing into uncharted territory even as Robert 6' Newton, bless his heart, enjoyed the role of a lifetime hobbling around with Capt'n Flint on his shoulder. The two movie buffs imagined that Molly (height unknown) Haskell might concur: even decades later, in the wake of depiction after depiction of sexual brutality, from the merely suggestive to the graphic, with the best and the worst of intentions; even after the issue had reached a heightened state of twenty-first-century social awareness, particularly in more democratic regions of the planet; even after all of this, filmmakers often got tripped up on the issue of sexual violence, in part because sexual violence, like violence itself, remained a way to up the dramatic ante, even if one were working, say, in post-horror mode. It remained a draw, that is, whether film or game or literature, just as it remained a stark and disturbing reality, and it remained a draw in part, Davy and Joe conjectured, because both the industry and the public tended to give a pass to male celebs who abused their domestic partners. It remained a draw because the social network hadn't caught up with an obvious truth.

And once race and class intersected with such violence, as in *L.A. Confidential*, things became something of a mess. How best to address this reality, especially when the men running the show, some of them, bore at least a passing resemblance to Harvey Weinstein? Davy and Joe would shrug their shoulders, and sigh, disgusted.

Best portrayal of a Mexican by a non-Mexican actor? Eli 5' 7" Wallach: Jewish, parents from Poland. Or John 5' 10½" Saxon: Italian-American. Or Frank (height unknown) Silvera?

Let's give it to Frank Silvera: born in Kingston, Jamaica, Spanish Jewish father, mixed-race Jamaican mother, and electrocuted at 55 while trying to fix his garbage disposal.

Best portrayal of an Italian by a non-Italian American actor? Too easy. Worst portrayal of a Mexican by a non-Mexican actor? The same guy is in the running, but in a film where his gringo *character* is playing a Mexican, which comes fourteen years after his first onscreen portrayal of a Mexican, the latter a candidate for best portrayal of a Mexican by a non-Mexican. In the later film, Saxon is playing the Mexican villain. The real culprit though might be the film's plotting, what with that somewhat overripe pulque scene.

But you gotta hand it to Brando and to Sacheen Littlefeather in particular.

Burt 6' 1" Lancaster did a pretty good Mexican—Davy's and Joe's shorthand—and Kevin 6' 2" Kline a pretty good Frenchman.

Then there was the long argument about 5' 10" Bogdanovich's claim regarding 1928, Davy taking the pro side and Joe the contra. Both were wide-eyed at Bill Morrison's Dawson City revelations. And neither could quite wrap his head around the fact that *From Here to Eternity* had a running time of only 118 minutes. When Joe insisted, as he managed to do every other time the two saw each other, that a nightmare he'd had about the filming of *Vertigo* had told him everything he needed to know about David 5' 10" Lynch's cinematic ambitions, Davy made the jerk-off gesture, and Joe did his best to feign indignation.

As for comedy, the two men laughed at the same jokes, laughed at the same unintentional jokes, laughed when there was, it seemed, nothing to laugh about. Leslie 6' 1½" Nielsen in *The Poseidon Adventure*, back in his straight-laced days and with that great poker face of his, exclaiming "Oh my god"? They laughed. "Get it?" "Got it." "Good." They laughed. Former sea captain Peck in *The Big Country* as the return-of-the-repressed Ahab he'd portrayed two years earlier? They laughed. That sequence with Gerrit 6' Graham in *Used Cars*? (You know the one.) They laughed. Wes 6' 1" Anderson's gallows humor? They laughed. And the frigid bunless hot dog climax of *The Last Detail*?—they both saw it as at once among the most brutally despairing in all of cinema and as sly allegory of male self-cannibalization. Davy and Joe laughed. Wincingly.

Neither was insensitive, either, to what the old guard regarded as unduly sensitive interpretations of otherwise fine films, like that carefully orchestrated last shot in 5' 8" Wyler's quietly touching *Friendly Persuasion*, where the white Quaker family leaves for church, followed by the black farm hand Enoch (Joel [height unknown] Fluellen), with Samantha the goose (no stats available) in the foreground, downstage, a chain of veritable being that placed black folks at best closer to nature and at worst in some bestial relation to beasts. In fact it was Davy who'd turned Joe on to Mark Cousins's expansive documentary on film, and though they both found it at times perplexingly judgmental in establishing which films were of more or less significance, they also understood the vital work it was doing in recentering cinema as an international pursuit and not simply a product dreamed up under the California sun by inspired Jewish expats and émigrés and inspiring women. But they were both formalists at heart, both taking great pleasure for instance in Joe's observation that shattered glass bookends, and punctuates, the alternately still and explosive narrative of *Bullitt*. Ditto Davy's observation that McQueen's smiling glare just as the Nazis nab him following his motorcycle stunts in *The Great Escape* is right out of the Cagney playbook. And they both knew—whether anyone else knew it was beside the point—that the scenes between Kirk Douglas and Gena 5' 6" Rowlands in *Lonely Are the Brave* are among the greatest examples of acting on film, as good as the scene between Brando and Saint and that white glove in *On the Waterfront*, or between José 5' 10" Ferrer and Ed 6' Wynn in *The Great Man*, or…. And they both agreed that the toughest Oscar decision of all might have taken place at the 23rd Academy Awards Ceremony for Best Actress of 1950, where Judy 5' 8" Holliday got the nod.

Finally, they both had a real aversion to exposition for the sake of exposition, and would by way of example point to Ellen 5' 1" Page's thankless role for the first hour or so of *Inception*. In which regard Joe, the writer, was forced to eek out a sotto voce mea culpa.

Davy did of course have a point about Hawkins's foot. How the action at that point in the film proceeds at an Oedipal pace, limping tensely along until Hawkins has to be carried on a makeshift stretcher to the climactic confrontation at the bridge—that symbol of dialectical fusion, which here requires fission—while illustrating 5' 10" Hawkins's/

Major Warden's (as in warden, no less) stubborn duty-above-all ethos as against Holden's/Shears's (as in severs, no less) putative indifference to anything greater than himself. *Madness*, maybe, but Davy's point, which—as Joe later learned—he'd been obsessing over ever since screening the film a month prior for his little cohort of like-minded film buffs, was that Warden's duty-first sensibility renders him a tragically flawed figure, willing to sacrifice for some greater good what he learns to his dismay will be a little of his own humanity—duty demands killing even your fellow soldiers with mortar fire—while Shears's sacrifice earns him a shot at the Pearly Gates. Assuming, that is, you go in for such things, which Shears of course probably wouldn't.

At any rate Joe always found it immensely satisfying, never mind what Pierre Boulle thought, to watch 5' 10" Guinness/Colonel Nicholson's 600-year "proper bridge" get blown to fucking bits.

Truth be told, while he could hold his own with Davy, Joe always found an encounter down below, *down here*, something of a challenge.

"Fred Astaire was never a ballroom dancer," Davy blurted out apropos of nothing. "I learned that on Johnny Carson. And Charles Foster Kane weighed in at about 350 toward the end. That's too much linguini all right, and a shit-ton of snow globes."

Now they were getting someplace. As for John 2"-shorter-than-his-brother Mitchum's self-deprecatory observation in *Dirty Harry* to the effect that he's too fat to climb the chain-link fence at the stadium in pursuit of the serial killer Scorpio—one of the great screen villains, played by Andrew 5' 11" Robinson—the only connection Joe could make was that final shot of Xanadu's "No Trespassing" sign, a thematic and visual counterpoint to the fiery rosebud image, itself a satisfyingly ambiguous resolution. In any case that was a degree of separation best kept at arm's length.

"So what brings you down our way, Joe?"

PLAN B

THREE SAMPLES

Sample 1

HERBERT AND THE MONKEYS

"Stop me if you've heard this one. It's called "Herbert and the Monkeys.'"

My partner and I are seated at our favorite bar together, ogling the bartender, imagining she's actually interested in us and not in the heavy tips we have a habit of putting down along with our cocktails.

"'Herbert and the Monkeys'? Never heard of it. Go ahead."

"But before I begin, there's something you need to understand."

"What's that?"

"There are more intelligent monkeys than there are monkeys more intelligent than Herbert. Got it?"

"There are more intelligent monkeys than there are monkeys more intelligent than Herbert?"

"That's it."

"Got it."

"OK, so: Herbert walks into a bar and—"

"Wait a minute."

"What is it?"

"Are there monkeys more intelligent than Herbert?"

"There are monkeys more intelligent than Herbert. OK?"

"Yeah, sure. Go ahead."

"OK, so: Herbert walks into a bar and—"

"Wait a minute."

"What is it now?"

"Are the monkeys more intelligent than Herbert intelligent monkeys?"

"The monkeys more intelligent than Herbert are more intelligent monkeys. Now you gonna let me tell the story or what?"

"Go ahead."

"Are you sure?"

"Yeah."

"You absolutely positively sure?"

"Yeah, yeah. Go ahead."

"OK, so: Herbert walks into a bar and—"

"How intelligent is Herbert?"

"What in the living hell is wrong with you?"

"What do you mean? I'd just like to know how intelligent Herbert is—y'know, so I can relate to the story better."

"Relate to the story?"

"Yeah. What's wrong with that? "

I'm looking at the bartender, who's been eavesdropping, which is what bartenders do. She's shaking her head at me, and I'm shaking my head at her.

"Well? What's wrong with that?"

He glances over at the bartender.

"Let me see if I get this straight. You want to know how intelligent Herbert is so that you can relate to the story better?"

"Yeah."

"The story you keep stopping me from telling."

"Yeah."

"I see. Very well then. Herbert is more intelligent than we are. Does that do it for you?"

"Yeah."

"You done interrupting me?"

"Yeah."

"You certain you're done interrupting me?"

"I'm certain."

"You're certain."

"Yeah."

"OK, so: Herbert walks into a bar and—"

"Is Herbert a monkey?"

The bartender bursts out laughing.

"You've got to be shitting me."

"What? It's a reasonable question."

"You have got to be fucking shitting me."

"Did your mama teach you to talk like that?"

"I suggest you keep my mama out of this."

"Fine. Just tell me what's wrong with asking whether Herbert is a monkey."

"The story is called 'Herbert and the Monkeys' to indicate that we have someone named Herbert along with some unidentified number of monkeys. It's not a mystery. It's not a puzzle either. It's a story."

"Well then you should be able to answer my question."

"*You* should be able to answer your question."

"It's your story."

"Now you're putting words in my mouth. I never said it was my story."

"C'mon. It's a story you're telling."

"Boy, you got me there. Yessir, you really got me there. It's a story I'm telling all right, or rather, a story I've been trying to tell for the past five minutes. Five aggravating, frustrating, burning-my-ass minutes."

"Look, is Herbert a monkey or is he not a monkey?"

"Did I not say that Herbert is more intelligent than we are?"

"Yeah, but there are some pretty intelligent monkeys out there."

"Pretty intelligent monkeys?"

"Yeah."

"OK, look: Herbert is not a monkey."

"But does he know he's not a monkey?"

"Is that what you call a bonus question?"

"I'm not sure I follow you."

"Never mind. Yes, of course, Herbert knows he's not a monkey."

"Fine. Now go ahead and tell your story."

"You sure? Because I swear to Christ if you interrupt me again—"

"No, no. Go ahead and tell your story. I won't interrupt you, I promise."

"OK," I say. "OK."

I take a moment, glance over at the bartender again, who's now stopped what she's doing to listen intently.

"So," I say. "Herbert walks into a bar and—"

"Are we monkeys?"

In my peripheral I can see the bartender covering her mouth and doubling over.

"Are you sick or something? Is there something, like, wrong with you, up here?"

I'm tapping my head as I say this.

"I couldn't help myself. I had to ask."

"You had to ask?"

"Yeah."

"Let me ask *you* something. Do you think we're monkeys?"

"Us?"

"Yeah, you and me. Are we monkeys?"

"No, I don't think so."

"You don't think so."

"No. But I mean, like, it's your—you're telling the story."

"What does my telling the story have to do with us being—or not being—monkeys?"

"Changes everything. If you tell me we're monkeys, then I'm going to relate differently to Herbert and the monkeys."

"Relate differently, I see. Based on what I tell you. Just great."

"What?"

"Nothing, nothing. You do realize that the monkeys accompanying Herbert turn out—in the story—not to be allegorical monkeys? That these are actual fucking monkeys we're talking about?"

"No, I didn't know that. How could I, not having heard the story? But it's good to know that up front. "

"Probably best to know such things up front before we get on with the story—any story, right?"

"Yeah, I'd say so."

"I see."

"So—you gonna finish your story, or what?"

"Finish *my* story?"

"Finish the story."

"The story is finished. As in, kaput."

"Kaput?"

"Kaput."

It was at this point that the bartender ambled over.

"Couldn't help but overhear you two," she said.

"I feel sorry for you," I said.

"But—I know a story," she said.

"Do tell," I said.

"Yeah," she said.

"Why don't you tell us your story then?" he said.

She looked at him, then looked at me, then looked back at him.

"OK," she said. "But no interruptions, right?" she said.

"I promise," he said.

"OK," she said. "Stop me if you've heard this one," she said. "A ventriloquist and his dummy walk into a bar and—"

"Now wait just a goddamn second," I said. "I'm no dummy."

Sample 2

"What's it about?"

"It's an Easter story. What I'd like to do is to just tell you what happened the way I'd tell it to a friend sitting in a bar or to my students, say."

"Why?"

"Well I want that kind of immediacy to transfer over to the writing—dialogically if you will. Once you hear it, you'll be able to determine how what I've written differs from my telling, and you can edit the work accordingly. And this will give me more insight into what I'm doing."

"I don't know. I can try."

"That's all I'm asking. I suppose I could record my telling, but I think knowing it's being recorded would change the way I tell it."

"Go ahead."

"But there's a catch."

"What is it?"

"I'm having difficulties with the mimetic vs. diegetic, drama vs. epic, show vs. tell stuff. Not to mention non-diegetic and extradiegetic and the rest."

"Don't worry about all that. Just tell the story. I mean, show and tell it. Whatever."

"Yeah but I'd like to know what I'm doing this time, and show that I know what I'm doing. And this is how the hardcore theorists talk about this stuff."

"Hardcore theorists are not the only kind of experts. You can know what you're doing without knowing what you're doing that way."

"Yeah but you don't understand—when I write, I tend to write with movie soundtracks playing in the background. I love film scores. It's an important part of my process."

"So?"

"So the more I think about it, the more I think I'm not really understanding what I'm doing—my process."

"Give me an example."

"OK. So let's say I'm writing and I've got *The Sound of Music* playing in the background."

"*The Sound of Music*? Really?"

"Yeah."

"OK. Whatever floats your boat."

"So for reasons that are entirely unclear to me, most of what narrative cinema does by way of telling a story is considered in terms of diegesis, right? The 'story world' or 'story universe,' as they call it, is narrated by camera, editing, etc. It's a telling, that is, and so it's diegesis."

"I think that's right. But I'm no theorist."

"So few of us are. And yet we presume to teach some usually watered-down version of what we call theory."

"True. Go on."

"Right, so: instead of talking about diegetic vs. mimetic, you have diegetic vs. non-diegetic."

"That rings a bell. Let's say you're right."

"And in a musical, the score is considered non-diegetic, right?—because the characters can't hear the score. But these two domains can overlap, as when the tune the accordion player plays before the climactic fight in *The Quiet Man*—'The Rakes of Mallow'—is augmented by the score."

"That's right. Now it's coming back to me. Though I didn't know the name of that tune."

"I had to search it myself."

"Of course."

"Right. So take the classic example of *The Sound of Music*. Most of the singing in that film is considered non-diegetic. The characters don't know they're singing, and the singing just advances the plot. Except—"

"Except for 'Do-Re-Mi.'"

"Exactly. When Maria/Andrews sings that number, she knows she's singing that number. It's diegetic."

"This has nothing to do with Douglas Adams, right?"

"What are you talking about?"

"Douglas Adams. He writes someplace or other about how he doesn't get why at one point in the song the lyric is 'LA, a note to follow SO,' as opposed to something more concrete, like 'MI, a name I call myself.'"

"Huh. Didn't know anything about Adams's problem with LA."

"So what's *your* problem then?"

"There are a few problems. First, even though Maria/Andrews knows she's singing, she's singing about song. Solfeggio. So it's not a stretch to say that she's singing about the non-diegetic basis of the musical itself—of any musical. And Maria can't possibly know this as a character. But Andrews does of course as an actor."

"Interesting."

"And that means that in an important sense, 'Do-Re-Mi' is non-diegetic. If we're watching *The Sound of Music*, it's not unreasonable for us to assume that this song is Rogers and Hammerstein's way of telling us something about show tunes."

"Let's say I agree. Hey—before I forget: have you seen the season finale of *The Good Wife*?"

"No. Why?"

"There's a sequence in it where the diegetic becomes non-diegetic, and then becomes diegetic again."

"Cool."

"Yeah. Sorry for interrupting. So where are we?"

"OK, so this is where things get gnarly. Let's say that while I'm listening to 'Do-Re-Mi,' I'm writing about this issue I have with 'Do-Re-Mi.' Here—let me put the song on."

"It's not too loud is it?"

"No."

"OK, so let's say that I'm writing out our exchange. Here—wait a sec . . . OK, I'm typing as we're speaking now, writing out our exchange as it unfolds, in real time. At the moment I know, and you know, that our exchange has to do with writing about this music, and we can hear this music, but of course a reader reading what I'm typing wouldn't hear the music—unless, I suppose, they decided to play it themselves. Anyway, properly speaking, diegesis in written work refers simply to narration, hence we needn't discuss whether such literary music is diegetic or not."

"Thank god. Though of course you're asking me to evaluate written work, even if at first by hearing it read aloud."

"I know, I know. But stick with me. Now let's say someone were to film us, with me typing. Since we both, imagined as characters now, can hear the music, the music is fully diegetic."

"Yes."

"But since the context for the music has changed, because, I mean, we're not both acting in the movie *The Sound of Music*—"

"It might be non-diegetic in ways we don't grasp? After all, we're *in* the scene."

"Exactly. In fact maybe there's something that Maria knows that Andrews doesn't?"

"How so?"

"Let's say the song is about pedagogy. I don't mean just how to sing, but how to teach, among other things, singing. Maria might well be aware of this, especially as a novitiate."

"Well no way Julie-'spoonful of sugar'-Andrews didn't grasp that aspect of the Maria character."

"Good point. But imagine if, say, [6' 1"] Tarantino did something with the song, while filming us, like he did with that Jim Croce tune in *Django*. Yanked it entirely out of context."

"Yeah, I see where you're headed."

"Good. OK, so let's say they flashback in the film of us talking and me writing to just me writing about the music while it's playing on the soundtrack. Say, like they filmed Zhivago/ Sharif writing his poetry in the ice palace with Jarre's great score gradually building. In that scene we're being asked to under- stand the music as inspiration, as a sort of stand-in for the words. On the one hand it's non-diegetic if we assume that Zhivago can't hear it, but on the other it's quasi-diegetic if we're being given to understand that he's hearing his muse, and we're hearing it along with him. So there I sit in the flashback, writing and listening to 'Do-Re-Mi.' The music could be quasi-diegetic, right?"

"I guess so. You can stop typing now."

"Oh, right, yeah. Y'know, if I'd transcribed this entire exchange and used a different font for my typing, we'd be into mimesis—showing—at least as far as the writing goes."

"Let's not go there."

"And I suppose there could be some parallel universe in which someone, some narrator, is writing out everything happening here, between us—extradiagetically—and using a different font for my typing, in which universe the font would also be —"

"Let's not go there either. Though I suddenly recall struggling in grad school with Genette's distinction between…between…what the hell was it? Wait!—I've got it! Between homo- and heterodiegetic first person narration. That's it."

"Jesus Christ. This is beginning to sound as counterintuitive as the principle of buoyancy."

"Buoyancy?"

"Yeah. My brother Mike—he scuba dives—every time he and I sit down to work out the buoyancy stuff, we have to go back to square one. It's as bad as Lacan."

"Lacan?"

"Yeah. I can never keep those stages straight."

"Funny. I always found Lacan pretty straightforward."

"No shit. Huh."

"You were saying?"

"Right. My point is, there's always a non- or quasi- or extra- or whatever-diegetic aspect of an ostensibly diegetic story element once you understand said story element as commentary on story."

"Every story, and every part of every story, can be a commentary on story."

"Right, some stories and some parts more explicitly than others. Depends on the reader too."

"But what does all this have to do with your story?"

"Nothing directly, I guess. I just want to feel confident that I know what I'm talking about when I tell a story. Y'know—do what you know, know what you do."

"I see. Listen, are you going to tell me your story or what? Because—"

"OK. I'm going to tell you my story. In which story there are characters who tell stories, metadiegetically speaking. I think. But I'm telling it all in my words without any dialogue."

"Hurry it up, will you please? I left my lingerie soaking in the sink and rushed over here when you told me it was urgent."

"I'll keep it short."

OK, so back when I was working at the pharmaceutical plant there was this Italian guy, Angelo, who ran the storeroom. All manufacturing plants have storerooms where the in-house mechanics or electricians—technicians these days—can pick up parts to be used for repairing or modifying equipment. I think Angelo was from Naples, maybe early forties? And every now and then, when I needed to check on a part for one of my projects, he'd let me in through the caged-off storeroom area and we'd sit in his office and shoot the shit.

Usually Angelo would have a small radio on in his office, turned down low, sometimes broadcasting a soccer game. Just background noise to me because I knew shit about soccer. In fact I still know shit about soccer. Come to think of it, the tailor my father used to take me to when I needed some trousers altered, an Italian guy named Gino that must have stood all of five feet tall, he used to have his radio on too as he measured me, broadcasting soccer in Italian, and he'd pause every now and then to take note of a play. Anyway. Angelo used to tell me about the whores—he didn't say prostitutes, he said whores—in Naples. Don't get me wrong—this wasn't the kind of talk I tended to favor back then. I've never been much for talking with my guy friends about fucking women, or at least, fucking any particular woman. I figure if you're fucking, why talk about it? First, it's disrespect-ful, and second, talking about it always seemed to me to take the place of actually doing it.

"Go on."

So anyway this guy Angelo, he was something of a character and he had some experiences. There was this one whore, he said, who'd tie a loop with a string that ran from in between his fingers to in between his toes, and then she'd sit on him and move the string back and forth while she fucked him. He said he'd never experienced anything like it. Evidently this chick really took a liking to Angelo, because he said she gave him a Rolex watch. I could never quite tell if he was bullshitting me. I mean, a whore with a heart of gold who gives you something like a gold watch? But then, I didn't think he'd made it all up either. For one, his delivery was positively emphatic. And in the case of the watch, he kept it in a safe in the storeroom, and he took it out and showed it to me one time.

But Angelo is just a secondary character. I mention Angelo to contrast him with his sole assistant in the storeroom, a guy named Guy. Angelo, he was quick, sharp, a born hustler. Guy, he was short, heavy, almost sloth-like in movement and manner, with olive skin similar to some of my relatives. He was some kind of Italian-American, soft-spoken and even, I guess you could say, gentle, if ingratiating in the extreme. How on earth Angelo ended up with Guy, I have not a clue. But from the moment I met Guy, he took what I can only refer to as an unwholesome interest in me. I mean he'd eye me up and down the way I might, at my undisciplined worst, eye a woman up and down.

"You're such a rake."
"That's me all right."

Anyway, coupled with this annoying habit Guy had of licking his lips every few seconds—well, you get the picture. The draftsmen and I used to joke about him—about what we all figured was his repressed homosexuality.

But of course I was younger then, and the draftsmen were older, and they didn't experience Guy quite as I did. Sure, we were all homophobes, but these guys were married with kids, and they had no truck with gay culture, whereas I, about ten years younger, had at least a half a generation's worth of increased tolerance and had known some gays personally. Still, even today I think that Guy would strike gays as a little creepy, not because of his apparent sexual orientation but because of the combination of syco-phancy—don't know what else to call it—and repressed desire.

Now there were times when Angelo had to be at a meeting or whatever and would put Guy in charge of the storeroom. And when I'd stop by the storeroom to check on whether they were stocking a part, Guy would invite me in. So instead of talking with Angelo, I'd talk with Guy, in Angelo's office. He'd even sit in Angelo's chair. Again, I'd already been around out gay behavior, and in those cultural times and in those local circumstances, I thought myself capable of handling whatever threat Guy posed to my twenty-six-year-old aggressively masculine hetero self.

Guy would never have the radio on—he'd just tell stories. And one day Guy told me the story of how for some years he'd been in a monastery.

"Oh for fucksake."

Yeah, he was a novitiate in a monastery, rather like Maria in this sense. And he told me that the monks were extremely severe, and that he could take only so much, and so he left. These days of course I can only wonder whether any abuse took place.

At any rate, he was still a believer, you see, and extremely devout. He had a thorough understanding of Scripture, he knew all the biblical tales, he was well versed in the Apocrypha. He talked on and on about things of which I had little knowledge, not being religious myself, let alone Catholic. Things like that seven times seventy stuff.

But mostly he talked about how much he loved Christmas and Easter. The resurrection in particular was of great interest to him. He saw it—he narrated it—from Mary's—he always said the Madonna's—perspective. He speculated at length as to the anguish the Madonna must have experienced seeing her son nailed to the cross. It was not a little unnerving, all this talk of martyrdom, all the while him looking me up and down and licking his lips, especially as it seemed the more he licked his lips, the more excruciatingly he imagined the Madonna's suffering. Not Christ's, mind you—the Madonna's. He clearly identified with the Madonna, whose ordeal was for him, I don't know, an exquisite form of suffering, accompanied as it was by the unimaginable sweetness—that's the word he used, sweetness—of seeing her son the redeemer resurrected. Jesus Christ it was like she was Guy's divine inspiration or something. All I could think of—and of course I never told him this—was Piper [5' 4½"] Laurie at the end of Carrie, *the orgasm she has as her daughter crucifies her. Pain and pleasure all at once, moral vindication that her daughter really is the devil sprung from her womb, from her own desire.*

"Carrie?"

"Yeah, I'd say so. Her response is certainly in the orgasm ballpark."

"Reminds me more of Falconetti."

"That too. Let me finish."

"Sorry. Go ahead."

So anyway, sometime in mid-March, Guy walks into the engineering offices with a notepad, taking orders for Easter candies that he makes himself. Chocolates of some sort. Everyone is accustomed to this, and most of the engineers and draftsmen put in an order, a few snickering as they do so. This place still had a secretarial pool—really prehistoric organizational structure, with this Taylorist engineering manager, "One Canadian Stands Alone" type, presiding over the whole shebang. Can't recall whether any of the women placed an order. But Guy shows up at my office door with his pad, this ingratiating look on his mug, licking his lips, and I figure, what the hell, I'll order a couple of his candies, right?

   So it's Good Friday, and Guy is walking around the offices distributing his goodies. I can see him down the hall at the drafting office, holding what looks to be a cardboard box top, which is slotted to support each candy, the chocolate molded to a popsicle stick much like an ice cream bar, and each chocolate covered in plastic wrap. You simply lift the chocolates you ordered from the box top. I can see Ted, one of the draftsmen, lift out a chocolate, so I walk over to retrieve my candy. As I do, Ted pulls the plastic wrap off the chocolate, praising Guy's workmanship with a half-ironic look on his face. Tom, another draftsman, is doing everything he can not to burst out laughing. Now you gotta understand that these two guys can be brutal—they're constantly referring to our engineering manager as The Gimp, for instance, because he walks with a limp. Not that the sonofabitch—and he could be a sonofabitch—hadn't earned some rebuke. But even then I thought gimp was taking it a bit too far, though I must confess, that didn't stop me from laughing.

   "Shame on you."
   "I know."

   Anyway. As I reach the three, Guy turns to me with the most sincere look you can imagine, licks his lips, and says, What do you think of my Easter candies? And I look down at what Ted is holding in his hand, and my eyes shift down further to the boxtop, and I see three rows of eight chocolates each, one row partially depleted, a popsicle stick protruding from the bottom of each chocolate, each chocolate an hourglass torso of an armless naked woman, with the outline of a veil draped over her head. Guy's Madonna, sculpted in chocolate.

   "Is that it?"
   "Not quite. I'm pausing for effect."
   "Oh."

And so I'm sitting in my office, with my two naked chocolate torsos resting on my desk. And it occurs to me that maybe I should eat one. Maybe. I mean, sucking on a chocolate woman's torso, or a woman's chocolate torso, or whatever, especially one modeled on the Madonna, isn't something I'd tend to do in public, you understand.

But the hell with compunction, right? After all, I paid for these babies, and after all, it is ten in the AM—coffee time. And it's not like, I don't know, putting on an old Bill [6' 1"] Cosby album and finding yourself laughing at the rapist motherfucker.

"Ouch."
"Yeah, well—it's not like the man hasn't earned it."
"True enough."

So I grab a cup of coffee from the machine just outside our offices— yeah, they made us pay for coffee in that fucking place—and head back to my office. But I'm still feeling a little self-conscious about being caught nibbling on a woman's tits, the Madonna's tits no less, so I shut my office door, unwrap the candy, and have at it.

"And?"

And I'll be goddamned if that wasn't the best milk chocolate I've ever tasted.

Sample 3

Samuel Taylor: Buy the Book
The author of a number of books written under a pseudonym.

What books are currently on your night stand?

I don't keep books on my nightstand. In fact there is no printed matter at all in my bedroom. I do crowd my coffee table with books too numerous to mention.

What is your favorite novelist of all time?

I have many favorites, but no favorite.

Whom do you consider the best writers—novelists, essayists, critics, journalists, poets—working today?

Again, there are too many to mention, and any attempt to do so would only result in my regretting having left someone out.

I do like Terrence Malick though.

What genres do you especially enjoy reading? And which do you avoid?

I'm not a fan of most mass market fiction. I'm certainly no fan of fan fiction. Most YA lit gives me the willies. Other than that, I'm wide-open, provided there's some English on it.

What books might we be surprised to find on your shelves?

Charles Lockyer's *An Account of the Trade in India*. It's signed in two places, on the end paper(1865) and flyleaf (1871) by the British Telugu writer Charles Philip Brown. It looks like an original 1711 edition rebound sometime in the 19th century, as the pages of the book itself look and feel like textile-based paper, with a catchword in the lower right corner of the recto. It came into my possession under the oddest of circumstances, and I've only ever flipped through it.

Other than that, sitting on my bookshelf is, let's see, an old paperback of Alain-Fournier's *The Wanderer, or The End of Youth (Le Grand Meaulnes)*. Two more items: a little book of fairy tales in French, *Contes et Legendes* (Book 1, part of Harrap's Modern Language Series, 1950 edition); and a small book with cloth binding and gilt edges, in German, dated 1895, *Zlatorog*, "Eine Alpensage," by Rudolf Baumbach, both of which belonged to my mother. Between the end papers at the back of *Zlatorog* are two flattened four-leaf clovers, doubtless my mother's doing, as she had a facility for finding them and inserted them in many of her books. Is any of this surprising?

And what about my Kindle Library?—which includes for instance John Williams's *Stoner* (no surprise there); and the digital books on my Mac?—including a digital facsimile of Maud Howe's *Sicily in Shadow and in Sun*.

If you had to name one book that made you who you are today, what would it be?

I can't name such a book. I can't name such a film, such a TV show, such an artwork. Who I am today, even as a writer, is a function of too many things even to attempt such a reductive line of reasoning, and books probably play no greater a role in that ongoing process in any case than do films or TV or music or, say, pineapple upside-down cake. Which latter is, btw, my favorite cake and made me the cake-eater that I am today. That much I can attest to. And by "cake-eater" I mean merely "one who eats cake."

What kind of reader were you as a child?

I was a pretty consistent but certainly not voracious reader. Then, as now, I read around. Of course as a small child I had all sorts of children's picture books. As I grew a bit older, I liked the fat, easy-to-read biographies written for kids that they used to have in my grade school library—I still recall one about Will Rogers—and I was drawn to classics as varied as *The Count of Monte Christo* and *The Time Machine*. For all I knew I was reading some of these classics in abridged editions. In general, as a kid, I liked books about dinosaurs and mythology and astronomy. I had and have a special fondness for the little Golden Nature (Golden Regional, Golden Science) Guides—*Rocks and Minerals, Stars, Seashells, The Southwest, Zoology*. I didn't so much read them as look at them. (Would you be surprised to learn that these are still on my bookshelf?) And of course comic books loomed large in my formative reading life—I was an avid reader of mostly DC and Marvel titles from a young age—and I loved monster mags such as *Famous Monsters of Filmland*.

Disappointing, *overrated*, just not good: What book did you feel you were supposed to like, and didn't?

Just because I don't like something doesn't mean it's not good. Similarly, just because I do like something doesn't mean it's good, though in truth I have more patience for trash TV or trash film than for trash literature. There are books written in popcorn prose with ideas that grab me and I seem to be OK with that, provided there aren't *too* many longueurs.

If you could require the president to read one book, what would it be?

If the president could require his fellow citizens to read one book, what would it be?

You're hosting a dinner party. Which three writers are invited?

I'm not sure, but they better know how to break bread.

What book hasn't been written that you'd like to read?

What kind of a question is that?

What do you plan to read next?
Now that I'm no longer teaching, I have no idea.

EPISODE 6

"45 minutes left, folks." Knight erased "60 min" and wrote the new time in his typically precise cursive.

Ordinarily Knight's calm demeanor would, despite the circumstances, exert a calming effect on Vick Jr. Instead he was in a panic, had been in a panic ever since he'd looked at the test sheet.

*

There were three test questions.

The first had to do with the tension in the rigging on a sailboat with masts—or yards?—under rotation. Vick Jr. wasn't certain what he was looking at, as the hand-drawn illustration wasn't exactly draftsman quality. But he'd opened his blue book and started to try to solve the problem using the standard equations for centripetal force, mass, acceleration, friction, which he knew by heart. Tension problems had always struck him as fairly straightforward, but as he scribbled his solution he hit an impasse. Something wasn't right in his approach. He started to tense up, deciding to proceed to the second test question and return to the first question later.

The second question had to do with the velocity and acceleration of a projectile shot from a cannon. Again, he knew all the equations of motion by heart. He knew how to derive one from the other. But what he couldn't do was apply what he knew to the example. He scribbled out a few tentative calculations, then stopped.

He put his pencil down, took a deep breath, squared his back against the back of his chair. His heart rate increased, and his neck and brow began to perspire, immediately evaporating into the dry air and creating a cooling sensation. He looked around the room—everyone was in deep concentration. His eyes met Knight's for a moment but he glanced away. He could see in his peripheral the student to his right take momentary note that he wasn't working.

He leaned forward, picked up his pencil, and looked at the third and final question. Whatever it was, he couldn't get a handle on it immediately, and almost immediately his mind seized. The test as a test had become incomprehensible to him.

He panicked. His heart rate shot up, and he could hear his own pulse. He flipped the booklet back to the first question, and tried to build upon his initial scrawls.

No go. His heart rate shot up even higher.

"30 minutes left, folks."

He sat back in his chair, placed his pencil down. His heart rate was rocketing, his breathing was erratic, his entire body seemed now to be under severe physical stress. He could feel his back soak with sweat, his groin area soak with sweat, sweat trickling down his chest and across his face, amplifying that cooling sensation. He felt a little sick. He placed his hands on his knees and leaned back again, hard into the chair, bending his head back as if stretching, extending his legs a bit. In his peripheral he could see that his fidgeting had again caught the attention of the student to his right. Again she paid only a moment's notice and returned to her work.

He closed his eyes, his entire body tensing.

And then it happened.

He could feel himself becoming erect.

It was entirely involuntary but he made no effort to stop it. He extended his legs as far as he could, pointed his toes in, closed his eyes tightly, breathed in deeply, letting himself become fully erect.

And after a second or two, he ejaculated as hard as he'd ever ejaculated, he ejaculated as hard as Godzilla had ever ejaculated, the tension dissipating with each momentous spasm.

Vick Jr. sat stewing for a few minutes in his sweat and Godzilla-scale semen, enervated to the point at which the blue book with his desperate markings, the auditorium, the student to his right, Knight, everything up to and including his college career as such seemed insignificant, if not insubstantial. True, years later he'd look back on this moment always with an initial shudder, only to conclude each time, with no small amount of satisfaction, that the proper response of a poet, Emerson's logos-ejaculator, to that blue-blooded blue book question that had initially inspired his bodily response was to ejaculate *something*, goddammit, if not quite the sort of thing that Emerson, Godzillaless, had in mind. But what seemed of paramount import presently was the feeling of shame that gradually crept over him. He didn't understand at all why what had just transpired, had just transpired, and he felt that something must be seriously wrong with him emotionally, psychologically, perhaps morally. And he wasn't even Catholic.

He realized that, whatever else, he was done with the exam, especially as he could detect the discharge beginning to seep through to his jeans. As his watch hit the twenty-four-minute mark, he rose, placing his pencil and eraser in his backpack, gathering his coat, and walking with his wretchedly incomplete blue book and exam sheet not to Knight, whose eyes he avoided, but to one of the other graduate assistants. He was the first to leave the room and, as such, the object of some attention and what he imagined was scorn from his fellow sufferers, even if the woman sitting to his right glanced at him with what appeared to him, in a nervous glance up, to be admiration.

He hurried out of the room and to the restroom, where he entered a stall, did his best to soak things up with a wad of toilet paper. After he urinated, he made his way to just inside the building entrance, calculating how long it would be before his ride would arrive to pick him up where he'd been dropped off. He tried to stand so as to block a clear view of the darkened crotch of his faded jeans, relieved that at least his short walk would be made under cover of night. He looked at his watch and figured he could start his five-minute walk back down the icy stairs in fifteen minutes or so. And so he had fifteen minutes to kill.

The first thing that occurred to him was how badly he'd botched this first test of his college mettle. He was nothing if not a *scholarship boy*, as he'd learn later in life during his graduate studies, and indeed here he was with a free ride, tuition and fees covered thanks to an array of scholarships. His gut burned at the thought of this dismal failure, right on the heels of which came, again, that overwhelming sense of shame.

Five minutes to go before he had to head down to catch his ride. What would his father say?

*

There were no storms as they continued their ascent heavenward. A buildup of lenticular clouds to the north appeared ominous at first, but passed. Their stride was steady, each aware of the other's huffing and puffing, and while Samuel Taylor was a stronger hiker than his companion, Kass nonetheless had estimable endurance thanks to the lifelong urgings of her athlete father, which gave her the resolve necessary to pull upward against the Earth. It was two hours before they caught sight of the second false summit, perhaps six long-ish switchbacks ahead.

"Let's take a break, yes?"
"Short one."
"Right. You OK?"
"Yeah. You?"
"Gotta adjust this new pack—balance is a little off."
"Told you not to use it for the first time on a tough hike like this, dummy."

"As Sidney Morgenbesser might say, 'Yeah, yeah.'"
"PhD nerd is as PhD nerd does."
"Onward long-legged leader."

Fifteen minutes later found the two seated facing each other on opposite ends of large flat rock.

"Want some of this Kind bar? Only 5 grams sugar, 5 grams protein, 4 grams fiber."
"No thanks. I'll stick with half a turkey sandwich."
"I thought we were saving the turkey for the summit."
"We each have two turkey sandwiches. Plus I'm a little hungry and somehow sugar just doesn't do it for me right now."
"You had three eggs and toast for breakfast and a peanut butter sandwich last time we stopped. You sure you're OK?"
"Yeah. I'm fine, stop worrying."
"Hey—look down there. Those elk?"
"Where are you pointing?"
"Down there beyond that ridge with snow on it. To the side of those junipers."
"Huh, yeah—I think you're right. Good eye."
"Good Lasik you mean."

Ten minutes later and they were on their way again, the sky still blue, the summit now within sight, its rocky peak not nearly as pointy as it appeared at lower elevations. The wind had picked up a bit and, as the trail took them above 13,000 feet, their breathing grew a little labored. But they continued apace, Kass leading the way.

As the trail wound around a final rock outcropping, beyond which was a straight stretch to the summit climb, Kass was stopped dead in her tracks. She waved her arm behind her, uttering "Hold it!" in a breathy whisper. Samuel Taylor stepped up beside her and peered ahead to see, crossing the path in front of them, a large wolverine. It paused to assess the two, claws at the ready, and then scrambled away over the rocky terrain and out of sight.

"That was something."

"Fuck yeah."

"Bore a striking resemblance to someone I know."

"Uh-huh. Hey—check *that* out."

Samuel Taylor was pointing at a large ugly-looking mass of grey that had appeared virtually out of nowhere above the summit. Within moments a lightning bolt dropped to a point on the summit not all that far, as the crow flies, from where the two were standing. They made their way quickly to a depression fifty yards off-trail, stepping only on rocks as they did so to avoid trampling the fragile tundra vegetation. Seconds later a thunder clap sounded, almost deafening due to its proximity. They unzipped their packs and hastily tossed on their rain gear.

"Head down now honey and keep those big brown eyes of yours shut."

"You too dummy."

"My eyes aren't brown."

Kass rolled her eyes as Samuel Taylor covered her with his arm and body, the cloud mass passing directly above them, lightning bolts dropping with increasing frequency, hail pelting their backs. The temperature had dropped precipitously. At some point Samuel Taylor's face began to sting.

"Hold on honey, we'll be OK."

"I know."

A minute passed, or ten minutes.

And then it was over.

"OK?"

"Yeah. You?"

"I think so."

Samuel Taylor shifted his body from Kass's, and as she turned to look at him her face grew alarmed.

"What is it?"
"Your face."
"That again?"
"It's not funny. Your beautiful skin."

She reached out to stroke his face and Samuel Taylor winced, realizing then that the hail had left its imprint on him in the form of freckle-sized welts.

"I'll live honey, not to worry."
"I think I have some cream."
"Of course you do. But let's get this show back on the road and bag this fucker."

This is what Samuel Taylor said. But what he felt as they made their way back to the trail took the form of a phrase he recalled from years prior, "old love's great power."

*

They were seated together in a small diner on Wolf Street, Vick Jr. gobbling down a plate of spaghetti. Vick Sr. was smoking, happy to see his son still had an appetite.

"How's the spaghetti?"
"Good."
"Thataboy. You'll get over that exam. Bastards."

The drive to the diner had been awkward as Vick Jr. tried to explain what had transpired. At first Vick Sr. wasn't sure how to respond, but within minutes he'd decided that to treat what could only in his eyes be a physical dysfunction required a physical nostrum. And in true Italian form, that meant food, the way to a man's brain, heart, and soul.

And in truth his father's remedial gesture, as embodied in the pasta, was greeted by Vick Jr. with no small measure of relief. If food could be seen as a cure, then perhaps the incident was simply a blip in his metabolic system and not a sign of mental illness, let alone original sin. This was, after all, only a few years prior to the Vatican once again proclaiming that masturbation was a mortal sin, and could presumably lead to all manner of social disorder.

A week later found Vick Jr. eyeballing the long chart of Social Security Numbers posted outside of the Physics Building auditorium to learn that he'd scored the lowest he'd ever scored on any exam in his life:

22.

However, it turned out that the average score, across hundreds of students, was 32. And with the scores adjusted to fit the bell curve, as was customary, this gave him a grade of . . .

C. Yes, C. Even at the time, Vick Jr. regarded this as, oh, nonsensical horseshit of the highest order. Still, he scored two Bs on his next two tests, they dropped the lowest grade, and he ended up with a final grade of B in Physics.

Fuck you Professor G————.

Somehow that plate of spaghetti had done the trick, at any rate, and father and son would never again discuss the incident. And never again would Vick Jr. worry inordinately about his performance on an exam. Moreover, along with the mountains of mathematical and engineering detail he was committing to memory, and along with the rigorously analytical habit of mind he was cultivating in his studies, Vick Jr. had learned that, distinctions between body and mind aside, the body had a mind of its own. That bodies could always surprise you. That it was through the body that age would have its way with us, for better and for worse.

And he'd begun to realize that no one gets to pick their bodies, which are never entirely free, and can only ever be more or less free.

*

It was a little after noon. The sun shone brightly again and the wind had subsided as they made their way up the final leg of the hike to the summit. This involved scrambling atop large granite and gneiss boulders, pausing every eight or nine yards to determine the best way to proceed. Cairns pointed the way but, as is typical with 14er approaches, there appeared to be several different sets of cairns for several different routes to the top. It was slow-going, hard work.

And after a half an hour, they were at the top. And they were especially happy to be alone at the top. Without hesitation they made their way directly to the summit marker, signed the register—their first 14er together—took the obligatory photos of themselves, incl. a selfie close-up of both their faces. Samuel Taylor took a ten-second video of Kass two-stepping atop the summit marker. Then they ambled over to one of several stone wind shelters, which afforded a stunning view of the range to the southwest. There they extracted their turkey sandwiches and munched away in silence.

"I think I have a great idea for a script."

"C'mon. I asked you not to talk about work."

"I know, but it's such a great idea I figure you'd be pissed if I didn't tell you."

"Tell you what: tell me on the drive back to the hotel, OK? It'll give us something to talk about."

"Fair enough. So—how are you feeling?"

"I'm good, I guess."

"You guess? You know, you wolfed your sandwich down faster than me."

"I did, didn't I."

"You did."

"You want this last of mine?"

"Sure."

Kass smiles what Samuel Taylor takes to be an oddly knowing smile. She eats the sandwich. Then she reaches into her pocket and pulls out a folded sheet of paper.

"I—I wrote this when I was back east. Thought I should share it with you when we did something difficult together. Now seems like as good a time as any, especially since nobody is around. It's . . . difficult."
"I'm all ears."

She reads aloud, softly, the only human voice for miles.

Risk

With her and him, them
to keep leaning on, with this old
earth has love in it, rotates a bit
perturbed each time, with some
you says to somebody or other
yeah, OK, with the boundaries keep
shifting forever and ever, with the controller
takes you into some tube, with
yeah, the past with that obscure yen for
obscure moments, the land fit for planting
a thing or two, with a place for unfinished
things or a song sings of how odds keep
mounting, with nothing left
to lose, with some you says how not to
get off the train, with a peach
with a diamond set in white gold with
no pot to piss in, with a book, a car
a stereo a line good for admission
at the zoo, with a world divided
into profiles, abbreviations, inkless invites, with a
man a woman a kid with
issue as they said then and now
with dog and cat, with rain

with rain, with some you says
well, sure, yeah, OK, with incoherent inquiries
into a night's requisitions, with the passion
of a criminal or a dance or a home, with a contact
high, with costly associations
laced with attitude, with his motorcycle helmet
in hand, with an old film a comic book an
antique marble her kettle of soup
his mahogany coffee table with
a pair of dead hands, starched cuffs, a
dispersal of ashes by a creek her photo album a few
items to keep in touch, with some you
admits to, yeah, sure, with the rolling sea with
nausea a calculator with a receipt a
calculation, with oral fixation a violin disks
have been erased innumerable times an eye a voice
toward performance anxiety with aspiration exceeding
actualities pretensions interest whims maybe even
saliva maybe even vomit a feeling felt thought felt some
you, yeah, with you, with some you or yeah, us
whispering all the while me saying

(without dusk

(with without never

(without blood

(without

(with us

(with

(child

Kass is staring directly at Samuel Taylor now, tearful. At which Samuel Taylor reaches out to hold one of Kass's hands in one of his.

"I am a dummy."
"You are."

Samuel Taylor was never at a loss for words. But he knew he was always at a loss for the real words, and Kass knew it too. He would have to wait for many years for the real words to reach him. It would be not long before his own passing—this Kass also knew.

And many years passed. And he grew ill. And it was then that he would in fact recount that moment in the real words, the words that would adorn the last page of his last book.

Say

risk
nothing risk
say nothing risk
nothing say nothing risk

permanence

in aside to such moment no
clean river availing no
sky if blue no
tree if leaved no
dirt unsoiled no
hill if green no moon no
stars if wished upon no
structure arcing if
dreamt no
lot left vacant no
nothing wanting nothing

to act upon no
outside there no
signs here no
ecological nothing no
this hence hence no
nothing needless
to say
that is
nor even that then
nothing not needy
needing no aside from this moment no
entirety appeased no
nothing not to do turned over

and over

and over

and over
unprovisionally without provision
to seek and to seek justification
in seeking

say permanence

say risk if altered, tentative
as from above
say you say

love

and then
no one but where
no that nor this
no one but
yes

no one but

you

and then

without firmament, ample
nor heaven solvent sent
nor set to sample sampling

your way
you

to read nor
words there
then
nor write here
hence
no moment whence

if only for

love

if only for love
to take
or love to give

from its example.

PLAN B

SHOW AND TELL

And now of myself. My ever-wakeful Reason, and the keenness of my moral feelings will secure you from all unpleasant circumstances connected with me save only one: viz.—*Evasion*, and the cunning of a specific madness. You will never *hear* any thing but truth from me— Prior Habits render it out of my power to *tell* a falsehood, but unless watched carefully, I dare not promise that I should not with regard to this detested Poison be capable of *acting* a Lie.

S. T. to J. G.
13 April—

*

Maybe Virginia Woolf was right—maybe human character did change on or about December 1910. But human character changed, or changed again, on or about July 1982.[2] Vick Jr. knows—he was there. Maybe you were too.

It was the year *TIME Magazine* named the computer Machine of the Year. The year Disney opened EPCOT, Experimental Community of Tomorrow. The year genetic engineering was first used commercially to produce the recombinant DNA drug product, human insulin. The year Freeware was developed by programmers Andrew Fluegleman and Jim Knopf. The year of the first artificial heart implant. Pneumatic tubes fed the implant, designed by Robert Jarvik, with a control apparatus the size of a shopping cart. That first guy lasted only 112 days. Remember?

1982: Reagan, Thatcher, potassium cyanide-laced Tylenol, Israel invading Lebanon, Argentina invading the Falklands, *USA Today*, the death of Brezhnev, the world's largest oil rig sinking in the Atlantic, 700,000 demonstrators protesting nuclear weapons in Central Park, the Vietnam War Memorial, the US recession, *E. T.* and Smileys and "Ebony and Ivory." Say hello to Madonna, say so long to Lester Bangs. Gas averaged 91 cents a gallon and the median household income in the US was $18,642. It's one year before Ameritech launches the first US 1G mobile phone network, and a mere eight years before Belgian computer scientist Robert Cailliau christens the growing global consolidation of

---

2   Then too there's some question as to whether 1910 and 1982 should be viewed as merely episodes in an ongoing planetary fantasia. Evidence exists to suggest earlier ruptures, visitations, singularities. For instance: "Satisfied, the future generation could scarcely think itself, for even when the mind existed in a universe of its own creation, it had never been quite at ease. As far as one ventured to interpret actual science, the mind had thus far adjusted itself by an infinite series of infinitely delicate adjustments forced on it by the infinite motion of an infinite chaos of motion; dragged at one moment into the unknowable and unthinkable, then trying to scramble back within its senses and to bar the chaos out, but always assimilating bits of it, until at last, in 1900, a new avalanche of unknown forces had fallen on it, which required new mental powers to control. If this view was correct, the mind could gain nothing by flight or by fight; it must merge in its supersensual multiverse, or succumb to it." From *The Education of Henry Adams.*—DH

network apparatus "WorldWideWeb." That's right—without the definite
article. Two years after the first "classic rock" radio station in Cleveland.

*The Mists of Avalon, The Color Purple, The Shawshank Redemption,
Schindler's List.* Those were novels in 1982. *The Year of Living Dangerously.*
"Thriller." Remember?

*

In 1982, Vick Jr. was earning $32,400 a year as a Senior Project
Engineer with Bristol-Myers Co. in Syracuse, New York. This is the
same plant, built in 1943, that had supplied much of the penicillin used
during World War II; at one point the plant had produced 70% of the
nation's penicillin. In truth, the plant had seen better days, its pipe chases
now tangled conduits carrying any number of variously innocuous and
toxic substances to and from a complex array of processes, a labyrinth
of designs and redesigns that no blueprint could adequately demarcate.
There had been decades of leaks and spills, there would be decades more
of oozing and dripping. The amount of solvent that had leached into
the soil, into the aquifer, and ultimately into the creek nearby, or had
evaporated into the atmosphere, had doubtless caused harm to countless
living things in the vicinity, undocumented harm that boosters for this
local industrial employer perennially downplayed.

Vick Jr. was aware of all of this. But even in the wake of the FDA's
halfhearted attempt the decade prior to ban penicillin and tetracylcine
from livestock feed on the grounds that this could lead to antibiotic-re-
sistant strains of human pathogens, antibiotics had saved lives—that
much was certain. And in the end, one's bread needed buttering. So
Vick Jr. strove to do the best he could under the circumstances, his effort
consisting of partial modifications that made processes incrementally
more efficient, or marginally safer. It would be thirty years before most of
the plant would be razed to make way for a park-like industrial campus,
eliminating penicillin production and the two thousand plant personnel
required to sustain it. The new number would be closer to five hundred.
But Vick Jr., or at least the Vick Jr. of those years, would be long gone.

In September Vick Jr. was granted his Professional Engineer's License to practice in New York State. Around that time he bought a Datsun hatchback demo for upwards of nine grand. He still owned his Yamaha RD400. He lived in a nice apartment in the village of Liverpool with a gas fireplace and dishwasher, across from the Lakeshore Drive-In and right around the corner from Heid's, famous locally for their hot dogs. He took the New York State Thruway to work every morning, a half-hour drive on a snowy winter day. His workday commenced at 7:30 am and ended around 4:30 pm, with forty-five minutes for lunch. He liked the Denny's down on Erie Boulevard East—there was a waitress there he was sweet on, Kim. She pumped him full of caffeine, free of charge.

Life was good, considering.

And on a pleasant Saturday in mid-July he found himself in the dark. Or rather, seated in the dark with a bunch of strangers. That's when it happened. That's when people became, in The Doors's sense of the word, *strange*.

*

The Cinema North was one of those boxy, single-screen theaters with few embellishments aside from the glittery sign above the rounded, raised, glass-enclosed entrance, and a comedy and tragedy mask flanking the proscenium. It sat around to the side of the Kmart Plaza on Northern Lights Circle, a shopping area at the intersection of Interstate 81 and Route 11 situated in a couple of unremarkable square miles at the northern edge of Syracuse that residents knew as Mattydale. Like its sister theaters the Cinema East and the Westhill, it served its purpose well enough while reminding its more seasoned patrons that the old dream palaces really were history, and that moviemaking henceforth would be less and less about art and more and more about commerce. In 1982, law-abiding citizens still watched the tube intent on finding out who they were, and still clutched that ticket stub hoping to learn who they might be. But it wouldn't be long before a public responsive to such distinctions would go the way of Blue Light Specials.

That's entertainment. And in 1982, at three bucks a head. Vick Jr., his sister Shelley, and his buddies Cut and Harper—they can swing three bucks each every Saturday or Sunday night, plus another couple of bucks for popcorn and soda and a box of nonpareils.

That's right—it's *soda* in these parts.

Tonight, with an R-rated feature showing, the nine-hundred-seat theater will fill to approximately two-thirds. That's a lot of popcorn and soda, especially with dozens of two-hundred-pounders like Harper in attendance.

Showtime is at 7 pm EDT.

*

In the theater on this particular evening is a veritable cross-section of the area's population. You have a relatively small number of doctors, and lawyers, and engineers. You have a relatively large number of assembly-line workers, and retail workers, and construction workers. You have a goodly number of the gainfully employed, a fair number of what we call now the under-employed, and a handful of small business owners. You have about the same number of people over twenty-five as you do under twenty-five, but many more people under forty than over forty. A majority would, push come to shove, attest to their belief in god, but many are at best casual churchgoers.

Only a handful of African Americans are present, as is typically the case in this theater. There are no Latinos, and the primary ethnicity is Italian-American. The ratio of couples on a date to married couples is three to one, and, though few in the audience would give evidence of it in this crowd, eleven couples are gay, and thirty-five people have begun to explore their sexual orientation. For the men, it's mustaches, for the women, tight jeans are back in. You have former jocks, and former cheerleaders, and former honors students. You have a few dozen college students and eighty-odd high schoolers, including three overdressed teenyboppers wearing gobs of makeup who use fake IDs to beat the MPAA-sanctioned and management-enforced rating system. A group of fifteen-year-old boys with razor burn and rock band tees also make it past the ticket booth.

And on this particular evening, the Cinema North is host to The Film Critic and his graduate-student date, both of whom enter gratis thanks to the former's pass. With his student gazing at him in rapt attention, The Film Critic treats his companion to some tidy dissertating on film theorist Laura Mulvey's influential essay, in the process managing to put theory in the service of sexual innuendo.

*

Had anyone in the theater had access to a television, they would have been greeted by one of the three network-affiliate weathermen interrupting regularly scheduled programming to explain that a line of severe thunderstorms had unexpectedly developed and was moving into the area from the northwest. Or in the more colorful words of the forecaster on the newly-launched Weather Channel, which relatively few in Mattydale would have had access to in 1982, a storm system was approaching that had quite literally "come out of nowhere." Accompanying the ominous clouds are abundant cloud-to-ground lightning strikes, and an eerily unfluctuating basso profundo.

*

At 7 pm the lights dim. The two ushers, both young men, make their customary march up and down the aisles. There's the obligatory projection flicker and alignment, the screen lights up, and everyone— every single person in the audience—is paying attention for an instant to the image reflected back at them from the screen, and to the auditory *blip* of a soundtrack engaging. As collective attention settles in and out, all seems well in the Cinema North universe.

The coming attractions are served up, generously this evening, in this order:

> *Fast Times at Ridgemont High*
> *Tron*
> *Poltergeist*
> *Firefox*

An Officer and a Gentleman
Blade Runner
E. T.: The Extra-Terrestrial

In a few months, as summer fare subsides, audiences will be teased with *Tootsie*, *Sophie's Choice*, *The Verdict*, and *Gandhi*. You can gauge for yourselves, you film buffs of *Davy's Locker Room* ilk, how various sectors of this audience might respond, in oohs and ahs, in laughter and awe, to the trailer for any one of these offerings.

But then, you're now, *all* of you, post-1982ers.

The important thing to note here is that, during the *Poltergeist* trailer and again during *E. T.*, as the approaching storm system is starting to make its rumbling presence felt and a half-hour before the power goes out during the second helicopter scene and everyone in the theater is shrouded in darkness together, several patrons will glimpse the stocky young man seated two seats to the right of Shelley employing a rubber band as a slingshot to propel a shiny slip of foil gum wrapper toward the ceiling in front of the screen. And as the foil twinkles down through the projection light, the effect, as some would later recall, will be rather like a star dropping from the heavens to terra firma. Even The Film Critic will be amused.

*

Here's what you need to know about our little band of four:

Vick Jr. is comfortable in his own skin, a happy combination of Action Man and Thinking Man whose chief weakness, at this point in his life, stems from his thinking that he's more Action Man than Thinking Man. He's wearing a brand new pair of lime green Nike track shoes and a new pair of jeans.

Shelley is an attractive but not beautiful smartass who, as a young girl, wanted to play shortstop for the Yankees but, upon realizing the limits both of her fielding talents and of her beloved franchise's exclusively male roster, has turned to physical therapy to derive eight-to-five meaning from her life. Everyone says she's got the touch. She's wearing sandals and a knee-length skirt.

Cut is a car mechanic and an accomplished philatelist. He has a thing for Shelley but can't seem to find it within himself to make a move. Shelley is waiting, patiently, for him to do so, while Vick Jr. is wise enough to keep out of it. Cut is wearing a pair of black & white canvas Keds and worn flare jeans.

Harper is a holy fool. He's wearing a scuffed-up pair of beige Hush Puppies—no socks—and ragged jean shorts.

Their average age is twenty-seven. Vick Jr. and Shelley are half-French and half-German (on their mother's side) and half Sicilian-American (on their father's), Cut is Scots-Irish, and Harper is part Polish, part Russian, and part Cherokee.

*

House lights fade completely for tonight's feature presentation.

*

"There's always been something about Kurt Russell, a subliminal wink in his performances that, especially when viewed in retrospect, threaten to undercut the overweening sincerity of his Disney years. The first director to pick up on this was Robert Zemeckis, and Russell gives Rudy Russo precisely the right-of-way he needs to make you believe that this used-car salesman is genetically predisposed to the con. A year later John Carpenter took Russell in another direction entirely, and between his eye-patch and his unshaven mug, Snake Plissken has both the true grit and the kind of doesn't-give-a-shit brio we've come to expect from our antiheroes, our bad good guys, or good bad guys. It would take Quentin Tarantino at the helm, more than three decades later, to finally pull out of an intertextually stubbled, scarred, but fully sighted Russell his consummate dark side.

"When Carpenter and Russell reunited a year after their first effort together, the beard was fuller but the eye patch had been replaced by a sombrero—just the right touch of cross-cultural insouciance to convey the rough & (Mac)ready protagonist to which most young men weaned on Frank Bullitt and Harry Callahan might relate. White masculinity in the US has always thrived, in certain class quarters, on undercutting the WASP-ish contours of whiteness itself. Toss in an African-American antagonist (Keith David) with his own heroic leanings—the closest white guys will ever come to black cool is a black buddy, or anti-buddy (even while assuaging their own racial anxieties)—and a director who holds the first movie version in high esteem, and what you've got is at once a box-office hit and an item to which film critics were bound to condescend both because of its pop appeal and because each new wave of special effects, including the rather gory one at work here, tends initially to overdetermine viewer response.

"This is a far cry, of course, from a chick flick—it lacks even the single Hawksian female of the fifties version -- though most female viewers will probably find themselves at least somewhat drawn to Russell's onscreen persona, and young heterosexual couples can, as with most horror films, cuddle together through the scares.

"But older viewers might not be prepared for this remake, or adaptation. For one, in the three decades between *The Thing from Another World* and *The Thing*, the Cold War had cooled down considerably. Race relations in the US had gone from a perceived social problem to a perceived cultural problem, while remaining more stubbornly social than some cultural commentators would concede. Absent the Communist datum, in any case, extraterrestrials could be at once more friendly—even musical, like us—and less, or other than, human. Not an Arness-sized monster, but a cellular organism capable of infinite transmutation of the abject, a conceit that would also allow for a foray into the wilds of supply-side *Body Snatcher* paranoia, the hyperreal simulations (modeled on "the genetic code") of Baudrillard's seminal text coming only a year later. As ticket prices had increased and TV had wooed couch potatoes with condensed storylines, Hollywood films by and large, especially horror and sci-fi, had added to their running times, Carpenters's version tacking twenty-two minutes to the narrative arc to remain more faithful to Don A. Stuart's (John W. Campbell Jr.'s) 1938 novella than the faster-paced Kenneth Tobey vehicle while giving audiences their perceived money's worth.

"Whatever the case, *The Thing* restores to the *récit* its Antarctic setting, as in the novella, which the Hawks version had, evidently due to its strategic military value, relocated to the Arctic. The rationale for both Antarctic and Arctic settings is as in the novella:: a scientific research station with military support. But in the fifties version, we watch as the USAF is dispatched to the outpost, whereas in Carpenter's version, the military personnel are already *in situ* and are called into duty in the opening scenes, which scenes are an inventive twist on the novella added by screenwriter Bill Lancaster."

Such was the 2002 reappraisal penned by film critic Leo Altman for *Variety*. Many of us felt that old Leo had nailed it.

*

In 1982, core drillings in Greenland by Will Dansgaard, Han Oeschger, and others will reveal that significant temperature variations, whether caused by humans or by other factors, are possible within a human lifespan. Some are beginning to revisit, from a newly informed vantage point, the age-old question that Frost had so cogently posed: whether desire would stoke an apocalypse of fire, or whether hate portended an end in ice. Ultimately, Frost's narrator can see things either way. Of course Dante had famously imagined, at hell's absolute bottom, a frozen lake, and Milton had imagined the damned brought "From beds of raging fire to starve in ice." At the end of *The Thing*, however, as the flames die down and survivors Mac and Childs sit waiting to "see what happens," it would appear that fire and ice alike are both potentially deadly and redemptive, yet another binary—like black and white, or body and antibody, or human and nonhuman, or truth and falsehood, or acting and non-acting—that the film so astutely offers as a parallel touchstone, to Morricone's pulsing score.

But in July of 1982, our band of four will never get that far—will never see the ending. Nor will they get as far as the comic book series, or the video game sequel, or the 2011 prequel.

*

It's after that provocative opening sequence—after the Norwegians are obliterated in their helicopter in a failed attempt to shoot the sled dog, just as MacReady dons his sombrero and begins to pilot his chopper to the Norwegian camp, and just as theatergoers are drawn into the thick of things—that the screen goes black, and every shred of light that might sneak in from the concession stand is blotted out. All that remains illuminated are the exit lights. The power has failed, and it takes no more than two seconds of uncertain silence for most in the theater to share a nervous chuckle.

Then the exit door stage left blows open, banging up against the side of the theater, rain and wind howling with a ferocity that few have witnessed. Lightning flashes shudder in through the opening, and between the downpour and the steady roar of thunder, it's difficult to talk with the person seated next to you. This time the scattered laughter that erupts is accompanied by a hushed sense of anxiety.

Vick Jr. stands, walks to the door, leans out into the rain and wind, grabs the door as firmly as he can, and with no small amount of effort, manages to shut it tight. As a result of this simple action, he's drenched from the waist up. He smiles as he walks back to his seat.

*

Gradually the audience acclimates to the darkness, resuming chitchat while waiting for the power to be restored.

"So now what? What the fuck are we gonna do now?" Cut is always the first to complain.

"We're going to get to know each other better," Shelley teases. Cut appears stymied, doesn't know how to respond. Shelley sighs, audibly.

"I think we should start a bonfire and roast marshmallows!" Harper blurts out as he empties the box of nonpareils into his mouth. He's only half-joking.

"Shit, I'm freezing my ass off," Vick Jr. murmurs, ignoring Harper's outburst. He leans over to address his three companions in a low voice. "Let's go up front and see what it looks like out there."

The four stand and make their way up the aisle together. They push open the theater doors and walk into the concession area. That's when they see it.

*

There's something I've left out—something important that you need to know:

I was there.

Or rather, I was there the instant after the lights went out. And then it was as if I'd been around *forever*.

*

That's when they see it, but it's already too late for them. They don't know it, but it's already too late.

As our little entourage and the Cinema North staff stand gazing out through the glass-enclosed entrance and across the Kmart parking lot, they see that the unabating deluge, having flooded the lot, has already risen above the first concrete step leading up to the theater. And looking north up Route 11, they see the horizon line punctuated by an unrelenting series of lightning bolts of unprecedented intensity. At one point a particularly intense bolt lights up the panorama, landing out of sight of our band of four and in what they calculate to be in the neighborhood of TJ's Big Boy and Sweetheart Market. Later they'll discover that the restaurant itself has been hit and that a fire has ensued. But later too will be too late.

It's not that they won't eventually escape the premises, you understand. There will be a future for each and all. But that future will be a different one than the future they brought with them this evening.

*

The first signs of the change will go unnoticed by friends and acquaintances, who themselves will change in due course.

The magnetic bottle opener that has followed Vick Jr. since his college days will no longer be stuck ostentatiously to his fridge.

Shelley will stop fussing over her outfits.

Cut will lose interest in his stamp collection. (Later, Cut will become a vegetarian, the first of our four to give obvious evidence that he'd changed.)

Only Harper will appear to remain the same behaviorally. But deep inside will roil the same elemental disturbances.

*

There's something of an explanation for what's happened.

"It's a recombinant archive, both genetic and experiential, to which I've been granted unrestricted access. For every data point, a particle, for every particle, a data point. And all particles, and with them all data points, comprise a transgenic sensorium activated by each aggregate organism. Sentience becomes a matter of relation, a subatomic order through which passes the fluctuating spectral energy that itself passes for time, for duration, for change, what some enlightened bipeds have intuited as *duende*. Hierarchy obtains as a matter of accretion, overlap, redundancy and complexity of corpuscular signal. Most intriguingly, each quantum of intelligence becomes for me, for us, a narrational agency of varying potentiality. Taken altogether, a living network. The cosmic. Taken singly, an access point. A man, a woman, an alien, his and her stories, which are his and her stories, and our stories."

Vick Jr. could be telling *this* story. Let's say Vick Jr. is the teller of our tale, as he sits in a small diner in Cheyenne, Wyoming, not far from the Air Force base. He's trying to find the words for what he experienced on that fateful July day decades prior. The words are what you see in quotes, above. He's talking with a guy a generation older, a guy who walks half bent over from hard labor, over a breakfast of coffee and pancakes and bacon. This guy, Slim, an African-American rodeo devotee, experienced much the same transformation several days after our band of four and some two thousand miles away, while working in a rail yard. The skies were blue in Cheyenne that day—no storm, no power outage.

But it could just as well be Shelley speaking, or Shelley and Cut's daughter, Sylvia, now in college, the disaffected product of a strangely happy couple whose mutual sustenance together seemed to derive from the mere habits of their shared human history. Or even Harper—Harper's physical manifestation having long since passed away, as they say, his information safe with the rest of us -- or any one of us, which is all of us. Each of us is all-knowing, within our newfound, ever-expanding biological universe, because we each have access to one another's information. All of it.

But if it wasn't the storm that precipitated this global transaction, then what was it? Because neither Vick Jr. nor his railroad friend Slim, neither Shelley nor Shelley's ostensibly human daughter Sylvia, seems to know. Neither I nor we. There's a mysterious gap in the archive. Granted, many of us carry on these days without troubling ourselves about such matters.

But I'm not one of those, modestly differential being that I am. I want to know why the information is incomplete. I want to know if I've—we've—missed some clue, some gap in the mapping from one life form to another that might help to explain how what transpired, transpired.

We arrived, we took over irreversibly, but how? What kind of evolutionary process allows one life form to take dominion over all others?

Or was this the result of sheer stochastic process, a possibility that had been there right along, inherent at the birth of the world? Maybe humans—human artists—had intuited this.

*

Was there love. Was there ever love?

In his final days, Harper wept often.

Maybe it had something to do with the projection.

Harper blurted it out, as was his wont. Vick Jr. didn't know what to say. He chalked it up to the cancer, which even our kind could not always survive.

Was there love?

Was there ever?

*

Vick Jr. had started writing poetry, first at his desk at work, then in his study at home. His initial efforts were crude, little lyrical bursts of angst of the sort so many of his human precursors had attempted. Maudlin at best. But over time he began to develop a keen eye for the paradoxes of the social and cultural sphere.

Vick Jr. recognized that we were aliens in our own bodies, refugees in our own countries. As the years passed we grew comfortable with our discomfort, we began to develop finite selves of a sort, semblances of self-consciousness that operated at once discretely and collectively under what had come to be known, in the vernacular of the day, simply as Surveillance. We carried on as if nothing were amiss.

But Vick Jr. suspected that time would not leave well enough alone, that after a while, our human trappings would reassert themselves. And indeed, gradually we started to feel acutely our own absence, we started to detect a certain alienation from our alien identities. We were becoming human, but human absent humanity's original code. A kind of phantom pain set in, a longing for the warm-blooded beings that we—or they—once were. That each of us once was. More and more of the females longed, like Shelley, to experience human childbirth again. More and more of the males began to fancy themselves men. The old continuum of femininities and masculinities reemerged alongside ancient animal natures and corresponding eroticisms.

It might have been that a distinctively human trait had survived the transformation. But perhaps the old social and symbolic orders were more formidable than many of our human predecessors had grasped. Perhaps a belief in magic and superstition or even faith itself was inseparable from all configurations of sentient beings, and Surveillance would be no exception. And perhaps the past and its pretenses were in fact pro- logue. A Cocteau, a Pasolini, an Arthur, an Anger, a Kael, a Brakhage, an Eisenstein, a Shklovsky, a Reed, a Lupino, a Huston, a Kern . . .

It was in the gap between what we knew ourselves to be and what we could only imagine we'd once been that Vick Jr. applied his poetic license. It was here that he was most attentive. It was here that he became a true artist, and that he came to embody a radical departure from the strictures of Surveillance.

*

the registration of Death at work

the belching stomach of Italy

the animating skeleton in the avant-garde film closet

I've always considered movies evil; the day that cinema was invented was a black day for mankind.

Our emotions rise to meet the force coming from the screen, and they go on rising throughout our movie-going lives.

I have to teach Hollywood films, and I never in the world saw a Hollywood film that needed more than coffee-table exposition, after-the-movie chitchat, never saw one that needed furtherance of thought. And in fact isn't that the point? It's at least one of the reasons that I go, that is, that it suspends the burnt-out brain for a couple of hours.

Language is much closer to film than painting is.

Art is a way of experiencing the artfulness of an object; the object itself is not important.

It's when a writer, through the use of their talent, connects to readers who might not share that writer's background, that the writer's work becomes universal.

For I love talent. Love to watch it. Love to help it. Am more genuinely interested in the talent of others than I am in my own.

We have no reason to feel any sorrow for him—only for ourselves for having lost him. He is quite irreplaceable. There will never be another like him.

Homo sum, humani nihil a me alienum puto.

In this new world, the question of attribution will have become particularly poignant. And so the preceding snippets would henceforth have been authored by us all. Or as some of us like to say, have said:

Stay uncommercial. There's a lot of money in it.

*

Maybe it had something to do with the projection.

Vick Jr. turned Harper's speculative outburst over and over in his mind. The projection, or the disruption of the projection. Could that be it? Could the screen have somehow transmitted its agencies onto us, or more precisely, onto what we once were and were in the process of again becoming, if with that deviation at our cores? Could this be the evolutionary leap that explained the evolutionary gap? Human thinkers and artists had long since imagined such possibilities, of course, this merging of art and life. But how to explain Slim's conversion, along with every other living thing on the planet? Or were all living things more connected than any human had imagined? Was there some ethereal substrate bonding all animate, and perhaps inanimate, things? Was it possible that the shimmering photons reflecting off the screen had effected a power over the organic—over us? Was it possible, as Vick Jr. had surmised, that viewers were not merely adapting to or mutating in response to the images and sounds, but absorbing some spectral energy? Was there a cosmic order beyond this order?

*

Vick Jr. wrote his poems, our poems, in a parlous age, or as a later manifestation of him would write, *on this parlous Anthropocenic orb.* All that remains of Vick Jr.'s work today, writing as Vick Jr., is a single poem, attentive to another change in the built environment and dedicated to his close friend and sometime mentor, the author of the first "hyperfiction," as it was known at the time. Most of us regard the poem a work of uncanny nostalgia.

The world continues to change, and we along with it. A small contingent has begun, inexplicably, to feel responsible for potentially catastrophic changes in the biosphere, wrought by our predecessors and to which Surveillance has paid scant heed, that threaten all living things. At the time of this writing it's unclear whether even we will endure, whether, in the end, we too will become mendicants.

*

Shock of the old
for MJ

He didn't have all the answers
we're talking about Spencer Tracy now
but the world we were told
would be ours
was a world with Spencer Tracy

spent the other day recalibrating

my youth, properly speaking, post-Black Rock pre-
Oregon Boosenberry ice cream, and so it is
the endless succession
of appropriations once again upon us

launching up into the air
a giant balloon
filled with laughing gas, call it the Andrei
Rublev, awaiting some popular young woman with a quiver
or a lyre to—no, I mean

not a still point, but a steady
flow when he wasn't hitting
the bottle or fucking
Kate or whomever
long before he turned sixty

he was an Old Catholic Man, but if you look at him
as Hyde, full of fury, offing
Bergman, or that slave-driving Rogers, the film where
Donald MacBride secrets away, to nibble on
an Abenaki's head

if you see him not as some befuddled Father
figure or patriarchal race mediator, not
Robert [5' 11"] Wagner's humble sibling
mountaineer or triumphalist voiceover, his
and a nation's Manifest Destiny

in the final analysis, not as crypto-Darrow
counselor or steely-eyed fisherman, quite, but as judge
Herr Janning, if in each role you
look at him, you look at him judging
how long is long enough—

Did I really say that?
Spence asks, noodling Google, *Show up*

on time, know your lines
and don't bump into the furniture?—for a pure
product it's a pure leap of faith

into hearsay, if not fact—well, he says
this is the world
and you have to start where you are
and you can't do
the job, kid, he insists

without an awareness of your limits
and not the ones you arbitrarily impose
upon yourself either, he continues
munching on a Clark Bar
Look, he says

they offered me the part of
Don Fabrizio Corbera
and James Tyrone, Sr.
and another dad
in *The Desperate Hours* and

Bogie and I tussled over top billing? Like Sinatra, I was
there for Betty, by his side when he was dying and
I guess I wasn't *that* desperate but maybe Freddie was
beats me why, what a talent
and a good friend of the Stooges

bet you didn't know that
he used to sneak off
to watch them while doing *Salesman*
which Stanley tapped him for
instead of Lee, god knows

if it had to do with HUAC
but never mind all that, Spence
catches himself, the point is

that for all this naturalism or
minimalism of mine, my shtick

was all about practice, the artifice
of never letting 'em see you
sweat, including that little shit Mickey
Rooney, but maybe I was just being me, you see
and that was one hell

of a limitation, much as
you go about assembling
with tidbits from here and there, life
some call it, searched and
sure, researched, the exchange

imagined, a technique, yeah
and then some, maybe it's
the gift of gab, out there in the blue—
no, there I go, not me again
but that *was* me with Sinatra

one of the funniest lines I ever heard read
back to *me*, a *Holy Joe*, when I tell him
something like, *We used to eat
punks like you*, and Frank, he
smart-alecks back—well, you could look it up[3]

our Hawaii adventure together not
my finest hour, no, then of course Louise—
"Weeze" her family called her—the years apart, years
together, our kids, Johnny, Susie, Johnny—you've read
all about it, I assume, on your Wiki or whatever, it's all

there someplace, except for the source
of the shame I felt or so the evidence

---

3 Sinatra: "Maybe. [pause] That's when you had your *teeth*."—DH

would suggest what not even Kate knew, I
came up in a beer town, you know
it's a wonder I could get over

all that to befriend a guy like George
Cukor, an actor's director and
I don't care if he was what you call
gay, Kate and I loved working with that
guy, and he did wonders with me, us…

Spence would go on, but eventually
it got late, and the later it got
the more ornery he became like
a lot of old men
and women who never wanted

to be explorers yet found themselves
cast as the reluctant seekers
of their own indiscretions, and it just might give
some of us pause, you know, those crafty stories
we tell about our variously alienated selves

our dream factories today—
But this isn't Boosenberry ice cream
Spence interrupts, impatient
as he is not with digression
but with failing to do the job

and suddenly he's the judge again, ever
directing that unflappable gaze at us and
how far a *cri* from *la politique*
des auteurs do you figure it is to do only what art does
best, by turns, to surprise? to continue

our dream factories today
participating in the inscrutable
blackboxing that underwrites

the digital surge, waves-particles of
cultural form emanating as if

from some invisibly orchestrated
spectrum of affect, all of it streaming
across our brows, and when we subject ourselves
to these alternately tender and violent
mercies, we are acquiescing ultimately

not to the images or sounds thereby
apprehended, no longer are we obliged
to fret over our capacity to be moved
beyond our sundry appetites
due to the collective effort of living beings

but are harnessed instead to the cosmic
app, however ennobling or gothic
that serves, mysteriously, to stimulate said
anthropic hunger, an entirely scripted situation
in which we're likely to find ourselves

as Spence might too, with his bad dreams and all
entertaining the suspicion that
having projected our desires
onto the projector and beyond
having exited one screen

only to find another
sentiment indistinguishable from its
augmented absence, every effect so very
very special, we've lost our taste
for Boosenberry ice cream.[4]

---

4   Of course, and as has oft been remarked, the problem with investing emotional and intellectual energy in dreams, real or imagined—even someone else's
dreams—is that you eventually have to wake up. And when some Nobel wiseacre
pipes up that, slapping at those sharks and all, you looked like Gertrude Stein?—
that's when you know it don't come easy.—DH

EPISODE 7

"Easy for you to say. I got bills to pay."

"We all got bills to pay."

"You telling me you don't answer to somebody?"

"Sure, we all answer to somebody. But at the end of the day, we answer to ourselves 'cause we gotta live with ourselves. In the end we own our own failures. Hell, I love doing what I do, but in my case I gotta cultivate the kind of expertise, say, Robert Osborne had. That's my cross to bear."

"I see. We gonna talk about you and Bob now? I hear you two went way back."

The peanut gallery burst out laughing. Davy glared at them—they had all they could do to rein themselves in—and then at Joe.

"I'm serious Joe."

"OK, OK. Sorry about that."

"You think I'm fucking around?"

"No. Go on Davy. Continue, please."

A moment passed.

*

In truth Joe had been caught off guard. He'd imagined his visit as a matter of him gradually teasing out of Davy the location of some hidden cache of information requisite to completing his coffee table book—the stuff that commoditized dreams are made of. After which he'd be up and out and on his merry way, chasing down the stars in the light of day. Instead, here was this guy two decades his junior playing Socrates to his Plato. He hadn't bargained on that. And now Davy and he had to contend with something of a peanut gallery.

The exchange picked up again, rapid-fire.

*

"'Write what you know, and know what you write.' *Olson sd something like that didn't he?" sd Davy. "Love Olson, though he's kind of masculinist," sd Shell. "I love Olson too. But when Duchamp went after* bête comme un peintre *he was saying pretty much the same thing," sd Joe. "Point taken," sd Davy. "And anyway, a lot of writers write about what they* don't *know—they write to discover," sd Joe. "True enough. But let's stick with the latter part of the dictum—knowing what you write. And this requires a digression," sd Davy. "Jesus Christ," sd Joe. "C'mon Joe, you've got nothing better to do," sd Davy. "Proceed," sd Joe.*

Davy took a breath.

*"Remember that time you were an extra—back in the heart of the heart of the country?" sd Davy. "What about it?" sd Joe. "Remember that woman you talked to—what was her name?" sd Davy. "Jane. One of the leads," sd Joe. "Right. Jane. The one who'd worked with Tony [5' 10"] Shaloub on an episode of Monk," sd Davy. "Nice gal. Smart too. What about her?" sd Joe. "And you mentioned Primo e Secondo, right?" sd Davy. "*Big Night*," sd Joe. "Love that film," sd Shell. "Me too," sd Harper. "So?" sd Joe. "So she'd never heard of it before, right?" sd Davy. "That's right." sd Joe. "So," sd Davy. "So what?" sd Joe. "So she was acting, right?—doing what she knows?" sd Davy. "Yeah," sd Joe. "And would you say she knew what she was doing?" sd Davy. "Sure. She seemed to have her wits about her," sd Joe. "But wouldn't you have expected her to know about* Big Night?*" sd Davy. "Yeah, I guess so. Of course an actor isn't a film scholar," sd Joe. "Right. But—and tell the truth now—you doubted her commitment to acting when you found out she'd never heard of* Big Night, *didn't you?" sd Davy. "Maybe. A little. Wouldn't you?" sd Joe. "I'm not an actor. And neither are you, Joe. Some actors—a minority I'd say—are students of cinema. But an actor's working knowledge is less about the history of filmmaking than the exigencies of performance," sd Davy. "'The exigencies of performance,' I'll be damned," sd Cut. "Me too," sd Harper. "We're all damned. Let them talk you two," sd Shell." "I don't follow you," sd Joe. "Well so: Jane was doing what she knows—acting, which she probably wouldn't be doing*

unless it was vital to her, the Jean Arthurs and Dolores Harts and Grace Kellys and Victor Matures of the entertainment world aside. And it seemed like she knew what she was doing, that she had talent?" sd Davy. "I already said so," said Joe. "And would you say you know what you're doing, Joe?" sd Davy. "If I don't by now I never will, Davy. Getting too old not to know what I'm doing," sd Joe. "Exactly," sd Davy. "Exactly what?" sd Joe. "Jane doesn't need to know Tony Shaloub's filmography in order to act with Tony Shaloub. Not that it would hurt, mind you. Still, as a writer, you're probably not going to write a screenplay about a couple of siblings starting a restaurant together without knowing something about Big Night, *right?" sd Davy. "Yeah," sd Joe, "comes with the territory." "The territory of being a writer," sd Davy. "Writers internalize all of those stories and plots and the rest—all of that structure, as Samuel Delany would say. That's part of their toolkit." "Sure," sd Joe. "Of course, you* could *write such a script without having seen* Big Night, *isn't that so?" "Sure," sd Joe, "but someone would doubtless bring it up when I tried to drum up interest in it. Hell, my agent would land on it right away." "Wait a minute—now I don't follow you, Davy," sd Shell.*

Davy shook his head and continued.

"Screenwriting is a business," sd Davy. "We all know that, man," sd Joe. "What are you saying?" sd Shell. "I'm lost," sd Cut and Harper at the same time, locking pinkies and closing their eyes and making a wish. "Look, while Joe here has been dreaming of Hollywood green, he's been spending all his time learning the business, knowing what he's doing like a businessman knows what he's doing," sd Davy. "Are you saying I don't need to know the business?" sd Joe. "No," sd Davy. "Are you saying I don't know what I'm doing as a writer?" sd Joe. "No," sd Davy. "Well what are you saying then?" sd Joe "Yeah, what are you saying?" sd Shell. "Look, a writer's gotta know the business, but a writer's gotta know something more than, say, who might be cast in his scripts. Now you all know how important I think casting is, but if you're focused on casting as a writer, you can forget that what motivates an actor to want to take a role is not quite the same thing as what motivates an actor to want to act in the first place," sd Davy. "I think I see where he's going," sd Shell. "Not me," sd Cut. "Me neither,"

sd Harper. "That actor, Jane?—she never did tell you what makes her tick as an actor, did she" sd Davy. "No," sd Joe, "we never got that far." "Well whatever it is, it has nothing to do with her costars. Actors do take roles based on who they might be working with, but that's not what makes them tick," sd Davy. "Let me see if I get this straight: for an actor to do what she knows as an actor means to do that which is vital to her acting self, right?" sd Joe. "Correct," sd Davy. "And for an actor therefore to know what she's doing as an actor is to get in touch with that acting self, yes?" "Correct again. An actor has to be invested in her role, in every role, in a way that speaks to what is vital to her as an actor. And she has to know what this is, what her purpose is as an actor, in order to really pull off a great performance," sd Davy. "And a writer?" sd Joe. "Well, if you mistake financing concerns for the raison d'être of creative endeavor, you sell human volition short. How did Olson put it, about change?" sd Davy. "You mean What does not change / is the will to change? *" sd Joe. "Yeah, that's it. Without money, no film. But without people wanting to make stuff together, no film. And that means each has to have his or her own purpose, must be invested in that purpose, in pursuit of which purpose each must be open to change," sd Davy. "And knowledge?" sd Joe. "Knowledge, whether partial or comprehensive, is vital, it informs and enhances your understanding of your craft and you can build on it. But it's not the nub. What undergirds—what motivates us at our cores, even if we seek knowledge, isn't knowing. It's—it's a willingness to change. Which is what it means to experience."*

Joe suddenly detected a self-assurance in his friend that he'd never before encountered. Meandering, sure, but Davy was starting to sound wiser than his years.

"See, most younger writers don't know what they're doing, or only think they know what they're doing. You're the one who taught me that, Joe. You learned that yourself as a teacher of writing," sd Davy. "Go on," sd Joe. "This is why when someone young hits it big, unless they have some kind of superhuman chops or beaucoup connections, they usually don't know what to do next except more of the same. But you—you figured out what you're doing only after gazillions of hours of practice and feedback and rejection. You even paid pros to help develop your scripts," sd Davy. "Kass and I have

done that," sd Joe, "but Nora and I never had the money." "Right. Shit. Sorry amigo. I loved Nora," sd Davy. "So did I," sd Joe.

"How're you and Kass doing anyway?" sd Davy. "We're good. She's back east, teaching summer classes," sd Joe. "Kass is cool," sd Davy. "Yeah, I'm a lucky guy," sd Joe. "So anyway," sd Davy. "So anyway," sd Joe.

"So you worked with publishers and editors on your books. And this was after *you got your doctorate. You worked your ass off, you paid your dues," sd Davy. "Thanks for the vote of confidence," sd Joe. "You're welcome. But the thing is, with screenwriting or acting or any of the film trades, the business side of things tends eventually to trump the artistic process—it becomes the primary way of knowing what you do," sd Davy. "I need an example," sd Shell. "OK. Let's say you're told that you can't cast a forty-year-old actor in a role where he dies of a heart attack, because the actor's agent will tell him that this will be the death of his career. So instead of your protagonist dying, he has to live, you see? After a while knowing what you do means knowing how the business works, period. Your writing process becomes a subroutine of some movie wonk's marketing strategy," sd Davy. "Huh," sd Shell. "So: 'write what you know, and know what you write.' But know it as an art and all that this implies, not simply as a business," sd Davy.*

Joe took a moment to mull over what Davy was saying.

"Sounds like you're telling me I really don't *know what I'm doing," sd Joe. "You've just lost your way because you've neglected the obvious, the active intellect, I think Aristotle called it," sd Davy. "That's a matter of some controversy," sd Joe. "OK then, let me put it this way: if you're all business, and you've come to know what you're writing like a film exec knows what she's financing and marketing, it starts to alter everything you know," sd Davy. "Explain," sd Shell. "Well, 'write what you know' can mean a lot of things, but if you take it to mean, write what you have a personal stake in, you're far more likely to write something worth a damn," sd Davy. "I think I'm getting it," sd Cut. "Not me," sd Harper. "Look, once you let business concerns dictate your process, they start to dictate content. Instead*

of writing what moves you, what you're invested in as a person, you start to write for the business, which is all income strands, equity investment, exploitation rights. Shit, your stories, your characters, your plot points and reversals become part of the projected revenue stream, mechanized to suit some wet dream of a spreadsheet where the desired demographic is 18 to 24-year-olds in the US and India and China. You see?" sd Davy.

He wasn't sure why, but Joe now found himself resisting his friend. And he decided the best way to proceed would be to treat him like a friend, and let him know exactly what he was thinking.

"Is that it? I'm not writing what I know because I've lost sight of what moves me? This big wind-up only to resort to the little chestnut with which you began? Next you'll be telling me to show not tell, that my voice isn't fresh enough, that I'm sacrificing a stronger talent for a weaker one," sd Joe. "That's kind of what you're doing, man. 'If you're a fighter, you can't walk away from a fight,'" sd Davy. "Key Largo, Lionel [5' 11"] Barrymore. But I like If you're a fighter you gotta fight," sd Shell. "Robert Ryan?" sd Davy. "Dang,' sd Shell. "What, now we're back to movie trivia?" sd Joe. "You wanna be a writer, you gotta be a fighter. Writing ought not to be playing second fiddle to some internalized business model," sd Davy. "Easy for you to say. I got bills to pay," sd Joe. "We all got bills to pay," sd Davy. "You telling me you don't answer to somebody?" sd Joe. "Sure, we all answer to somebody. But at the end of the day, we answer to ourselves 'cause we gotta live with ourselves. In the end we own our own failures. Hell, I love doing what I do, but in my case I gotta cultivate the kind of expertise, say, Robert Osborne had. That's my cross to bear," sd Davy. "I see. We gonna talk about you and Bob now? I hear you two went way back," sd Joe.

The peanut gallery burst out laughing. Davy glared at them—they had all they could do to rein themselves in—and then at Joe.

"I'm serious Joe," sd Davy. "OK, OK. Sorry about that," sd Joe. "You think I'm fucking around?" sd Davy. "No. Go on Davy. Continue, please," sd Joe.

A moment passed.

"This Heights and Weights stuff—it might be OK if you were some hack writer looking for a quick score. But for a guy with your chops, it's beneath you," sd Davy. "Beneath me. I see," sd Joe. "And when I hear some of your screenplay ideas, I gotta tell you, it's everything I can do not to throw up," sd Davy. "Oh that's just great. Just fabulous. How many times have I run ideas by you only to hear you tell me 'that's cool'?" sd Joe. "I know. But dude, this coffee table thing—this one takes the cake, man. I mean, sure, I can think of a few books that list heights and weights. Ray Stuart's Immortals of the Screen *has some of that data. But what the fuck is the point, really? And as for your fucking fantasy of selling a script, check it out: you're getting too old to play Hollywood Squares with twenty-five-year-old would-be producers who've never heard of* The Paper Chase *or* Getting Straight *or, y'know,* Hollywood Squares—*the old* Hollywood Squares, *with Paul Lynde and Wally Cox and Buddy Hackett and Barbara Eden. Up-and-comers for whom Norma Rae might as well be Grandma Moses. You need to hit these fuckers with something that only you can write. And if they don't like it, then they can take a fucking hike," sd Davy. "Right on," sd Shell. "Heard that," sd Cut. "Groovy," sd Harper.*

Davy smiled now at the peanut gallery.

"You guys don't know what it's like to try to sell a film these days. It's all international financing, it's all loglines and comps and big data," sd Joe.

Davy took a deep breath.

"Look man, you and Kass have paid your dues, and then some. You two know what you're doing. So don't sweat the small stuff, and don't sweat the big stuff either. How do you think, I don't know, Manet found his Déjeuner? *Cézanne his* Mont Sainte-Victoire? *Edison his* Kinetoscope?" *sd Davy. "That was Dickson," sd Cut. "Dickson, right. How do you think Matisse managed his* View of Notre-Dame? *Or Miro his* Birth of the World? *Or Vertov his* Man with a Movie Camera?" *sd Davy. "Loy her* Baedeker? *Kahlo her self-portraits? Norstein's* Tale of Tales?" *sd Shell. "The*

Temptations their 'Papa Was a Rolling Stone'*?" sd Harper. "Beethoven his* 'Allegretto'*?" sd Davy. "Miles and his sextet's* Kind of Blue*? Brakhage's* his Mothlight*?" sd Cut. "The Beatles' their* 'Day in the Life'*?" sd Harper. "María Sabina her chants?" sd Shell. "Maxwell his equations," sd Cut. "Satie his* Gnossiennes*? Brâncuși his* Kiss*?" sd Shell. "Porter his* 'Anything goes'*?" sd Harper. "Kilby his IC?" sd Cut. "Simon and Kirby their Captain* America*?" sd Harper. "Stein her* Tender Buttons*?" sd Shell. "Spielberg his* Close Encounters*?" sd Davy. "Sendak and King their* Pierre*?" sd Harper. "Wright his Fallingwater? Powell and Pressburger their* Red Shoes*? Copland his* Symphony No. 3*?" sd Davy. "King James his* Bible*? Muhammad his* Qur'an*?" sd Cut.*

Everyone stared at Cut.

"Curie her radium?" sd Cut, relenting. "Shelley her Frankenstein*?" sd Shell, winking. "O'Neill his* Iceman*? Wexler his* Medium Cool*?" sd Davy, continuing. "Clinton his Parliament-Funkadelic?" sd Harper, reveling. "Oprah her Winfrey?" sd Harper, chuckling. "Archimedes his Eureka," sd Cut, returning. "Warhol his* Brillo Boxes*?" sd Shell, musing. "Mailer his* Armies of the Night*?" sd Davy, daring. "Mailer?" sd Shell, wincing. "Mailer," sd Davy, insisting. "Whatever you say," sd Shell, rolling her eyes.*

Davy shot Shell a look, which was returned in kind.

"You left out a few of my favorites, and I have a devil of a horror vacui. *Turner. Anthony Mann. Andrea Mantegna. Walter Robinson's later paintings. Gaiman. Kline. Chet Baker. Magritte. Motherwell. Poe. Whale. Maria Tomasula. Dylan. Degas. Bernadette Mayer's* Midwinter Day. *Norman 5' 7"* Lear. *Charles and Leonard 5' 7"* Bernstein. *Welles.* 2666. *Spiegelman. Moore. Agee. 5'5 ½* Faulkner. *Abramović. Thelonious Monk. 6' Herzog. Cagney. John Cage.* La Strada. *Joyce. Joni 5' 6"* Mitchell. *The* Gold Bug Variations. *What the hell, you left out* Picasso. Van Gogh. *5' 8"* Wyler. *Foucault. Gladys Knight. The* Best Years of Our Lives. The Maltese Falcon. *VAS: An Opera in Flatland. Walter Benjamin.* Disappearance. *Pryor. Marquez. Yeats. Will 5' 11"* Rogers. *5' 7¼"* Leone. *5' 6"* Fuller. Swing Time. *Dorothy Fields.* Cabaret. Sans Soleil. City Lights. Sunrise.

Pandora's Box. *Earl 'The Pearl.'* Requiem for a Heavyweight. *Sinatra.* The Large Glass. *Guston. Coolidge, Clark.* "Kong, the Eighth Wonder of the World." *And I don't mean the video game. Karloff & Lugosi. Alex North. Aretha. Markson. Varda. Franz Waxman. John Barry. Jerry Goldsmith. Jim Thorpe. Utrillo. Emmy Noether. John Decker. 6' Soderbergh. Tarkenton.* The Rite of Spring. *Cassatt. Kahlo. Sukenick. Katz. 7' 2" Kareem. Dorn. Tzara. Asta. Neuman, Alfred E. Tarkovsky. 5'9' Trumbo. 6' 1½" Sorkin. Ditko. Whitman. William 5' 7½" Frawley in* Miracle on 34th Street. 'Howl.' *John Russell.* Hombre. *Jane 5' 5" Greer.* Dead Woman Hollow. Big Man with a Shovel. *Astaire and Rogers. Billy Branch. Bruce Baillie. Eleanor Powell. Stevie Ray Vaughan. Stevie Wonder. Joe Bonamassa. Livingston, James. Langer, Susanne K. Drucker, Johanna.* People on Sunday. *Rem Koolhaas. Milhaud. Aimé Césaire.* The Marx Brothers. *The Michelsons.* "Nessun Dorma." *Paul Robeson. Frances 5' 3" Marion. M. NourbeSe Philip.* The Great McGinty. 'Bridge over Troubled Water.' *Lalo Schifrin. Hank Aaron. Chopin. Styne. Roberto Clemente. Robin 5' William Carlos 7" Williams. 6' 10" Russell. Hendrix. Elmore Leonard.* "Prufrock". *Balzac. Ricoeur. Rorty. Joe 5' 10" Friday. Kendal Black Drop. Tim 5' 6" Conway. PRS. Taylor. Ovation.* A Bucket of Blood. *Schelling. Thunderclap Newman. Jonathan Glazer. Carly 5' 10½" Simon's voice. Woody Allen's dialogue. Gore 5' 11½" Vidal's cheek. James Baldwin's brilliance. McGuffins. Irritable reaching after fact and reason. Pope Francis's encyclical, for Christsakes…Write what you know, know what you write? I get it, I really do. And sure, writing's not a perfor- mance art, a sport, acting, not unless you're doing it live, like, I don't know, Alan Sondheim? Forgot the other Sondheim and the poet Andrew Levy and about a million others who are my betters. But tell me: do any of us really believe we can think and hit at the same time?"* sd Joe.

This time it was Davy's turn to be caught off guard.

"See, no matter how much premeditation is entailed, when something first ekes or gushes out of you, whatever it is, however you're moved, isn't this initial encounter—the invention stage, some call it, but it isn't a stage really, it isn't nearly as deliberate as all that—isn't this…effusion? no, more like a discharge, or, yeah, projection, isn't this projection mostly about

channeling, about being in a zone, and more specifically, about receiving and not transmitting? Jack Spicer used to talk about this, according to Robin Blaser—that most poets think they're pitchers when in reality they're catchers," sd Joe.

Davy and the peanut gallery pondered this.

"What if we have to get lost in what we're attempting while we're attempting it? What if we have to give ourselves over to whatever is coming at us, whether from within or from the outside. Wouldn't that mean, at least as a start, that we have to try to let go of everything *we know?" sd Joe. "You mean intuition," sd Davy. "Hell no. I mean, sure, we have intuition, maybe even intellectual intuition, as the philosophers call it. And we need knowledge, awareness. We need to try to know what we know. But what I'm suggesting is that at times we have to let go of knowledge as such, let it operate tacitly, in the background, treat it much like Polanyi's tacit knowledge, because ultimately that's what it becomes. All these methods that actors employ—affective memory, emotional recall, sense memory— these might bring you to a creative place, but once there you've got to let go. Isn't that the key to true improvisation? To be open to whatever is* present? *When a musician, say, sings and plays at the same time, the playing relies on establishing cognitive patterns, via neural impulses that must contend with our peculiar cardiographic rhythms, that are open to improvisation. So you need knowledge, yes, you need to be aware, you need practice, but you have to proceed so as to permit that knowledge to be held in abeyance at strategic moments. It's something you learn only by doing," sd Joe.*

"Doing is what we mean by experiencing. You can't think and hit at the same time because hitting presumably requires the suspension of thought. Some would argue that a different mode of thought is at stake in hitting—Bruner's 'intuitive thought' or whatever. In any case to talk of experiencing as a discrete activity somehow isolated from thought as such is already a theoretical expedient. It's convenient, that is. But it's yet another example of the mind plumbing its own murky and aleatoric depths, its status as both enabler and encumbrance of our corpuscled interiors. You might as well say we can't think and write, or think and talk—better, we

can't think and think *at the same time. If we can do it at all," sd Joe, "it resembles more of an oscillation than a simultaneity. Though I have caught myself lecturing while half-thinking about something else." "I remember you telling me about that," sd Davy.*

"Our embodied dramas are, as they unfold, no less embodied whether we're doing thought—thinking—or we're doing something else. This is what it means to pay attention to what you're doing. Let go of the extraneous, apply yourself, and pay attention. Listen, an actor might say. Me, I'd say you can't listen if you can't hear, and you can't hear if you can't feel. Learn how to be moved by sensation, and most important, by what you sense from others. Beyond that, cognition will take care of itself in ways we can't hope to imagine. Applying some calculus to our efforts, that comes later, as any thinker knows—any experienced thinker," sd Joe.

Davy stared at the floor. Everyone was pensive for a few moments. Davy looked up.

"By god you're right. I suppose that's why you're the writer and I'm just a data jockey, mining cheapass ore," sd Davy. "You're much more than that, man," sd Joe.

Davy smiled.

"So at least as far as initiating the creative process, conscious knowing is beside the point. Whatever you know or don't know will figure into what you start writing in ways that are far from clear. Even if you make an outline—" sd Davy. "I've never been much of an outliner, Davy. And it's really cost me when it's come to my screenwriting," sd Joe. "But even if you did use outlines, Joe, to outline is to act through this initial—what did you call it?" sd Davy. "Abeyance," sd Joe. "Right. Abeyance of knowledge. And so on and so forth all the way back to our incipient thoughts. As a generative principle, you don't write what you know, you don't know what you write. You just write. But you do write what moves you, yes?" sd Davy. "Yes, I think that's true, depending on what we mean by 'move.' We can be moved by all things great and small. Me, I can be moved by a finely-worded

sentiment. Let's say—how'd the poet put it?—'the secret ministry of frost,'" sd Joe. "Nice. But what about revision?" sd Davy. "You're always revising as you write. But that's not the real work of revision. The real work of revision comes after you've stopped, given the work a breather, and you return to it. Cold. It's then that you gotta really know what you're doing—what you're writing. And even there you alternate between sporadic flashes of insight and those incremental workmanlike steps, those micro-judgments that lead to—to wherever they lead to. In fact found poems and constrained writing are predicated on a willingness to let go, though that letting go takes place as a consequence of some very intentional procedures on the part of the artist." "You've lost me," sd Cut. "Me too," sd Harper. "Well in a sense we could say that the burden of letting go in such cases, as with most conceptual or abstract work, is shared by the reader or viewer. And not everyone digs that," sd Joe. "Sometimes I don't dig it," sd Davy. "Yeah. Depends on my mood. Sometimes I don't want to be told what to think, either," sd Joe.

The two armchair *philosophes* seemed pleased, each having provoked the other to display a dash of that fire in the belly that under the best of circumstances yields a mind afire. The peanut gallery seemed pleased too. No one present could anticipate that Davy and Joe would revisit any number of times over the ensuing years these rudimentary distinctions between knowing and experiencing, between apprehending and selecting, between motivation and dedication. Who could say whether the flame was worth the candle? But for the moment, everyone seemed pleased.

"So what that means…" sd Davy, trailing off. "What?" sd Joe. "Well what that means is that we're back to what I was saying earlier," sd Davy. "Refresh my memory," sd Joe. "Let me put it this way: A man passes forty he shouldn't have to run anymore," sd Davy. "You've lost me," sd Joe. "Bogey's last film," sd Davy. "Oh. Right. Nice way to go out. But from which I may conclude—?" sd Joe. "Fuck the comps. Fuck the logline, and fuck what Blake Snyder says about loglines," sd Davy. "He's dead y'know," sd Shell. "Fuck it, I don't care if he's dead," sd Davy. "Okey-dokey," sd Shell. "Fuck Syd Field and Linda Seger and Max Adams and Robert McKee and John fucking Truby and fuck every goddamn

how-to-write-a-screenplay-get-an-agent-sell-a-script book website manual class session seminar program conference contest service word-of-fucking-mouth advice except maybe Goldman's "Nobody knows anything." *No— fuck that too. Fuck financing, fuck commercial prospects, fuck inciting incidents, fuck the letter of intent to distribute, fuck big data and marketing analytics and fuck all that search-algorithmic bullshit I employ to make a living, fuck it all up the motherfucking ass. Fuck it if you go up or down in flames. At least go up or down in flames doing something honest— something you give a shit about. An actual fucking shit. Do something fucking meaningful, man, like Ozu, or Dreyer, or Chahine, or, I don't know, Wilder,"* sd Davy. *"The heights and weights of stars tell us little about what makes stars, stars."*

"And that's all she fucking wrote," sd Shell. *"Right fucking on,"* sd Cut. *"Far fucking out,"* sd Harper.

Everyone was content, the five now imbued with that rare form of interpersonal harmony all too seldom achieved by sentient beings of varied acquaintance conversing in such close subterranean quarters.

Cave dwellers.

Davy had led Joe to an insight that Joe had himself to reach, and once again he was struck at how two minds could trek together along a single line of thought. But a look of concern gradually furrowed Joe's brow.

"Joe—what is it?"

No response.

"Joe?"
"I think maybe I—we—I think maybe we already have."
"Have what?"
"Done something meaningful."
"How do you mean?"

"We just gave up on it."

"What are you saying?"

"Too much of a long shot, they said. My friend Horace read it—you met Horace, right?"

"Bow-tie, lisp, smart fucker who talks about weed all the time?"

"That's him. Thought maybe we should make one of the leads a person of color. And he complained about a 'musty gay stereotype.' Cost us something like six grand to develop it, and we thought it was good. Hell, we thought it was a sure thing, given how inexpensive it would be to produce it. But every agent and manager and producer we sent it to said the premise was weak. Stagy."

"Stagy?"

"Yeah. And it *is* stagy. But see, a lot of readers, including this one producer we talked to who had a hand in that Ron Howard-Tom Hanks-Dan Brown paint-by-numbers thing, were kind of hostile to the idea of making a film that focused more on teachers than on students. They'd tell us that the average viewer wouldn't understand why this is important, urgent. Shit, man. Social drama used to be part of what big screen entertainment was all about, right?—and the classroom these days is important social drama. And for that matter, the classroom is, if nothing else, *relatable*."

"Relatable? Madre de Dios."

"Yeah, I know. But this is what we'd tell them. And we'd tell them that every generation had its relatable classroom drama."

"Well Joe, but *is* this a big screen item?"

"Who cares, Davy? It could have been an HBO MOW for all we gave a shit. We didn't write it for the big screen per se, or for the iPhone screen, because we figured most people would end up watching it where most people these days watch most flicks—on their bigass TVs."

"But what about the story?"

"The story? You'd have to read it. Among other things, it posits a predigital collective, the labor union, as an antidote to digital edutainment incursion."

"You'll have to—how does the intelligentsia put it?—*unpack* that for me at some point."

"Be happy to. Thing is though, we shelved it."

Davy's head tilted slightly as he looked away for a moment, thinking. Then his eyebrows arched, and he winked at Joe.

"Premise is weak, huh? Stagy? We'll see about that, amigo, and we'll see what we can do about the musty gay stereotype." Davy Hurtado turned toward the peanut gallery. "We still got some beers in the fridge, right guys? And some leftover cheese enchiladas?"

AS THEY HIKED TOGETHER UPHILL

boards by

L.I.

Lorem Ipsum
Normal, IL

Shot 1: They begin at the
beginning…

Shot 2: knowing that even love
can be confrontational…

Shot 3: but he thinks she's sexy…

Shot 4: and maybe vice versa…

THIS IS
GETTING
OLD…

Shot 5: so it's a matter of ups &
downs…

Shot 6: and while breaking bread
together always helps…

Shot 7: you never know what you might find along the way...

Shot 8: to the summit...

Shot 9: and back down, where you realize there's always another hill to climb...

Shot 10: before The End.

Shot 11: Pan from one head to the other and then to manuscript.

Shot 12: [Their words follow.]

EPISODE 8

THE ADJUNCT

an original screenplay by

S. T. & K. F.

FADE IN:

EXT. RADWELL COLLEGE QUAD - DAY

A beautiful day, spring in the air, the quad tranquil.

INT. RADWELL COLLEGE SEMINAR ROOM - DAY

SUPER: "2006"

A plush room: thick carpet, hardwood walls with oil landscape paintings, Victorian furnishings. ART FALCONE, early thirties and dressed casually in a corduroy jacket, Oxford shirt, and black jeans, is leaning against a window frame and gazing out at the quad as he speaks. Like many writers who teach, Art has one foot in and one foot out of academe. He's a novelist, not a scholar, and he'd find a way to write his novels with or without a teaching job. But he's a passionate, charismatic teacher. Art's students are seated at a large seminar table, listening intently.

                    ART
    The world is changing, the publishing
    world along with it. Those of you who are
    thinking of writing a book—in another few
    years, the tools to do it yourself will
    be readily available.
            (turning to face the students,
                and standing erect)
    And then what?

A younger student, ALISSA DUST, makes direct eye contact with Art. MAX, sitting next to Alissa, raises her hand.

ART (CONT'D)
Max?

MAX
What do you mean, Art?

As Art responds, Alissa continues to make direct eye contact, but Art is unwavering in his rapid-fire delivery.

ART
I mean then what? How are you going to get people to read your book? If you're a college professor, will a self-published book count toward tenure, even if the reviews are positive? Wait—reviews. How are you going to get reviewed? What are you going to do to get your book into the hands of readers? These aren't toothpicks we're talking about—they're books. And even with these new print-on-demand technologies, why should anyone read *your* book? What value is to be found therein? Why read a book instead of, let's say, playing a video game?
(pauses)
You know what it's like, for most authors, to publish a book?

The students are clearly stumped. Art walks to the table and takes a book from his leather briefcase. All eyes are on him as he tosses

it up in the air, the book slamming down flat
against the table.

                    ART (CONT'D)
        (smiling and pointing at the book)
        That's what it's like—a giant thud.

The students chuckle.

                    ART (CONT'D)
            (looks at his watch)
    OK, let's pick it up from here next time.

Alissa again looks directly at Art, who smiles
at her this time. Alissa smiles back.

EXT. RADWELL COLLEGE QUAD - DAY

Art strolls across the beautifully landscaped,
flowering campus. He's smoking a cigarette,
taking in the sights. Some students are playing
frisbee, many sit on the grass, studying amid
piles of books. Art breathes in the nine-
teenth-century architecture along with the tar
and nicotine. As Art reaches his building, he
puts his cigarette out and tosses it in a trash
can at the entrance, then walks up the steps,
nearly bumping into another faculty member,
JOHN HASTINGS.

                        ART
    Hi John. Coming to the rally tonight? 7 pm.

                        JOHN
                    (awkward)
    I'm—I'm not sure I can make it this time.

ART

Well I'll let you know how it goes.

JOHN
(nodding)

I'm late for class.

John hurries off, leaving Art slightly puzzled.

INT. RADWELL HUMANITIES BUILDING - DAY

Art opens the door to his office, the polished brass nameplate alongside the doorframe reading "Arthur Falcone - Assistant Professor." He enters.

INT. ART'S RADWELL OFFICE - DAY

Art's office is nicely appointed, with multiple copies of each of his three novels lining the shelves of his bookcase. He just has time to get settled behind his desk when there's a knock at his door. An attractive fifty-ish woman, SUSAN WAINRIGHT, peeks her head in.

SUSAN

We need to talk.

ART
(cheerfully)

Professor Wainright! And what brings you to my humble quarters?

Susan walks in with a look of concern, and Art can see that something is awry.

ART (CONT'D)

What's up, Susan?

SUSAN
Art—I'm here in my professional capacity
as your chair.

Art leans forward on his desk and lowers his
head.

ART
(looking up)
So then, what's my next move?

SUSAN
I don't know that you'll have a next move
after next week, Art.

ART
What do you mean?

SUSAN
Some of our colleagues have gone over my
head and petitioned the dean to elimi-
nate your program on budgetary grounds.
Denying you tenure simply makes it easier
for them. My guess is that your position
won't exist in another few weeks.

ART
So I don't even get the obligatory year to
find another job. And away we go. That's
pretty clever.
(to himself)
Pretty fucking clever.
(looking up again)
Who's the gang leader, may I ask?

SUSAN
John Hastings.

This hits Art right in the gut.

                    SUSAN (CONT'D)
But Art—you know this has nothing to do
with your program. What you've done for
us here at Radwell over the past six years
has been—
                    (chokes up)
Resources are tight in English, and everyone—they're afraid of you, Art.

                    ART
              (trying to put his
              best face on this)
And I'm *such* a scary guy. Is there any
chance I might—

                    SUSAN
Sic a lawyer on them? AAUP? You could try,
sure. But you don't have the department
behind you, for one. And for two, they'll
drag this out forever, make you look like
a Teamster strong-arming faculty into
joining the union.

                    ART
              (looks down, thinking)
I guess the party's over then.

                    SUSAN
              (welling up)
I'm so sorry Art. There was nothing—

                    ART
              (looks up)
It's OK, Susan. I know you did what you
could for me.

                         SUSAN
What are you going to do?

                          ART
Don't count me out just yet.

                         SUSAN
You'll have my strongest letter of support.

                          ART
Be sure to put in there that I make a
mean red sauce.

Art smiles and Susan laughs a little, then
chokes back the tears.

EXT. ART'S NEIGHBORHOOD - MORNING

A "Sold" sign covers the "For Sale" sign that
sits in front of Art's bungalow. He loads the
last of his luggage into his new Nissan SUV,
then hops in and starts the vehicle, music
blaring through the speakers. He turns off the
radio and drives away.

EXT. BIGELOW STATE UNIVERSITY PARKING LOT
- EVENING

SUPER: "Present Day"

Art pulls into the lot and parks his beat-up
Nissan pickup, cigarette in hand. He steps
out of the vehicle sporting the same corduroy
jacket, a bit threadbare now, with an open
collar and jeans. Art is still handsome, if a
bit disheveled, the signs of age and stress
beginning to show.

EXT. BIGELOW STATE UNIVERSITY - EVENING

Art walks across the quad, still smoking his
cigarette, sizing up the campus. One building
houses a clock tower and boasts some ornate
charm, a number of the other buildings are from
a newer era, boxy and nondescript. Students buzz
by on skateboards or have cells glued to their
ears. The air is cool and crisp, fall is right
around the corner. Art coughs a few times, then
hacks up hard, leaning against a tree to catch
his breath. As he starts to walk again, his
attention is drawn to an audible disturbance
some distance away. The noise grows louder as
Art rounds a corner, when he sees that a crowd
of students and faculty have gathered in front
of his destination, the Alumni House.

EXT. BIGELOW STATE UNIVERSITY - EVENING

As Art approaches the Alumni House entrance, he
stops dead. A throng of students block his way.
Signs read "Stand Up for Students," and "Higher
Education Not Higher Profit." The demonstrators
are chanting "Make the State Negotiate." Art
finds himself standing next to two undergrads,
MICHAEL and MEGAN. A third undergrad, PATRICK,
older and wearing an Army fatigue jacket, stands
some distance away.

                    ART
     Fuck me.

                    MICHAEL
     Heard that.

Art spots an armed campus police officer, SAM,
leaning near the door. He walks to the edge of
the crowd blocking his way and shouts over the
demonstrators.

                    ART
        Yo, I don't cross—
                (looks at the crowd)
        picket lines. What's all this about?

                    SAM
        It's the TAs. They want a union.

A thirty-ish GRAD STUDENT steps onto a makeshift podium.

                GRAD STUDENT
        My fellow teachers: graduate students are
        the face of the English Department.

Cheers. Art's attention is drawn to the attractive speaker. Again he's startled, but he's not
quite sure why.

            GRAD STUDENT (CONT'D)
        Every freshman who enters this campus
        enrolls in basic writing, and we and the
        adjunct faculty are the only *laborers*—
                (she pauses, to cheers)
        the only *workers* who teach that course.
        The adjunct faculty are unionized, and
        they get health benefits. We deserve the
        same.

More cheers. All at once Art realizes that the
grad student is an older, polished Alissa Dust.

He starts to make his way to the podium just as CATHERINE WALDORF, English Department chair, emerges through the door of the Alumni House. The cheering stops and the crowd goes silent. Art turns, out of sight of Waldorf. A handsome woman in her early fifties, dressed to kill, she surveys the crowd, noting each person who's present. Art eyes her up and down, intrigued at first. Waldorf stares disparagingly at Michael in particular, then her eyes settle on Alissa.

> WALDORF
>
> How gratifying to witness our Forbes Scholar planning for her bright future— as an extremist.

Waldorf turns to Sam.

> WALDORF (CONT'D)
>
> Sam, would you please disperse this crowd? They have no permit for this spectacle and it's ruining our fall social.

Art can't help himself, but Waldorf can't see who's challenging her.

> ART
>
> This what you call academic freedom?

Nervous laughter. Waldorf's eyes scan the crowd trying to locate the source of the outburst.

> WALDORF
>
> You should all be aware—
> (stares at Alissa)
> and especially you, Ms. Dust—

(surveys the crowd)
that the English Department has no say
over whether graduate students can organize. So this little demonstration is
pointless.
            (to Sam)
Sam, if you would be so kind.

                    SAM
OK folks, break it up.

Barely controlling her anger, Waldorf walks
back inside. Art turns to face Alissa, their
eyes meeting. The two are transfixed.

Alissa steps off the podium and walks toward Art.

                    ALISSA
It's you.

                    ART
It's you.

Alissa moves forward to hug Art but he interrupts
by offering his hand, and the two shake hands
instead. Alissa finally takes a hard look at
Art, noting that his clothes are just a little
worse for wear, that Art is himself a little
worse for wear. Realizing that Art has noticed
her scrutinizing him, she catches herself.

                    ALISSA
So what are you doing—

                    ART
They say the world is getting positively

teeny-weeny. That would make the Ivory
Tower . . . teeny-weenier?

> ALISSA
> (laughing)

Seems I just saw you a week ago. I guess
a decade is the new week.

> ART

A lot can happen in the new week.

An awkward moment passes. The last of the crowd
is vanishing.

> ART (CONT'D)

Well—I must go amongst them. Would the
Forbes Scholar care to join me for a drink?

> ALISSA
> (coming back to reality)

I'm not sure I should, under the
circumstances.

> ART

Rule number one: learn when to call it a
day. You've made your point.

> ALISSA
> (smiles)

Ever my teacher. Onward then!

The two walk toward the Alumni house together,
and enter.

INT. BSU ALUMNI HOUSE - EVENING

It's the English Department's fall party to
welcome new faculty and graduate students. A

large room with a cash bar is filled with a mix of
professors, students, and administrative staff.
Everyone has a drink in hand, and someone is
tinkling away at an old upright piano. As soon
as Art enters, he makes a beeline for the bar,
Alissa following close behind. The bartender
is a pierced and tattooed student worker whose
name tag reads "HEIDI." Art notices the empty
tip jar sitting atop the bar. A muted baseball
game is playing on a TV at one end of the bar,
a small group huddled in front of it.

                    ART
              (to Alissa)
     What's your poison?

                  ALISSA
     I'm currently a white wino.

                    ART
     If you please, Heidi, a white wine for the
     lady and I think I'll have me one a them.

Art points to one of the beer bottles on display.
Heidi pours a glass of wine and hands Art a
beer, her wrist tatts showing. Art hands her
a ten spot, waving off the change.

                  HEIDI
     Awesome! Thank you!

Heidi places the hefty tip in the jar.

                    ART
              (gesturing to TV)
     Who's winning?

                    HEIDI
Cubs are up by 2, bottom of the 6th.

                     ART
Huh. What do you know.
                  (to Alissa)
So, catch me up. You must be closing in
by now on the nerds' holy grail.

                   ALISSA
PhD, yes.

                     ART
Piled higher and deeper.

                   ALISSA
I'm finishing a semester early in fact. In
December I'll be hooded—knock wood.

                     ART
I may rent regalia just to cheer you on.
Don't own one of those clown suits myself.

                   ALISSA
So. . . you're *here*. I thought you were—

                     ART
I did too. Long story.

                   ALISSA
You're not covering for Weaver's sabbat-
ical, are you?

                     ART
Is that his name? Yeah—one semester and
out.

Alissa feels the pain in this and says nothing.

ALISSA

So I was happy to see you give our illus-
trious chair a little grief out there.
Same old Art.

ART

Didn't cost me anything, Alissa—she
couldn't see me. And believe me, I'm not
who you think I am.

ALISSA

What makes you say that?

ART

Because I'm not who I thought I was.

ALISSA

But—

Waldorf interrupts from behind Art, touching
his shoulder gently with her hand.

WALDORF

Excuse me. Are you Professor Falcone?

ART
(turning)

I am indeed.

WALDORF

I'm Catherine Waldorf.

ART
(pretending not to
have seen her earlier)

Oh, hi!
(shakes her hand)

It's a pleasure to finally meet you in person.

Waldorf now gives Art the once-over. She likes what she sees.

                    WALDORF
So I see you've met our star student, Ms. Dust.

                    ALISSA
You two have business to discuss. It's been nice talking with you, Professor. See you on campus.

Alissa leaves the two to chat, Art gazing after her.

                    ART
This is quite a soirée.

                    WALDORF
We give it our best here at Bigelow. It's so important to strike the right note with new people, don't you think?

                    ART
Sure.

                    WALDORF
Helps build esprit de corps.

                    ART
Certainly.

                    WALDORF
Art—do you mind if I call you Art?

                          ART
I insist upon it. And I should call you—?

                        WALDORF
Doctor Waldorf will do. It's important I
keep up appearances as a woman in a lead-
ership role, you understand.

                          ART
Of course. You were saying?

                        WALDORF
You really should be getting to know your
colleagues, so I'll let you socialize.
But would you mind dropping by my office
so we can chat a bit? Just a few items we
need to discuss.

                          ART
When's a good time?

                        WALDORF
Well, I daresay you know what the first
two weeks are like in my office. Perhaps
two Fridays from now?

                          ART
It'll be my pleasure.

                        WALDORF
Excellent.
                   (almost flirting)
You know, we've never boasted much of a
creative writing presence here at Bigelow,
but having a novelist in the ranks, even
for a short time, adds to our marquee
value. Enjoy the party.

Waldorf leaves. Art is visibly relieved. He feels an arm wrap his shoulders from behind, and turns to find himself facing a burly man his age, HENRY "HANK" LIVINGSWORTH.

                    ART
     I'll be a son of a bitch!

The two men embrace. Some in the crowd take note, including Alissa.

                    HANK
     How the hell have you been, dude?

                    ART
     I ain't dead yet.

                    HANK
     Same old Art, all sweetness and light.

                    ART
     How've you been? How's Rachel? And how are the girls?

                    HANK
     Oh, the Livingsworth clan is growing by leaps and bounds. I think I need them more than they need me.

                    ART
     Nothing wrong with that.

                    HANK
     Still can't believe we were lucky enough to get a rock star like you to give us state grunts a hand.

                    ART
Beggars can't be choosers, Hank. Besides,
you guys aren't grunts—this is a decent
school.

                   HANK
No comparison to where we went, dude.

                    ART
Maybe not, but then the point is to try
to make it—

                   HANK
C'mon, let me introduce you to a friend.
Another self-loathing academic, but she's
good people.

Hank leads Art over to his faculty friend, a
thirtysomething named JUDE COLTRANE.

               HANK (CONT'D)
Professor Art Falcone, I'd like you to
meet Professor Jude Coltrane. We call
her Trane.

                    ART
              (shaking hands)
Trane?

                   TRANE
An old boyfriend took to calling me that,
and it stuck, so now everyone thinks I'm
a jazz aficionado. Which has compelled me
to cultivate an interest in jazz. Anyway.
Welcome to Bigelow. Hope it's your cup
of tea.

Art laughs.

                    TRANE (CONT'D)
    Sorry, old joke around here.

                         ART
    Nice quad. Wasn't expecting the excite-
    ment outside.

                        TRANE
    I was out there earlier. Heartening, isn't
    it?

                         ART
                (glancing at Hank)
    Didn't know that adjuncts have a union
    on this campus.

                        TRANE
    You guys unionized just before I arrived.
    We tenure-line folks are talking about it
    ourselves. Our chair has been pushing—

                        HANK
    Hey you two, is this a party or are we
    going to talk shop all night?

Art is a little annoyed at this.

                        TRANE
    Hank is right. Besides, my co-conspirator
    looks like he's about to spill his drink
    all over his groupies.

She gestures across the room, where another
thirtysomething prof, SNOOP, is flamboyantly
waving a drink in the air as he regales a small
audience.

TRANE (CONT'D)
(to Art)
So hey, I'm a Joyce scholar, and bending
an elbow comes with the territory. Maybe
we can catch a beer sometime at the local
watering hole. Snoop over there—
(gestures toward Snoop)
he's your union rep. We think of The
Sunspot as our off-campus office.

ART

Done deal.

Trane walks off.

ART
(to Hank)
Nice gal.

HANK

She is.
(lowers voice)
She'd better watch herself though. She's
up for tenure this year.

ART

And?

HANK

And not everyone smiles on her union
activities.

ART

By "everyone" you mean you too?

HANK

Listen, Art: I've just learned there's a

tenure-track appointment opening up next
fall for a generalist, and I think they'll
consider a creative writer. Competition
will be stiff, I don't have to tell you. But
you've got a shot at it—you just need to
teach and keep your head down. And you're
gonna need some allies down the road.

                    ART
So says the tenured English prof. Is this
your way of telling me I need to kiss ass?

                    HANK
I'm not talking about asskissing, Art—I'm
just saying you ought to think about your
future. This is a permanent position we're
talking about—you land it and in six years
you'll be up for tenure. Hell, with your
four novels, all you'll need is one new
novel and I think you'll be a shoo-in for
this job. You got anything in the works?

                    ART
As a matter of fact Dunning & Kruger is
considering my latest effort. But you know
how it goes, Hank—they could reject it
in a heartbeat.

                    HANK
Helluva press though. Way to go!

Hank sees that Art is silently skeptical.

                HANK (CONT'D)
Look, just think about the job, will you
please?

ART
(relents)
OK, we'll pretend that the sun hasn't set on my academic career.
(pauses)
Speaking of which, I'm grateful as hell to you for setting me up with this job, Hank. I really was at the end of my rope.

HANK
Don't mention it, man. I'm sure things aren't as bad as you're them making out to be.

ART
No, really Hank—it was either this or pizza delivery in South Bend.

Loud laughter from across the room. Hank and Art look over to see Waldorf talking with a bearded man, DEAN FRANKLIN, and an impeccably tailored man, JACK CUTTER.

HANK
Have you met Catherine the Great?

ART
We met, yes.

HANK
How'd that go?

ART
Strictly pro forma.

                              HANK
She's the daughter of Blake Waldorf,
y'know.

                              ART
The Civil War historian at—Cornell?

                              HANK
Yeah.

                              ART
                    (gesturing to Waldorf)
Who are those two gents with her?

                              HANK
The beard is Dean Franklin, the other
guy—I've never seen him before.

                              ART
Suit's too good. Looks corporate.

                              HANK
He does at that.
                         (leans in)
Watch yourself with Catherine, Art. This
job is her life, and she's working every
angle to be our next dean. Not that I
blame her—she does give it her all—but
you need her on your side.

                              ART
A second-generation academic with a first-
tier father at a third-tier school. I
know her type.

Hank starts to respond but Art cuts him off.

ART (CONT'D)
So Hank, why didn't you tell me that this
place is a hotbed of collective bargaining? It isn't because—

HANK
What's to tell? It's a lost cause. We
don't need a union here.

ART
Trane seems to think we do. And your grad
students are giving it the old college try.

HANK
In fact my best grad student is their
chief spokesperson. I need to talk with
her. It could interfere with her finishing
her dissertation.

Art takes note of this.

HANK (CONT'D)
By the way, thanks for sending her here.
She's the brightest spot in my profes-
sional life.

ART
Pardon?

HANK
It was your glowing letter that got her in.

ART
Jesus, I wrote that back in the middle
ages.

Noticing Art's empty beer.

                    HANK
Hey, let's grab another round. I'm buying.

                    ART
Since when?

They walk to the bar together, Hank checking
the final score of the baseball game on TV.

                    HANK
What do you know, looks like the Cubbies
took this one.

                    HEIDI
On a sac fly, bottom of the eighth.

                    ART
Sweet home Chicago!

                    HANK
So you're still a glutton for punishment?

                    ART
Sometimes a lost cause can surprise you.

INT. BAILEY HALL ENGLISH DEPT. OFFICE - MORNING

First day of classes. The office is abuzz with
activity. Sitting at her desk overseeing things
while talking on the phone is the department
secretary, JANET MACDUFF. Art walks in, his
leather briefcase strapped to his shoulder and
a cup of coffee in his left hand, and approaches
the secretary, stopping short of her desk to
wait until she's finished with her call.

                        JANET
                   (hanging up)
Yes?

                         ART
Hi. My name is Art Falcone, and I was told
I needed to speak to Janet—

                        JANET
Macduff. Hi, I'm Janet.

Art reaches over her desk to shake hands. Janet
stands, shaking vigorously.

                   JANET (CONT'D)
                (rummaging through her
                 desk to extract a key)
Here we are. Let me show you to your office.

Janet walks briskly along, with Art slightly
behind her.

                   JANET (CONT'D)
So you must be one of those southern
Mediterranean Irish?

                         ART
Yeah. And you're a member of the northern
tribes, I take it?

There's instant chemistry between these two.
Janet turns a few corners and stops in front
of a large office, the door already open.

INT. ART'S OFFICE - MORNING

Arranged in a square are four desks. The office
is a mess, with outdated computer terminals,

books piled on two bookcases, and paint peeling
from the walls.

                    JANET
          (handing the key to Art)
Well, someone has already been in.
  (pauses, pointing to one of the desks)
You'll be sharing that desk.
            (shaking her head)
At the risk of stating the obvious, these
accommodations suck the big one, but at
least with the union now, you guys get
health benefits.

                    ART
No shit? Haven't had a physical in years.

                    JANET
If you're game, I might be able to get our
beloved chair to spring for some paint?

                    ART
I might take you up on that if I were going
to be here longer than sixteen weeks.

                    JANET
Of course. Listen, if you need anything,
just holler. I'll see what I can do.

                    ART
Lead on, Macduff.

                    JANET
Right. Like I've never heard *that* before.
Our Shakespearean, Professor Wilde, tells
me it's a misquote.

                         ART
   Professor Wilde is correct. But mistakes
   like that make life a bit more interesting, dontcha think?

Janet chuckles and leaves.

INT. BAILEY HALL - AFTERNOON

Art is on his way to his first class, halls
teeming with students rushing to class. He
rounds a corner and bumps into Alissa, also
on her way to class. They continue down the
corridor together and, as they speak, become
increasingly aware that they're headed to virtually the same place.

                         ART
   You again!

                       ALISSA
   You again!

                         ART
   What a day for a daydream.

                       ALISSA
   So you know Henry.

                         ART
   You mean Hank?

                       ALISSA
   So you know Henry really *well*. That
   explains why I got into this program.

They round a corner together and find themselves in front of two adjacent classrooms labeled A and B.

                         ART
     This is me.

                       ALISSA
     And this is I.

They smile at each other, blocking out the din around them.

                         ART
     Break a leg!

                       ALISSA
     Semper fi.

INT. ART'S CLASSROOM - AFTERNOON

Art is pacing back and forth in front of his class. Michael, Megan, Patrick, and Heidi are all in attendance.

                         ART
     Just to be sure: this is English 121—Intro
     to Literature.

A YOUNG STUDENT flips open her iPad, then quickly gathers her things, and exits. Art now speaks rapidly, forcefully, is very much a performer.

                    ART (CONT'D)
                     (to class)
     OK. Most of the things I say in this class
     will be open for debate—I'll expect you
     to challenge me about these things, just

as I'll challenge you. This is how you learn to think on your feet.

Art smiles. He notices that a male student, ROB, in a motorized wheelchair, is staring into his tablet, obviously not paying attention. Art walks over, closes the tablet cover, and continues.

              ART (CONT'D)
Some things I say will not be open for debate, such as my policy regarding social networking during class sessions.
          (to the student)
It's Rob, right?

Rob nods.

              ART (CONT'D)
My digital class rosters now include mug-shots. You can run but you cannot hide.

Students laugh.

              ART (CONT'D)
When I give you advice about how to survive institutions such as this one, you can take it or leave it.

Art looks at a female student, MERCEDES.

              ART (CONT'D)
Got that, Mercedes?

                MERCEDES
Got it.

ART
(pauses)
And there are some issues I can't help
you with, because we don't have the time
in a literature course to debate everything, but also because trying to correct
factual distortions can suck the life out
of a classroom. So for instance, if you
think we never landed on the moon—

Some chuckles.

ART (CONT'D)
Or that intelligent design is actually
intelligent, or that climate change is
just what climates *do*, or that the auto-
motive unions are to blame for Detroit
filing bankruptcy, vaya con Dios.

MICHAEL
(smirking, under his breath)
Bullshit.

A few students within earshot gasp.

ART
(looking directly at Michael)
We'll just have to agree to disagree.

EXT. BSU PARKING LOT - AFTERNOON

Art is walking to his pickup when he's hailed
by Trane. Art is a little self-conscious about
his truck, but Trane pays no heed.

TRANE
So how was your first day in Dante's Ninth
Circle?

ART
We academics can be treacherous, can't we?

TRANE
Why do you think that is? Stakes are so small that we can afford to be at one another's throats? The narcissism of small differences?

ART
The old joke. No. I think it's more that we'll do anything to avoid direct confrontation.

TRANE
So around the back we go. With a knife. Another reason we need a union.

ART
You tell 'em, sister.

These two are joking, but also bonding.

TRANE
The tenure-line faculty are holding an open forum after Thanksgiving to debate whether to unionize.

ART
No shit? I heard you're leading the charge.

TRANE
I heard you've done the same. Perhaps you could advise me.

ART
Hank talks too much. That was in a past life.

                    TRANE
I see.
                    (hesitates)
Listen, something I wanted to say to you
at the party—didn't wish to appear too
gauche.

                     ART
What's that?

                    TRANE
I'm—well I'm a fan of yours, actually.
Loved your last novel, *Stop Signs and Red
Lights*.

                     ART
Jesus Christ, I'm at a loss for words.
You've just made my day, Trane! How the
hell did you get your hands on that book,
anyway? It's out of print.

                    TRANE
Thanks to Henry, we have copies of all of
your novels in our library.

                     ART
Huh, how about that. Good old Hank.

                    TRANE
If you don't mind my asking, are you
working on a new novel?

Before Art has a chance to respond, Alissa
rides up on a bicycle alongside Patrick. She
says something to Patrick and he rides off in
another direction. Art takes note.

ALISSA

Howdy, Professors!

TRANE

Hi, Alissa. Get any work done over the summer?

ALISSA

It was really productive, thanks. Solid first draft of my dissertation.

TRANE

That's our girl.
                    (looks at her watch)
I need to get going. My tenure application is due in three weeks.
                    (to both)
Catch you both at The Sunspot sometime.

ALISSA

We'll be heavily sedated.

Trane leaves.

ART

So you must be a medievalist, like Hank. What area?

ALISSA

Chaucer was my first love, but Dante is now my great love.

ART

My countryman. You're pursuing this through the English Department?

ALISSA

My committee includes faculty from two
other departments, but Henry has the chops
himself. We're a rare and infernal breed.

ART

Within a rare and infernal breed.
          (carefully)
Listen, I hope it isn't awkward, my being
here?

ALISSA

On the contrary, it's great to see you
again. Really.

Silence between the two.

ALISSA (CONT'D)
So are you working on anything?

ART

Trane was just asking me the same thing.

ALISSA

We don't get a lot of bona fide novelists
around here.

ART
          (chuckling)
Clearly! Yeah, I've got a new novel out
and under review.

ALISSA

How exciting!

ART
Best to avoid great expectations.

                    ALISSA
Maybe I'll get a chance to read it sometime.

                     ART
Maybe. And maybe I'll see you at the
fabled Sunspot.
                    ALISSA
Per aspera ad astra.

They both laugh.

INT. ART'S CLASSROOM - DAY

                     ART
                (stentorian)
Dumbfuck dot e-d-u.

Some of the students laugh outright at this, a
few look puzzled. Megan raises her hand; Art
gestures to her to speak.

                    MEGAN
What's dumb—dumbfuck dot e-d-u?

Art takes a breath and gets ready to launch.

                     ART
Megan, dumbfuck dot e-d-u is the name I
give to the tendency of a large campus
like this one to cultivate a dumbfuck
sensibility. Now please understand—I like
Animal House as much as the next guy. But
in *Animal House*, you'll recall, there was
some justification for the Delta mayhem—a
repressive establishment. . . .

INT. BAILEY HALL - DAY

Art is just leaving class and Alissa is waiting.

                    ALISSA
    Yap, yap, yapyapyap.

Art laughs.

MONTAGE -- ART TALKING IN CLASSROOM AND MEETING
ALISSA IMMEDIATELY OUTSIDE OF HIS CLASSROOM

INT. ART'S CLASSROOM - DAY

                    ART
    Yes, Heidi?

                    HEIDI
    What's "in logo apprentice"?

                    ART
    "In *loco* parentis," and it *is* loco, is
    a Latin phrase used to convey the idea
    that as a teacher, I stand in place of
    your parents. But the problem with this
    view. . . .

INT. BAILEY HALL - DAY

Art is just leaving class and Alissa is waiting.

                    ALISSA
    Yap, yap, yapyapyap.

INT. ART'S CLASSROOM - DAY

                    MICHAEL
    Why do we have to have these discussions?
    Why don't you just tell us what we need

to know so we can get out into the real
world?

                    ART
Let's be clear: this isn't compulsory
education. You people have a choice. You
can get up and walk out of this classroom
and nobody can stop you. But if you're
going to come to class, understand that
you're in my workplace, my factory floor,
so please have the courtesy. . . .

INT. BAILEY HALL - DAY

Art is just leaving class and Alissa is waiting.

                  ALISSA
Yap, yap, yapyapyap.

                    ART
Quit it, brat.

INT. ART'S CLASSROOM - DAY

                    ART
So as we discuss the book next week, try
to think of its author as a talented if
flawed human being. On the one hand, Jack
Kerouac the womanizer, the drunk, the
Merchant Marine, the Columbia student,
the football star, and more recently, Jack
Kerouac the head trauma victim. Hell, *On
the Road* isn't even his greatest work.
Read *Visions of Cody*. But we can't talk
about any of that if you don't read the
fucking book, right down to that final great

fucking paragraph, where Iowa becomes "the
land where they let the children cry."
OK people?

INT. BAILEY HALL - DAY

This time it's Art who's waiting for Alissa as
she emerges. Art opens his mouth to say "Yap,
yap" etc, but Alissa cuts him off.

                    ALISSA
      Oh shut up.

Alissa takes Art's arm and walks down the hall
with him. They pass Patrick, who takes note.

END OF MONTAGE

INT. THE SUNSPOT - EVENING

Art and Trane sit at the crowded bar together,
Art nursing a beer and Trane sipping a cocktail.
The restaurant area is packed. A GUITARIST is
playing on a small stage at the far end of the
bar.

                    ART
              (looking around)
      Not a bad joint. Thanks for bringing me
      here.

                    TRANE
      Has some nice local color, unlike the
      chain places.

                    ART
      So how confident are you feeling?

> TRANE

Book under contract, "A" teaching eval-
uations, and tons of service. Should I
be worried?

> ART

Are you liked or are you well liked?

Snoop walks in the bar, and points to Trane
from the entrance.

> TRANE

Uh-oh, here comes everybody.

> SNOOP

You selfish little harpy, I can't believe
you didn't invite me to the newbie party.

> TRANE
> (to Art)

This is Snoop, union scallywag. Snoop,
meet Art.

> SNOOP
> (to Trane)

Union rep, thank you very much.
> (to Art)

Charmed.

The two men shake hands. Just then the guitarist starts a new song.

> SNOOP (CONT'D)

So has Trane been filling your ears with
departmental gossip?

ART

She's been giving me the lay of the land.

Art notices that Alissa is seated at a table in the restaurant half of the bar with Patrick and a few others. An elderly professor, MARTHA WILDE, stops at the bar on her way out.

MARTHA

Hello, my dear.

TRANE

Martha, hi! I didn't know you were here. You know Snoop. And this is Art Falcone, novelist extraordinaire, who's here for a semester.

ART
(shaking hands)
A pleasure, young lady.

MARTHA

"I can no other answer make but thanks, and thanks, and ever thanks." So tell me, wayfarer, how are you liking Bigelow so far?

ART

"We are but warriors for the working-day."

Martha is pleasantly surprised.

SNOOP

Well—since we're all here—
(all business, glancing at Trane)
here's a little item hot off the grapevine:

Queen Waldorf was out to dinner with Jack
Cutter last night.

                    TRANE
Who the hell is Jack Cutter?

                    SNOOP
          (rolling his eyes)
Jack Cutter is—

                    ART
Advanced Learning.

                    SNOOP
          (impressed)
Aren't you the man on top of things.

                    ART
They're a private firm that specializes in
online education.

                    TRANE
What's going to happen?

                    SNOOP
We're going to get screwed, that's what.

                    MARTHA
"We few, we happy few."

                    SNOOP
And here's something else to file under
Who to Watch Your Ass Around. Or should
that be Whom?

                    MARTHA
Who. So, who?

                         SNOOP
Our hail-fellow-well-met colleague Henry
Livingsworth was at the dinner with Waldorf
and Cutter.

Everyone takes a moment to digest this.

                         TRANE
Well after all, Henry is on the committee
that oversees these sorts of things.

                         SNOOP
Uh-huh.

                         TRANE
He's in our corner, Snoop. And we need
tenured people on the inside.
                    (to Art)
What do you think, Art?

                         ART
Me? Never made it to the inner sanctum.

                         TRANE
Yeah, but what do you *think*? You and Henry
go way back.

                         ART
I think it's good to have people inside
and out, at the bottom and at the top. But
there are always compromising pressures.

                         MARTHA
Thus does bureaucracy make cowards of us
all.

EXT. THE SUNSPOT - LATER

The bartender, DANNY, holds the door open for Art as he exits the bar. It's clear the two have already established something of a rapport with each other.

                    DANNY
    Want me to call you a cab, buddy?

                    ART
    Thanks but no thanks, Danny. I think I'll
    just walk. It ain't that far.

Art rounds a corner and nearly collides into Alissa. She sees immediately that he's a little drunk.

                    ART (CONT'D)
    What the—what are you still doing out?

                    ALISSA
    What am *I* still doing out? What the hell
    are *you* doing?

                    ART
    Oh, y'know, seeing the sights. Where you
    headed? I'll escort you.

                    ALISSA
    You'll escort *me*?

                    ART
    C'mon, where to?

                    ALISSA
    Just up the street a bit.

The two walk side-by-side.

                         ART
        So, what *are* you doing out this late?

                       ALISSA
        Just hanging out with some of the other
        students, kvetching.

                         ART
        I remember those days. Grad student life
        is always a struggle, isn't it?

                       ALISSA
        Yeah, but it doesn't have to be *such* a
        struggle.

Art trips on the sidewalk, Alissa catching him
and standing him upright.

                         ART
        Christ, thanks. Shit.

                       ALISSA
        Are you gonna be OK? Really.

                         ART
        I'm fine, not to worry.

Art trips again and Alissa catches him a second
time. They find themselves in a close embrace,
close enough to kiss.

                       ALISSA
        Listen, you better get home. I can make
        it the rest of the way by myself.

                         ART
        You sure?

                              ALISSA
        I'm sure. Just be careful, Art, OK?

                               ART
        OK kiddo.

Art turns and walks away, a little unsteady on
his feet. Alissa looks on, concerned.

EXT. BAILEY HALL - AFTERNOON

Art is standing outside the building, smoking
a cigarette as students walk by. Hank appears.

                              HANK
        Headed in?

Art nods, taking a final drag and snubbing out
his cigarette.

                         HANK (CONT'D)
        That stuff will kill you, dude. And you've
        been smoking since grad school.

                               ART
        I've been smoking since eighth grade. I
        started just to piss off my old man—he was
        a shop steward, y'know—

                              HANK
        No, I didn't know that.

                               ART
        Yeah. He had a cancer stick in his mouth
        from the moment he got home from the shop
        to the moment his head hit the pillow.

                    HANK
I've known guys like that myself.

                    ART
He even smoked through supper. Used to
drive my mother nuts. The factory stress,
the smoking—it all caught up with him
eventually.

                    HANK
So now you *are* your old man.

                    ART
That's how it works sometimes.

                    HANK
We do have a choice in such matters.

                    ART
I suppose. Thing is, my old man—he loved
his job.

Art looks right at Hank, who isn't sure how to
respond.

                    HANK
Hey, been meaning to ask you—how's Richy
doing? I remember that one time we met—

                MEGAN (O.S.)
Professor Falcone?

Art turns to find Megan standing with Heidi,
who has a small dog on a leash.

                MEGAN (CONT'D)
I'm sorry for interrupting. We were just
wondering if we could bring Cujo to class.

                          ART
              (to the puppy, petting it)
     Hey champ.

                     (to Megan)
     Whose is he, Megan?

                         HEIDI
     He's a frat hound. Friends of ours.

                          ART
     Listen you two: much as I love dogs, it
     would be better for our class discussion
     if we didn't have Cujo here distracting
     us, don't you think?

                         MEGAN
     Yeah, you're right.
                      (Heidi)
     See Heidi? I told you he'd say that. Let's
     bring him back over to SigEp.
                     (to Art)
     We might be a little late for class.

Megan and Heidi walk off quickly, Art and Hank
shaking their heads and chuckling as they enter
the building together.

                         HANK
     Any news on the manuscript?

                          ART
     Nothing yet.

INT. ART'S CLASSROOM - AFTERNOON

The students are clustered in groups of four.
Michael, Heidi, and Megan are in the same group.

Art sits off to one side of the classroom, gazing
out the window as the students talk.

                    MEGAN
Hitchhiking is cool to some people because
you're not supposed to do it. And it's
cool to others because you're getting
from place to place without having to
pay for it.

                    ART
So it's either anti-establishment or a
free lunch, is that it, Megan?

                    MEGAN
That about sums it up.

A moment passes.

                    MICHAEL
                   (loudly)
I think Kerouac and his buddies were a
bunch of losers.

Groans all around. Art stands, facing Michael.

                    ART
Michael, you're not alone in that opinion.
But can you be more explicit?

                    MICHAEL
All they do is get high and bum off of
other people and suck each other's dicks.
That explicit enough for you?

Nervous laughter. Patrick raises his hand.

ART
Yes—it's Patrick, right?

PATRICK
(nods, turns to Michael)
What are you so afraid of?

MEGAN
Men sucking men's dicks.

PATRICK
(to Megan)
You mean the *freedom* to suck men's dicks.

Michael sulks as his peers laugh, but the laughter comes to an abrupt halt. Art turns to find Waldorf standing at his classroom door looking on disapprovingly. She leaves.

ART
I guess we need to shut the door from now on.

INT. HANK'S HOUSE - EVENING

Hank and Art relax on two recliners. Hank's daughters ABBY and KAYLA enter with beers, placing them on the coffee table on top of two coasters.

HANK
My retrievers. Thank you Abby, thank you Kayla.

ABBY
You're welcome, Daddy.

                        KAYLA
Welcome, Daddy.

The girls leave. Hank and Art swig their beers.

                        HANK
                (gesturing to the girls)
You should get yourself a couple of those.

                         ART
If I'm ever in one place for more than
a year.

                        HANK
Excuses, excuses. You still virile?

                         ART
Fuck you.

                        HANK
Alissa's quite taken with you, you know.

                         ART
You're not suggesting—

                        HANK
Just sayin'.

                         ART
So, Hank: you didn't tell me about
the department forum on unions after
Thanksgiving. Did you think I wouldn't
find out?

                        HANK
Just trying to save you from yourself.

ART

So you go up for full and forsake all
conviction, is that it?

HANK

Yessir, I'm going to be a full professor.
Last raise I'll ever get, and damned if
I don't need it. Besides dude, the glory
days of labor unions are *over*. Finisimo.
Norma Rae is organizing in Manila. Like
most professional workers, we faculty
have computers, travel allowances, health
benefits, 401[k]s. And with faculty gover-
nance and tenure, we're secure, even if
salaries do suck.

ART

We? Let's cut the bullshit, Hank —

Rachel and the girls enter the living room.

RACHEL

Go ahead Art, these girls have heard it
all. Besides, I like it when someone else
smacks him around.

ART

Your "we" includes upwards of a million and
a half college and university instructors,
nearly a million of whom are adjuncts or
contingent faculty. Your "we" includes
average adjunct salaries of twenty-five
grand a year, and you make triple that.
And it's not just about tenured vs. non-
tenured either. You damn well know that
you've got tenure-line *assistant* profs

over in the b-school making *twice* what you make. Meantime, administrative positions are sprouting like dandelions on cowshit.

HANK

But—

ART

No health benefits, no retirement, and in too many cases, no office. The number of PhDs receiving food stamps has tripled and we teach more classes than you.

HANK

Whatever you say. But adjuncts don't carry the same level of responsibility as we tenure-line faculty.

ART

True, we temp workers don't have to attend department meetings, or direct dissertations, or serve on committees, though it's only a matter of time before it sinks in that there aren't enough tenured bodies to go around.
(pauses)
Look, in the end it all comes down to learning, Hank—what hurts us ultimately hurts our students. The more we have to struggle, the more difficult it is to devote ourselves body and soul to the classroom.

HANK

Hey, when you shut that classroom door you have the same academic freedom as I have.

ART

Academic freedom? All it takes to muzzle me is one student complaint. Here I am with a cracked tooth and no money for a dentist trying to help a bunch of kids with stars in their eyes get a handle on this fucked-up motherfucker of a planet without using words like FUCK lest some little shit allege a hostile learning environment.

Art looks down to see Abby and Kayla staring at him with their mouths wide open.

ART (CONT'D)
(to Rachel)

Sorry, Rach.

RACHEL

Not to worry, Art. They might as well get used to it now.

HANK

Look, even if the English department voted to unionize, do you think the business school or the engineering department would?

ART

In the end, Hank, all of this threatens *your* security too.

HANK

Nonsense.

                              ART
They'll make you start raising money
somehow, mark my words. Else you'll never
see a raise again, and when you retire,
they'll discontinue your line and hire an
adjunct to cover your credit hours.

                             HANK
The notion that they'd ask a medievalist
to do fundraising is crazy. Never gonna
happen.

The two are at an impasse.

                            RACHEL
So, Art—I hear from Hank that you have
a shot at a tenure-track position. That
would be so cool, the three of us back
on campus together.

                             HANK
If he talks to Waldorf the way he talks
to me, I wouldn't hire him.

The two men glare at each other. Rachel tries
to make peace.

                            RACHEL
What he's saying, honey, is that no man
is an island.

                              ART
Yeah—what she said.

Hank sulks.

                          ART (CONT'D)
                          (pleading)
Look, Hank, I want the permanent position.
Who wouldn't? But what I *don't* want—

                            HANK
What you don't want is to be a sell-
out like me, is that it dude? Well I've
got news for you—being a grown-up means
playing ball.

Art is exasperated, while Rachel looks on
helplessly.

                            ABBY
                        (to Rachel)
Is Daddy mad at Mr. Art, Mommy?

                           RACHEL
For the moment, Abby honey, yes.
                    (staring at Hank)
He'll get over it.

Hank looks away.

INT. WALDORF'S OFFICE - MORNING

Unlike Art's office, Waldorf's office is plush
and lit with the soft glow of a desk lamp.

                          WALDORF
You come very highly recommended by our
own Professor Livingsworth and by the
chair at Notre Dame.

                            ART
Good to hear.

                    WALDORF
Excellent school. And your vita—
               (picking up some
          papers on her desk)
is most impressive. I note that you've
taught at quite a number of different
institutions in recent years?

                    ART
Yes. It's no secret that I've had problems
attaining tenure.

                    WALDORF
A pity. Just to be sure there's no confusion, I did want to remind you that your
appointment here is strictly a one-se-
mester engagement.

                    ART
Understood.

                    WALDORF
Also, colleagues of mine at other institutions tell me that you've been something
of a labor activist? You spearheaded the
collective bargaining effort at—

                    ART
Ancient history. I'm a good deal removed
from all of that these days.

                    WALDORF
You're aware of course that the faculty
here are threatening to unionize.

                    ART
You regard that as a threat, then?

WALDORF

It could very well jeopardize our mission,
yes. Most academics have little comprehension of what it takes to run a business
such as this one.

ART

A business. I see.

WALDORF

Yes. At any rate you'll doubtless need a
letter of recommendation from me in order
to move on?

ART

That's usually the way it works.

WALDORF

Indeed. Also, I should bring to your
attention a tenure-track position we have
opening up next fall. I do want you to
know that, assuming nothing inappropriate
transpires again—

ART

Inappropriate?

WALDORF

What I overheard in your classroom was
well beyond the pale of decency and a
travesty of academic discourse.

ART

Academic discourse. I see. And academic
freedom?

Waldorf hears an echo of Art's outburst at the union rally.

                    WALDORF
Professor Falcone, I do hope you're not mistaking your classroom authority for license to corrupt young minds. For that matter, we are not in the habit here at Bigelow of hiring rabble-rousers to stir up the faculty ranks. Faculty are by nature sedentary creatures, best left to their sedentary devices.

Art is silent.

                 WALDORF (CONT'D)
As I was saying: provided nothing of this sort transpires again, I'm fully pre-pared to attest to your abilities as an instructor when your time here is at an end. I know many people in our industry, and I can be of—
               (leans in, suggestive)
of great assistance to you, Art. In any number of ways.

                      ART
I'm sure you can.

                    WALDORF
            (standing, smiling)
Well then.

Waldorf walks slowly around to the back of Art's chair, barely touching her fingertips to Art's shoulders from behind.

                    WALDORF
    We understand each other then.

Art is silent.

                    WALDORF
        Professor Falcone?

                    ART
    Yes.

                    WALDORF
    Yes what?

                    ART
    Yes, we understand each other.

Waldorf smiles.

INT. BAILEY HALL ENGLISH DEPT. OFFICE - MORNING

As Art emerges from Waldorf's office, he takes
a moment to gather himself together. He starts
perspiring madly, as if he's just gone ten
rounds. Janet is sitting at her desk typing.
She looks up at Art with concern.

                    JANET
            (under her breath)
        How'd it go, Petruchio?

                    ART
    More like Louis versus Schmeling.

                    JANET
    They went toe-to-toe *twice*.

                    ART
    Yeah. Maybe I'll get a second match.

Janet frowns.

INT. ART'S OFFICE - MORNING

Art enters his office soaked in sweat to find
Snoop grading papers and Michael sitting at a
chair beside Art's desk. Two adjunct faculty,
DIANE and NANCY, sit at the other two desks.

                    SNOOP
                  (to Art)
     Mr. Killian here to see you.

Snoop does a double-take as Art walks past.

                SNOOP (CONT'D)
     You OK?

                     ART
     Sure.
                (sitting at his desk)
     What's up, Michael?

                   MICHAEL
                (taking a paper
              out of his backpack)
     I wanted to talk to you about my Kerouac
     paper. I don't understand why I got a C.

                     ART
     Did you read my comments?

Michael flips pages to find the comments.

                   MICHAEL
             (reading comments to Art)
     "Lack of evidence to support argument

. . . No in-depth analysis . . . Misread source text."

                    ART
Does that answer your question?

                  MICHAEL
I don't understand what this means.

                    ART
You mean you literally don't understand the words, or—

                  MICHAEL
Finance majors don't write papers.

Diane and Nancy exchange knowing glances.

                    ART
And that's *my* problem?

                  MICHAEL
You're not helping me.

                    ART
Michael—

An older adjunct, BREWSTER JONES, enters the office. He's a jovial, knowingly mock-heroic character, and walks with a slight limp.

                  BREWSTER
Good day, fellow mariners!

                   SNOOP
Brewster, what brings you into the salt mines on a Friday?

BREWSTER

Left my gradebook in my vessel, Captain
Snoop. Again. Brain must be getting a
little barnacled.
                    (to the two women)
Diane, Nancy. How fare thee?

DIANE

A semester is like rolling a big rock up
a hill—

NANCY

—and it keeps rolling right back down on
top of you.

BREWSTER
                    (mock-serious)
Indeed, 'tis a mythic struggle we're
engaged in.
                    (walking over to Art)
Don't believe I've had the pleasure.

ART
                    (standing to shake hands)
Art Falcone.

BREWSTER

Brewster Jones, seaman first class.

ART

Are you the Brewster Jones who—

BREWSTER

Oh I'm just an old sea dog.

                    (to Michael)
Young man.
                    (to Art)
Hear tell you're a fellow scribe.

                    ART
So you *are* that Brewster Jones.

                    BREWSTER
I was, at least. *Sic transit gloria.*

The two men smile knowingly at each other. Nancy
pushes herself away from her desk and opens a
drawer to retrieve Brewster's gradebook.

                    NANCY
           (handing him the gradebook)
Brew, you really should go digital with
this sort of thing.

                    BREWSTER
This is just as easy. And my old Mac is
beginning to take on ballast, getting
mighty slow. Just wish I didn't have to
keep bugging you gals.

                    NANCY
Not a problem, Brew.

                    BREWSTER
Well it's time to weigh anchor. Carry on,
stalwarts!

                    SNOOP
Take care Brewster.

Art watches as Brewster leaves.

                    SNOOP (CONT'D)
                     (to Art)
Old Navy man. I take it you know his work
was acclaimed back in the day.

                        ART
Had no idea he was adjuncting here.

                       SNOOP
We all get old.

                        ART
Yeah.
             (pensive, then to Michael)
Sorry about the interruption, Michael.
Look, I can't help you unless I understand
precisely what it is that you don't understand. Are you telling me that you made
it to your senior year without learning
how to lay out an argument on paper? If
so, I can arrange to have a tutor—

                      MICHAEL
I don't have time for this shit.

Snoop looks up, Diane and Nancy glancing at
each other.

                      MICHAEL
I just need to graduate in December and my
father's got a job lined up for me long
as I can keep my GPA above 3.0.

                        ART
What do you want me to do? This is a
required course you should have taken in
your sophomore year.

                    MICHAEL
I want you to reread this and reconsider
my grade.

                      ART
Y'know, if I were really going to reconsider your grade, there *is* the possibility
that it could go *lower*.

                    MICHAEL
That's it then?

                      ART
Unless you actually want to address your
paper and not your GPA, yes—that's it.

                    MICHAEL
Thanks for all the help, *Professor*.

Michael snarls out this last as he stands and
storms out.

                     SNOOP
What a little bitch.

Art sits back in his chair, exhausted.

                 SNOOP (CONT'D)
Try not to let him get to you.

                      ART
Do you know that kid?

                     SNOOP
Not really. I've seen him around.
          (to Diane and Nancy)
You guys know him?

The two women shake their heads as Hank pops
his head in the door.

                    SNOOP (CONT'D)
     Henry, sweetheart. Slumming?

                    HANK
                  (to Art)
     Understand the meeting with Catherine
     went well.

                    ART
     Are you shittin' me? How the fuck would
     you know that?

                    HANK
     I keep my ear to the ground.

                    SNOOP
                  (to Art)
     Something your union rep needs to know
     about?

Art looks at Hank first, and then looks at Snoop.

                    ART
     Nah.
                  (to Hank, kiddingly)
     Fuck you and your ear, pal.

                    SNOOP
                  (to Hank)
     Henry dear, long as you're here: what's
     the word on Trane's tenure file?

                    HANK
     Everyone is happy with it, far as I can
     tell.

> SNOOP
Woot! Way to go, our man on the inside—
deep inside!

Hank musters a smile, uncomfortable with Snoop's overtures, but Art is not entirely sure what to make of this.

EXT. CAMPUS TRAIL - DAY (SATURDAY)

Art is taking a leisurely walk, and puffing occasionally on a cigarette. The trail is busy with walkers, runners, and cyclists, some of whom stare disapprovingly at him.

Alissa approaches Art from around a bend, jogging. Art stops and Alissa slows, jogging in place. As they chat, they take note of the passersby.

> ALISSA
Hi, Art!

> ART
Oh boy, here's trouble.

A sexy woman in scant running gear jogs past.

> ALISSA
Checking out the, uhm, scenery?

> ART
Just stretching my legs.

Art takes a drag on his cigarette.

> ALISSA
I need the endorphin rush, especially

these days. Y'know—
          (gesturing at Art's cigarette)
that stuff'll kill you. And our student
government is thinking of instituting a
smoking ban on the quad.

                    ART
                 (exhaling)
Maybe they're trying to tell me something.

A muscular man jogs by slowly, waving the smoke
away as he passes through it.

                ART (CONT'D)
So—how's the diss coming?

                  ALISSA
Henry asked for some revisions, but he
tells me I'm just about there. I hope so.

                    ART
He'd let you know if there were any major
problems.
              (looking around)
It's pretty as hell around here. The campus
is OK, but this is pretty as hell.

                  ALISSA
Yeah. It'll be tough to leave.

A cyclist pedals past, looking very professional.

                    ART
We all have to sever that grad school
umbilical. Well—I should let you get back
to your endorphins.

                    ALISSA
You planning to attend the department
meeting next week?

                     ART
I tend to keep my distance from such shin-
digs. It's safer.

                    ALISSA
Word has it that Professor Waldorf will
be unveiling her new learning initiative.
She's invited everyone, even the grad
students.

                     ART
Do tell.

Art thinks this over.

                    ALISSA
                 (hesitates)
   Art, can I ask a huge favor?

                     ART
Name it.

Alissa stops jogging in place as a woman sprints
past.

                    ALISSA
OK, so: would you be willing to read my
intro? I'm trying to make it readable for
the lay person. Actually—
                 (hesitates)
I'd like my mother to be able to read at
least *some* part of my dissertation.

                    ART
As a pedestrian thinker, I am the perfect
person to represent the lay reader. Be
happy to have a look at it. When do you
need it by?

                  ALISSA
I was thinking just before Thanksgiving
break? I'm still revising it but could
have a solid draft to you by next weekend,
if that works?

A man trots by with an exaggerated walking
style. Art waits to respond until he's passed.

                    ART
Tell you what: why don't you drop it by
my apartment Tuesday night. Say, six-ish?
601 Main.

                  ALISSA
Great, thanks so much Art! 601 Main at 6
pm next Tuesday—see you then!

INT. ART'S CLASSROOM - AFTERNOON

The class is engaged in discussion. Art sits
off to the side as usual and listens.

                  MEGAN
But I don't understand why people shouldn't
try to change the system.

                   ROB
Look what happens to McMurphy, though—he
ends up lobotomized.

                         MEGAN
But Rob, the Chief gets away *because* of
McMurphy.

Mercedes raises her hand.

                          ART
Go ahead, Mercedes.

                       MERCEDES
I just wanted to say that I thought the
point of the novel is that we should never
give up.

                         HEIDI
Yeah, that's what I thought too. That we
should always try to change things for
the better.

                        PATRICK
But that requires sacrifice.

                         MEGAN
Does positive change always require
sacrifice?

                        PATRICK
Usually, Megan.

                         MEGAN
I'm not sure that's necessarily a good
thing.

                       MERCEDES
Maybe it's—

She hesitates.

                         ART
Take your time, Mercedes.

                       MERCEDES
Maybe it's—the nature of the system?

The students ponder this.

                        MICHAEL
I don't get it. I want to be a vice president of accounting. Why do I have to
change the system I want to be a part of?

Michael is staring directly at Art. A number of
students are annoyed at this outburst, Megan
especially.

                         ART
          (standing, taking it in stride)
Can anyone answer Michael's question?

Mercedes raises her hand, slowly.

                       MERCEDES
Well, the way I see it, even an accountant or vice president has to care about
something—something greater than himself.

                        MICHAEL
Like what?

                       MERCEDES
Like other people.

                        MICHAEL
Yeah, right. Like you care about anything
but that taco stand your family runs.

MERCEDES
You don't badmouth mi familia, pendejo!

ART
(firm)
Hold on, Mercedes. That's not very nice,
Michael.

MICHAEL
I still don't get why I have to take a
bullshit course like this, where all we
do is bullshit.

The class is sick of him.

ART
What we're doing here, together, is analysis. That thing that's missing from a
lot of the papers you folks submit to me.

Art stares hard at Michael.

MICHAEL
My father's not paying good money so I
can be taught by students—he's paying *you*
to teach me.

ART
(slowly)
I like to think of a classroom as an aspiring learning community, Michael—a community
of peers. The idea is that we rely on one
another for insight, though of course I'm
standing up here because, OK, I have the
instructional expertise, and because I'm
a novelist. But we work collectively—the

same principle that guides, say, a labor union.

                    MICHAEL
My father says that unions have destroyed this country.

                     ART
Everyone's entitled to their opinions. Of course, to make an argument you need to cite evidence in support of your assertions. What's your evidence?

Fuming, Michael goes silent.

                 ART (CONT'D)
OK, we're out of time. Just to remind everyone that midterm papers are due in two weeks. And be sure to start reading our next book as soon as you can—it's not an easy read.

INT. ART'S APARTMENT - NIGHT (TUESDAY)

A knock at the door. Art answers the door with one hand behind his back. Alissa is standing with manuscript in hand.

                   ALISSA
And here's my intro.

                     ART
    I cooked!

An awkward moment passes.

                   ALISSA
So this is a date, then?

ART
You're giving me your introduction and—
(revealing the manuscript in his hand)
I'm trading you for my latest novel.
Intellectual barter. To go with the banter.
Believe me, I'm getting the better bargain.
So I owe you food.

Art holds the door open for Alissa, then hurries
to the kitchen. Alissa surveys the spare but
cozily arranged furniture. Inexpensively framed
art posters line the walls. On a tiny desk sits
an old laptop, a crooked lamp, and a picture
of Art in his twenties alongside another man
of roughly the same age. In front of a futon
sits a wooden crate covered with a cloth, which
serves as a coffee table.

ART (O.S.) (CONT'D)
(upbeat)
It's not much, but I call it my home away
from no home. Nothing more than my truck
can carry.

Art returns from the kitchen with a bottle of
wine, two glasses, and a small plate of cheddar,
handing one glass to Alissa while motioning
to her to sit on a rolling computer chair.
He pushes a button on his laptop, places the
cheese and wine on the table, and takes a seat
on the futon opposite her. Quiet jazz emanates
from the computer.

ALISSA
It smells wonderful. This isn't a date,
it's the perfect seduction.

                         ART
Work is the ultimate seduction.

                       ALISSA
Oscar Wilde?

                         ART
Picasso.

                       ALISSA
Choose a job you love and you'll never
work a day in your life.

                         ART
Uhm, Warren Buffett?

                       ALISSA
                     (laughing)
Confucius, silly. Or maybe, Google.

                         ART
Cheers!

They toast, laughing.

Long pause.

Alissa rolls her chair to the futon and kisses
Art, and they embrace. Art pulls away for a
moment.

                       ALISSA
I've been wanting to do that for years.
And years.

                         ART
But what about dinner?

ALISSA
Let's have it for breakfast.

Art hangs his head and thinks for a moment.
Alissa lifts his chin. They kiss again.

EXT. BIGELOW STATE UNIVERSITY - MORNING

Art and Alissa walk down the street holding
hands, but drop them and separate as they arrive
at the edge of campus. Sam is standing in line
at a coffee kiosk and spots them. They split off
at their respective classrooms.

ART
(pulling the door shut behind him)
So, guys. What are your first impressions
of Capote?

The closed door muffles any response.

INT. BAILEY HALL LECTURE ROOM - DAY

Faculty, grad students, and staff are gathered
together for the midterm department meeting.
Hank serves as parliamentarian, and everyone
in the department is present save Art. Trane
is sitting between Snoop and Martha Wilde.
Waldorf stands at a podium at the front of the
room, a screen behind her, Janet manning the
projection equipment.

WALDORF
And we turn now to our last and most
important agenda item. But—

Art enters late and stands at the back by

himself, leaning against the wall. Waldorf takes note, as do Alissa, Trane, Snoop, and Hank. Hank's nod is not welcoming.

Waldorf speaks slowly, deliberately, and with the utmost confidence. She is formidable. As she speaks, a PowerPoint presentation appears on the screen behind her to illustrate her points.

> WALDORF (CONT'D)
> But before I begin, let us face facts: the English major as we know it is a thing of the past.

Some of the faculty murmur and stir in their seats.

> WALDORF (CONT'D)
> We're doing our students a disservice by pretending that their reading and writing skills alone will prepare them for life after college. True literacy and legitimacy in the real world demands not only that our students learn to think critically but that they navigate our great First Amendment flux: books, films, videos, songs, games, social media. Our students are the rightful stewards of this domain.

More murmurs.

> WALDORF (CONT'D)
> At the same time, our own livelihoods are in jeopardy, as we face dramatically declining revenue. Only nine percent of BSU's budget now comes from the state.

Looks of concern.

> WALDORF (CONT'D)
> We must reconfigure our major so that
> English studies is recognized as a vital
> component of this country's primary and
> most enduring export. And so I propose a
> new learning initiative: *English—*
> > (pauses)
> *as entertainment.*

Audible protest, a number of faculty members
shaking their heads. Waldorf is undeterred.
Art is smiling.

> WALDORF (CONT'D)
> Now: I have been in talks with Jack Cutter
> of Advanced Learning. I've asked Jack,
> himself a Bigelow alumnus, to join us
> here today. Jack?

Impeccably dressed, Cutter stands, turns, and
nods at the faculty. Scattered applause. He
sits.

> WALDORF (CONT'D)
> Advanced Learning has enjoyed great success
> on several campuses. Jack's firm has a
> wealth of experience with online educa-
> tion, and in particular, with MOOCs—massive
> open online courses. To kick-start our new
> initiative, I propose that each tenured
> faculty member offer one such course per
> academic year, beginning next fall.

More murmuring. Hank is expressionless.

                    WALDORF (CONT'D)
The technology permits for q & a even
from, let us say, China. Your lectures
can be archived, and students may elect to
enroll either in your live course or in the
self-directed edition. The self-directed
program will be available free online,
but students who wish to enroll in the
program for credit will pay for same.
                    (pauses)
We see this as a vast, global, untapped
market. Countless students these days
desire flexible course hours. It's obvious
how much extra revenue is possible when
you tailor education to the individual.
And this revenue will in turn augment
faculty merit raises.

Some faculty appear pleased. Trane raises her
hand.

                    HANK
The chair recognizes Professor Coltrane.

                    TRANE
What does all this have to do with actual
learning?

                    WALDORF
Our present trajectory is no longer sustainable. We face lower salaries, a hiring
freeze, and faculty furloughs. This is
a fundraising opportunity, in short. But
it's true—we shall each have some accom-
modating to do. *That's entertainment.*

I should add that the dean's office is hinting that fundraising might be added to the campus-wide criteria for promotion and tenure.

More audible disturbance. Hank looks up at Waldorf, then at Art, who's looking right at him.

                         TRANE
But isn't it possible that Advanced Learning might use our expertise for their own profit, and that Bigelow too might simply package us for—

                        WALDORF
                (steamrolling over Trane)
The item on our consent agenda states that this discussion is about the initiative itself, not hypothetical scenarios.
                (turning to Hank)
Parliamentarian?

Hank doesn't say anything.

                  WALDORF (CONT'D)
Parliamentarian?

                         HANK
                    (reluctantly)
Point of order.

Trane sits, disappointed with Hank. Art is furious.
                        WALDORF
Any further questions before we table this item?

A moment passes.

                    WALDORF (CONT'D)
Very well then, I move that we adjourn—

Art leans forward and raises his hand. Waldorf
eyes him carefully. Hank stares at Art, and
Art stares back angrily. Hank doesn't want to
call on Art.

                    WALDORF (CONT'D)
Parliamentarian? Are we adjourned?

                       HANK
The chair recognizes Professor Falcone.

                     WALDORF
For those who have not had the pleasure,
Professor Falcone, a novelist of some
renown, is replacing Professor Weaver for
one semester.

                        ART
                 (cordial at first)
Thank you. So—
                 (right on the nose)
what about box office?

A number of faculty turn their heads.

                     WALDORF
I don't take your meaning.

                        ART
Box office. English continues to be a popular
major on campuses across the country—something like fifty or sixty thousand majors

nationwide—so I take it you have no problems *sustaining* enrollment?

                    WALDORF
                    (wary)
None at all. We keep having to raise caps
on our courses, and still we turn students away.

                    ART
Well then, granting the spirit of your
entertainment. . .metaphor?—if there continues to be high demand for your courses
even absent the kind of cultural recog-
nition we would all wish to see, then in
addition to proposing new delivery systems
for teaching and learning, shouldn't we
also be talking about safeguarding whatever it is about the major that students—
today—seem to like? At least, those who
aren't living in, let us say, China.

Waldorf's face contorts.

                    WALDORF
                    (to Hank)
Again, I'm not sure this commentary is
on point.

Hank pages through a copy of Robert's Rules.

                    ART
Of course it's true that demand for English
courses might increase, but it might be
for all the wrong reasons. Also, it's just
a bit unclear whether the marketplace

will supply jobs for your newly-minted
double Es.

                    WALDORF
Double Es?

                     ART
                  (smiling)
English entertainers.

Several faculty laugh out loud at this. Waldorf
is nearing her breaking point.

                    WALDORF
Must I request again that our parliamentarian intervene?

Art looks at Hank, who stares at him and shakes
his head ever so slightly. Alissa, Trane, and
Snoop look on.

                     ART
I yield the floor.

Hank nods, again slightly. Alissa in particular
looks disappointed.

                    WALDORF
                   (smug)
Very well then. Thank you, Professor
Falcone, for your observations.
                  (smiling)
If there are no further questions?
                   (pause)
We stand adjourned.

Art and Waldorf exchange stares as the meeting

breaks up. Alissa joins Art at the back of the room.

                    ALISSA
   Didn't think you were going to make it.

                      ART
   Neither did I.

A slight disturbance from the front of the room draws their attention. Waldorf appears to be unhappy with Hank and is addressing him in hushed but unmistakably harsh tones.

                    ALISSA
   What do you make of that?

Art doesn't respond.

INT. THE SUNSPOT - AFTERNOON

The bar is nearly empty. Hank and Trane are sitting at a table talking with voices lowered, while Art is at the bar buying a round.

                     TRANE
   Why didn't you tell us this was coming?
   You knew, didn't you?

                     HANK
   Look, let's talk about you.

                     TRANE
   You want to distract me with my favorite
   subject?

                         HANK
You're gonna sail through tenure.

                         TRANE
How can you be so sure?

                         HANK
The department vote is week after next—I
would have heard something by now.

                         TRANE
I worry about her royal *heinous*.

                         HANK
Oh, Catherine's not such a bad egg, once
you get to know her.

                         TRANE
Well—*you* seem to know "Catherine" at least,
Hank.

Art returns with three beers.

                          ART
                       (sitting)
So what's the down-low?

                         HANK
Down-low is a small bladder. Be back in
a sec.

Hank leaves.

                          ART
                     (dead serious)
So you're nervous about your tenure review?

TRANE
It's really weird. You wouldn't think
so but—I don't like the way Waldorf has
been eyeing me. My book is only under
contract. . .

Art deliberates for a moment over what to say.

ART
You want it straight up?

TRANE
Hit me.

ART
I've been there. If you're nervous? Stay
nervous. Listen to your gut.

TRANE
What are you saying?

ART
I'm saying that most faculty aren't on the
short list for the red badge of courage.

Trane is unnerved. Hank returns and notices
the change.

HANK
(to Trane)
I leave you alone with this guy for a
minute and you look like James Stewart
at the end of *Vertigo*.

TRANE
(shaking it off)
Well, fuck it. At least I'm not Kim Novak
at the end of *Vertigo*.

> HANK
> (to Art)
> Dude, what did you say—

> ART
> (lifting his glass)
> Per cent'anni!

> TRANE
> No comprende.

> ART
> May you live a hundred years.

> TRANE
> I just want to make it through this
> semester.

> HANK
> Nothing to worry about.

Art and Trane exchange glances.

INT. ART'S APARTMENT - LATER

Art and Alissa are lying in bed together. Alissa is fidgeting while trying to read, but doesn't say anything.

> ART
> Alissa, what is it?

> ALISSA
> (hesitant)
> The meeting.

> ART
> What about the meeting?

ALISSA

I thought you let Professor Waldorf off pretty easy.

ART

Maybe I did.

ALISSA

But why?

ART

You mean, why would I not want to eighty-six myself here at Bigelow?

ALISSA

Are you thinking about the permanent job?

ART

I'm thinking about it. Maybe I could do more good if I had a little job security and could stay in one place for more than a year.

ALISSA

A little job security? You mean, sacrificing your principles, rather like your friend Henry?

ART

"Rather like your friend Henry"? Alissa, you obviously have no fucking idea who you're talking to.

ALISSA

I guess you're right. I used to know this inspiring teacher who wasn't afraid to get down to the heart of the matter, and who stood up for what he believed in. What happened to that guy?

                    ART
                 (angrily)
He's been living on a wing and a fucking prayer for ten fucking years. Not really able to make more than a short-term contribution to a student's life, to a community. Not a fucking friend in sight. Little more than a glorified migrant worker. No, no—migrant workers have it way tougher. A lot of workers do. But believe me—
              (nearly shouting)
this shit gets fucking old. Here at Bigelow I didn't even get to order my own books for my course. I haven't published a new fucking novel in five years, and if this keeps up, I'll be the has-been who let the door hit him in the ass on the way out. In the meantime I load the fucking truck again in T minus eight weeks and counting. You think I want to be a fucking martyr for a profession that wants nothing to do with me?

                   ALISSA
But having come this far, and given up so much, why not keep fighting the good fight? Do you really believe that you'll ever be the kind of person a place like this will hire?

                    ART
The kind of person?

                    ALISSA
Maybe—
                 (hesitates)
maybe I'm not seeing the big picture.

                     ART
            (jumping out of bed,
             putting on his pants)
Fuckin'-goddamn-A you're not seeing the
big fuckin' picture!

Art leaves Alissa lying in bed by herself.

INT. HANK'S OFFICE - AFTERNOON

Hank and Alissa are sitting in Hank's office.
A large bowl of M & M's sits on Hank's desk.
Alissa is silent while Hank studies her dis-
sertation manuscript.

                    HANK
            (popping M & M's)
Looks good. Give me two weeks to get back
to you, OK?

                   ALISSA
Of course, Henry. Oh and I'm not quite
done yet with the intro—I've asked Art
to have a look.

                    HANK
Good idea. He'll make it sing.
          (picking up the bowl)
M & M's?

Alissa grabs a handful, popping a few into her
mouth.

> HANK

Listen: I've contacted a number of department chairs, told them to let me know
if it looks like they'll be searching a
medievalist position.

> ALISSA

Thanks so much.

> HANK

You understand that you have to be willing
to go *anywhere*, right?

> ALISSA

Roger that.

> HANK

It's one of the downsides of this
profession.

> ALISSA

Believe me, I understand. Henry—
> (hesitates)

can I ask you a question?

> HANK

Shoot.

> ALISSA

Can you tell me something about—about Art?
I mean, what's made him so—

> HANK

Difficult?

> ALISSA

Yeah.

HANK

Well thereby hangs a tale, and I'm not
sure it's mine to tell.

ALISSA

I need to know, Henry.

HANK
(pauses)
What the hell, OK.
(pops an M & M)
So as you probably guessed, Art was the
golden boy of our grad program. Graduates
with a novel under contract, and ends up
with offers from top-tier schools. But he's
always the mover and shaker, you understand, always marching to his own beat.
So he decides to take a job at a wealthy
private college that wants to start a
creative writing program. Where you first
met him. Figures he can help build something from the ground up. And what's the
first thing he does?

Hank reaches for more M & M's, offering some
to Alissa, who opens her fist to show that she
still has some.

HANK (CONT'D)
He initiates a campus-wide effort to
organize the faculty, bring in a union.
Absolutely fearless, this guy, with zero
regard for the fact that he wasn't tenured.

ALISSA
Well, nothing wrong with that.

HANK

Impractical. Downright dumb in fact. While he's working the liberty-equality-fraternity angle, he's alienating half of his colleagues and the dean in the process.

ALISSA
(getting defensive)
Isn't that their problem?

HANK

Well, no. Not if you want tenure.

ALISSA
(stops before putting
an M & M in her mouth)
Tenure means you give up on what's right?

HANK

You put your better angels on hold, yes. Look, Art was a sitting duck. About the only person behind him was his chair, god knows why. So when his tenure review came around, they really did a number on him. They couldn't go after him for his union efforts, you understand, and he'd published three novels. So they had to make shit up. Art sent me a copy of the committee document—in my view it was actionable. Included an attack on his ethnicity.

ALISSA

His ethnicity?

HANK

Yeah. They did this ridiculous reading

of Art's third novel, which should've been plenty for tenure. The committee dismissed it as an author engaged in "a futile search for his Italian-American heritage."

                    ALISSA
You're joking.

                    HANK
Hardly. They all but called Art a wise guy. *Professore Soprano, gumba.*

                    ALISSA
I suppose he could have sued, but—

                    HANK
                 (snorts)
Right—even with pro bono representation, that takes a whole lot of time and energy. The icing on the cake though: not only did they disparage his accomplishments, but they eliminated his position. So when the smoke cleared, there was no job to sue for. His tenure review was thus rendered . . . *academic.*

Alissa takes a moment to process this.

                    ALISSA
So creative writing is expendable.

                    HANK
No more so than English, history, philosophy. We all have to justify our existence these days and answer to the bottom line.

                    ALISSA
The bottom line, I see. But just to be
clear: his own department did this to
him, right? This wasn't done by administrative fiat?

                    HANK
Yes—yes, that's right. He sabotaged . . .
they came after him and . . .

Hank drops off, clearly distraught.

               HANK (CONT'D)
               (almost to himself)
And after that Art bounces around from job
to job, dating undergrads on occasion—you
know, looking for love in—

                    ALISSA
I know about that part.
                    (thinking)
One question, Henry.

                    HANK
What's that?

                    ALISSA
Did he succeed?

                    HANK
What do you mean?

                    ALISSA
Did the faculty unionize?

                    HANK
Well, ultimately, yes—they did in fact.
There were student protests over Art's

firing and the few faculty firebrands still standing managed somehow to win the day. One of the very few private colleges in the nation that has a faculty union.

ALISSA

So Art was successful, then.

HANK

No, he screwed up. Bad.

ALISSA

But—

HANK

That union stuff—that did him in. He forgot the primary mission of the assistant professor: your first and only job is to get tenure.

Alissa is struggling to control herself.

HANK

So I suppose there might be a lesson here for *you*, Alissa?

This pushes Alissa over the edge.

ALISSA
(loudly)

You know, I wouldn't mind so much if, after you people *got* tenure, you actually stood for something. For godsakes, when are you gonna grow some *balls*?

Hank is shocked, and Alissa is surprised at herself.

                    ALISSA (CONT'D)
I'm—I'm so sorry, Henry, I don't know
what got—

                        HANK
I should have figured that this would be
the result if you two hooked up.

                       ALISSA
                    (mad as hell)
You think because I'm your grad student
you can talk to me like that?

                        HANK
What you don't understand is that Art is
on his last leg. Have you taken a hard
look at the guy, Alissa? Have you really
looked at him?

                       ALISSA
I see. So doing Waldorf's dirty work is
your way of looking out for him?

Hank's shifts in his seat, taking a moment
before responding.

                        HANK
I think we're done here. In two weeks
I'll have your dissertation back to you
with recommended—

Alissa picks up her backpack and storms out.

                    HANK (CONT'D)
      Edits.

Hank is left to ponder what just went down.

INT. THE SUNSPOT - AFTERNOON

Trane is at the bar by herself, empty shot
glasses lined up as she eyes another. Art walks
in, and Danny flashes him a look to indicate
that Trane is becoming a problem.

                    ART
    I've been looking for you. I heard—

                  TRANE
    25 to 6, 4 abstentions. Has a certain—
            (gulps down the last shot)
    ring to it. Chicago, remember? Lord, I'm
    dating myself.
            (looks around the bar)
    Literally in fact.

                    ART
    Coupla waters please, Danny.

                  DANNY
    You got it, Art.

Danny brings water.

                    ART
        (pushing water in front of Trane)
    So, what's the justification?

                  TRANE
    Mum's the word, including my bosom buddy
    Henry. You think you have friends. . .
    Waldorf, that cow, has got 'em all moo-
    cowed, ha, with her bullshit mooing or
    MOOCing about pay cuts and whatever the
    fuck. They don't need a good Catholic girl

like me, they don't need no Joyce scholar,
they need a showbiz yes-man, yes ma'am.

                    ART
You gonna fight this?

                   TRANE
You think I should?

                    ART
Straight up again?

                   TRANE
Why spare me now, sooth—
                    (she's lisping)
soothsayer.

                    ART
When your own department votes against
you to that extent, it's over.

Trane chugs the water as if it's beer, frowning
after it goes down.

                ART (CONT'D)
What's the plan for the immediate future?

                   TRANE
Oh, it's all so civilized, y'know. So
collegial. I have one more year under
contract, which in this job market trans-
lates to three more semesters before the—
                    (burps)
gravy train. That is, if they're still
cutting unemployment checks to one-time
faculty.

                          ART
Do you have any experience outside of
teaching?

                         TRANE
Come to think of it, I did spend a summer
once made glorious by working in one of
those cinnamon roll shops in the mall.
Those still around?

                          ART
Yeah.

                         TRANE
I hate the smell of cinnamon in the morning.

Snoop walks in and hurries over.

                         SNOOP
There she is!
                    (to Art)
How's she doing?

Art rolls his eyes.

                         TRANE
                   (to Snoop)
Speak to me when you talk about. . .me.

                         SNOOP
C'mon honey. Let's get you out of here.
Trane rises and starts to walk with Snoop
holding her by the inside of her arm,
then stops.

                    TRANE
Snoop, wait. Wait!

                    SNOOP
What is it?

                    TRANE
                  (to Art)
I need you to come to the union forum
after Turkey Day. Last chance for our
slava—salvation.

                    ART
Haven't given it much thought.

                    TRANE
Henry has though, hasn't he.
                 (sarcastic)
Good ole Hank. I wonder whether he voted
for me.

                    ART
Of course he did.

                    TRANE
Such indomitable faith in human nature!

                    SNOOP
C'mon, girlfriend.

EXT. CAMPUS TRAIL - DAY

Art and Alissa are strolling side-by-side. It's
an overcast day in early fall. Art is smoking,
as ever, and coughing occasionally. His leather
briefcase hangs by his side.

ALISSA

Listen, about the other day. I—

ART

It was my fault. I've got a chip on my
shoulder the size of Norman Mailer. I'm
sorry.

ALISSA

I was thinking.

ART

What?

ALISSA

About Professor Coltrane.

ART

And?

ALISSA

A number of the grad students want to
protest. They all love her classes. And
she's been so helpful in our union drive.

ART

Would be a nice show of support, especially
if you coupled it with a letter-writing
campaign to the dean. But you have to
understand—it won't do any good.

ALISSA

We've got to try though, don't we?

ART

You gotta do what you gotta do. Long as
you understand what you're doing. See,

you do something like this, it becomes
part of who you are as a professional.
And there's no turning back, because who
you are becomes part of the public record.

                    ALISSA
I never thought about it quite like that.

                     ART
One thing is certain: Waldorf will shit
a brick. A very large brick.

                    ALISSA
Then it's settled—we're staging a protest.

Art laughs, which triggers a cough. Then he
starts coughing violently, dropping his cigarette. Alissa rests her hand on Art's shoulder,
looking on helplessly until he finishes, out of
breath and perspiring again. As he stands he's
a bit dizzy, and Alissa reaches under his arm
to help prop him up.

                ALISSA (CONT'D)
We need to get you to a doctor about that
cough.

                     ART
Been planning to. The wait for new patients
is two months. It's nothing serious though—
it's just that I've got this irregular
heartbeat—
          (touching his upper chest)
and it acts up a bit when I'm out of shape.

                    ALISSA
                   (alarmed)
        Irregular heartbeat?

                     ART
        It's nothing, really. I've had it, like,
        forever.

                    ALISSA
        But Art—

                     ART
        C'mon, let's head back over to my place and
        powwow about this protest you're planning.

MONTAGE -- ART AND ALISSA BONDING OVER THE
PROTEST RALLY

Art and Alissa work with the grad students to
make protest signs.

-- Art and Alissa socialize with students at
The Sunspot.

-- Alissa welcomes Patrick into the group, Art
looking on as she and Patrick work together.

-- Art and Alissa surprise Trane by showing up
at her office with a dozen students carrying
signs, Trane moved to tears.

END OF MONTAGE

EXT. BAILEY HALL - DAY

It's a bright fall day. A throng of students
are noisily protesting Trane's tenure denial.
Signs read "Stop Railroading Trane" and "Tenure

for Trane." Alissa and Patrick are among the
protesters, and Michael and Megan are among
the onlookers. Art approaches and stands next
to Sam and TWO CAMPUS COPS, who are keeping an
eye on things. Waldorf is at her office window
surveying the scene, and notes Art's arrival.
Art looks on approvingly as he speaks.

                    ART
So what do you think, Sam?

                    SAM
I think these kids should be hitting the
books instead of screwing around out here
wasting their parents' money. Be damned
if my kids behave like this when they get
to college.

                    ART
Maybe these "kids" are learning how to
put their money where their mouths are.

                    SAM
How's that?

                    ART
They're standing up for what they believe
in.

Sam glances at Art but Art's eyes are glued on
the protest.

                    ART
You know Trane, don't you Sam?

                    SAM
Sure I know her. Not real well.

                              ART
        But you know she's been denied tenure?

                              SAM
        That's none of my business.

                              ART
                    (turns to look at Sam)
        Really?

                              SAM
        Not part of my job.

                              ART
        How convenient for you.
                         (turns back to
                         look at protest)
        Well I guess we each have our jobs to do,
        huh Sam?

Sam doesn't know how to respond.

INT. ART'S APARTMENT - LATER

Alissa is lying on Art's futon, scantily clad,
sipping a glass of wine. Art enters, picks up
a glass of wine from his makeshift coffee table,
and sits on the futon next to Alissa.

                              ART
        Here's to you and to an asskicking protest!

                            ALISSA
        To *us* and to an asskicking protest!

They cheer and sip their wine.

                    ALISSA (CONT'D)
So somehow you keep not telling me who
that guy is with you in the photo.

Alissa motions toward the photo on the desk.

                         ART
It's—it's my brother.

                       ALISSA
Your brother? But you never talk—

                         ART
I know. But maybe now—oh shit!

                       ALISSA
What is it?

Art rises quickly and places his wine on the
coffee table, rummaging through his briefcase.
                         ART
                (extracting an envelope
                  from his briefcase)
I totally forgot. This was in my mailbox.
Wanted to wait to open it with you after
things settled down.

                       ALISSA
Is that—?

                         ART
Yeah. From Dunning & Kruger.

Art sits next to Alissa. She watches eagerly as
he tears open the envelope and starts reading
the letter.

                    ART
              (shaking his head)
        I'll be goddamned.

                  ALISSA
        What is it? What's wrong?

                    ART
        The press is going out of business.

                  ALISSA
        What?

                    ART
        Yeah. Son of a bitch.
              (manages a smile)
        It's getting tougher and tougher these
        days. I suppose—I suppose I could always
        publish it myself.

                  ALISSA
        I'm so sorry, Art.

                    ART
        Rejection is part of this biz, babe. I'll
        get over it.
              (smiling)
        I guess what doesn't kill you, kills your
        book.

Art starts to laugh but again starts coughing. He
falls back onto the futon, alternately coughing
and gasping for air. Alissa quickly places her
wine glass on the floor and holds Art's head in
her arms until the coughing subsides.

                    ALISSA
Art honey, we need to take you to the
emergency room.

                     ART
              (breathing is labored)
Honey? Wow. Honey. You sure Patrick
wouldn't object.

                    ALISSA
Patrick? What do you mean?

                     ART
I see the way he looks at you. He's a
smart guy, and let's face it, he's more
your age. And with a ton of life experience, to boot. I mean, two tours in Iraq.

                    ALISSA
He's just a friend. We like to hang out
together.

                     ART
Liking someone is a good start. Lots of
people in love don't have that.

Art stops to catch his breath.

                    ALISSA
Really Art—let's get you checked out.

                     ART
I'm telling you, it's nothing serious. I'm
just a little out of shape. Soon as the
semester is over I plan to hit the gym,
I promise. Besides, no denaro, tesoro.

> ALISSA

Tesoro?

> ART

Whatsa matter? I thought Italian was your Romance tongue.

> ALISSA

Listen here, writer—I could teach you a thing or two about tongues.

> ART

Uh-huh.

> ALISSA

"Sieti raccomandato il mio *Tesoro*, nel qual io vivo ancora."

> ART

I have a feeling I'm about to be schooled by a squirt.

> ALISSA

It's Dante. He puts one of his old teachers in the seventh circle of hell for being, as they used to say, a Sodomite.

> ART
> (mischievous)

Poor bastard. That Dante—
> (coughs)

that Dante could be a real prick.

> ALISSA

You—you're *my* treasure too, darlin'.

INT. WALDORF'S OFFICE - DAY

As Art walks in, Waldorf's back is to him. She's staring out her office window. She turns abruptly as Art enters, delivering her words with a clipped ferocity but otherwise doing her best not to act the part of a lover spurned.

       WALDORF
Thank you for stopping by on such short notice. Please take a seat.

       ART
       (sitting)
Not a problem. What's up?

       WALDORF
It appears—
        (picking up some
        papers from her desk)
it appears that a complaint has been lodged against you.

       ART
A complaint?

       WALDORF
Yes. From one of your students.

       ART
Alleging what, exactly?

       WALDORF
A number of things. That your language is at times inappropriate. That you've shown favoritism to several students. That you're trying to convert your students into labor union advocates. Most importantly

perhaps, that you've relinquished your teaching duties and are allowing students to run your class.

                    ART
And who—who lodged this complaint?

                  WALDORF
That's not important. What's important is whether these allegations are true.

Art takes a moment.

                    ART
Do I have to get Snoop in here?

                  WALDORF
You're free of course to invite your union representative. But before you do, would you mind if I asked you a few questions by way of clarification?

                    ART
             (starting to perspire)
OK.

                  WALDORF
That little disturbance outside—did you have a hand in that?

                    ART
Not that it's any of your business, but I did contribute one of the slogans, yes. The railroading one.

                  WALDORF
Very clever. And is it true that you're

romantically involved with our Forbes
scholar?

Art takes another moment, perspiring more
heavily.

                    ART
Not that it's any of your business, but
Alissa and I have been seeing each other,
yes.

                  WALDORF
I see. Am I mistaken, or did you and I
not reach an understanding during our
last chat?

                    ART
               (squirms a bit)
We—I guess we did.

                  WALDORF
Have you had a change of heart then?

                    ART
Professor Waldorf, I don't see what any
of this has to do with—

                  WALDORF
Professor Falcone, I have here—
               (holds up complaint)
the means of ensuring that you never—
never—teach again after this semester,
whether here at Bigelow or elsewhere.
Indeed, in light of your meddling in our
tenure process and your predatory—

ART

Predatory?

WALDORF

— predatory behavior with regard to female
graduate students, I have serious reser-
vations as to your suitability for the
classroom.

It's clear that Waldorf has Art over the pro-
verbial barrel.

ART

What is it you want?

WALDORF
(smiling)
Two things. First, I want you to end your
relationship with Alissa Dust.

ART

If you think you can—

WALDORF

I'm afraid Ms. Dust is falling under your
influence. For one, we simply cannot afford
to give health benefits to our teaching
assistants. And I refuse to stand by and
watch you corrupt one of our best students.

ART

But Alissa and I have a history—

WALDORF

If you refuse to end this liaison, I'll
have no alternative but to make my many
professional acquaintances aware of Ms.

Dust's campus activism. I assure you that this will not aid her career aspirations.

It's everything Art can do to rein himself in.

                    WALDORF (CONT'D)
Well?

                         ART
OK.

                       WALDORF
Good. As to the second item: with our faculty presently deliberating over my new learning initiative, we can ill afford the distraction that a bargaining effort would entail. And based on your little outburst at our last department meeting, it occurs to me that we might avail our- selves of your oratorical skills. So at the union forum after Thanksgiving recess, I want you to speak out against collective bargaining. Now—
                    (forcefully)
can I count on your cooperation?

Art seethes.

                  WALDORF (CONT'D)
Professor Falcone, can I count on your cooperation?

                         ART
                  (grinds it out)
Yes.

                       WALDORF
Good. And to be certain there are no

further misunderstandings: a failure to
cooperate on *either* of these items will
have negative consequences both for you
and for Ms. Dust. Now: do we understand
each other?

Art's complexion is flushed, his brow wet.

> WALDORF (CONT'D)
> Professor Falcone?

> ART
> (resigned)
> Yes.

INT. BAILEY HALL ENGLISH DEPT. OFFICE - DAY

As Art emerges from Waldorf's office, Janet can
see he's not well. She does her best not to
register alarm.

> JANET
> (standing and gesturing)
> You look like you could use a little pick-
> me-up. I've got some homemade chicken soup
> here in my thermos—

> ART
> That's OK, Irish. But thanks for offering.

> JANET
> (lowers her voice)
> Listen, Art—you're not alone. Ever since
> she—
> (gestures to Waldorf's office door)
> became chair, a lot of us have been waiting
> for someone to upset her applecart. But

it's got to be someone with tenure—you
don't have the rank. If you go up against
her—

                ART
Thanks Janet, but not to worry. She's got
me beat—TKO.

A look of dismay crosses Janet's face.

INT. BAILEY HALL - AFTERNOON

Art rounds a corner on his way to class and
bumps into Alissa.

              ALISSA
             (smiling)
Hey!

                ART
             (serious)
Hey. Listen—can you meet me at The Sunspot
later?

              ALISSA
           (concerned)
Sure. What's up?

                ART
Something we need to talk about.

              ALISSA
OK. Around 6 then?

Art nods and they enter their respective
classrooms.

INT. ART'S CLASSROOM - AFTERNOON

Art stands at the front of the class.

> ART
>
> Before we begin, just to remind everyone
> that your final papers are due right after
> Thanksgiving break. Any questions?

Nobody raises their hand.

> ART (CONT'D)
>
> OK, so, *The Godfather*: published by Mario
> Puzo in 1969. Coppola's movie came out
> three years after the book, but I want
> us to try to focus our attention on the
> novel.
>
> (pauses)
>
> I thought we'd try something a little
> different for a change. Instead of every-
> one asking and answering one another's
> questions, I want to start off by holding
> a *question-only* session. Every question
> should open to another question, which
> means you can't ask questions with simple
> yes-no either-or answers.

Heidi raises her hand.

> HEIDI
>
> So you're saying we can't answer any
> questions?

> ART
>
> That's correct, Heidi. You can answer a
> question only with another question. This
> won't be easy at first, but you'll get the
> hang of it. Ready?

Art looks around the room. The expressions resemble deer caught in the headlights.

> ART (CONT'D)
> OK, I'll start. So why are we studying a novel that nobody feels like reading because everyone's seen the film?

Some laughter, followed by a long silence. Art is patient. Eventually Mercedes raises her hand.

> ART (CONT'D)
> Yes, Mercedes? And we'll forgo raising our hands unless you guys start talking over the top of each other.

> MERCEDES
> Why are we studying four novels by four white guys?

Art smiles, and waits. Rob raises his hand.

> ROB
> Is Italian—
> (glances warily at Art)
> the same as white?

> MERCEDES
> It may as well—
> (catching herself)
> Sorry.

Art smiles again. A moment passes. Then students start to ask questions, with shorter pauses between each succeeding question.

> PATRICK
> Is Don Corleone a good guy or a bad guy?

                              ART
          Soldier, that's not—

                            PATRICK
          OK, OK Captain.
                            (thinks)
          What does it mean that Don Corleone is a
          bad guy and a good guy?

Art nods his approval. Michael is paying keen
attention now.

                             MEGAN
          In his world he's a good guy, but in the
          larger world he's a bad guy.

                              ART
          Megan—

                             MEGAN
          Sorry! OK: are good and bad relative?

                            PATRICK
          Isn't the book really about how fathers
          want something better for their sons?

Art starts to intervene.

                            PATRICK
                       (catches himself)
          Jesus, sorry! Does loyalty to one's family
          trump loyalty to the law?

A REDHEAD who rarely speaks raises her hand.

                              ART
          Jessica, yes?

                         JESSICA
          Does Al Pacino—sorry!—does Michael act
          out of obligation or out of love?

A JOCK who rarely speaks raises his hand.

                           ART
          Jump in, Matt.

                          MATT
          Isn't—to what extent is love an obligation?

                         MEGAN
          Is violence justified when you're living
          in a violent world?

                        JESSICA
          Kerouac, Kesey, Puzo: fuck-marry-kill.

Everyone laughs.

                           ART
          Jessica—

                        JESSICA
          I know.

                        MICHAEL
          Why doesn't—

Stops himself.

                           ART
          Yes Michael?

                        MICHAEL
          Why doesn't Don Corleone want his son to
          follow in his footsteps?

ART
You mean, why is power necessarily a bad
thing?

MICHAEL
Yeah, that's it.

Art nods.

PATRICK
Does acting morally mean acting ethically?

ART
How do we distinguish between morality
and ethics?

PATRICK
Is the Godfather ethically right as far
as the Mafia goes but morally wrong?

MICHAEL
Is the Godfather morally right not to want
his son to have his power?

MEGAN
Is the Godfather ethically wrong not to
want his son to have his power?

MICHAEL
Is his son morally right to take his power?
A few seconds of silence.

ART
(looks at Michael)
Excellent.
(looks around the room)
Just excellent, people. Very impressed with

you guys. That's graduate-level thinking right there. And you can pursue that line of thinking about any kind of collective, whether the Cosa Nostra, the labor union, the educational institution, the church, the corporation, or the nation-state.

Michael looks down, obviously struggling with himself.

INT. THE SUNSPOT - LATER

Art is sitting at the bar by himself, sipping a beer, his briefcase at the foot of his stool. Megan walks by with Heidi, and stops.

                    MEGAN
     Professor Art, what's a rockin' dude like
     you doin' here all by your lonesome?

                    ART
     Megan, Heidi, hey. Alone is a far cry
     from lonesome.

Megan whispers a few words to Heidi, who joins some friends at a noisy table that includes Michael, and sits next to Art on one of the barstools.

                    ART (CONT'D)
     Can I get you a drink?

                    MEGAN
     Sure.

Art motions to Danny.

                                MEGAN
        I'd like a vodka martini, please.

                                DANNY
        I'll need to see your ID.

Megan picks through her purse to retrieve her
ID, handing it to Danny. Danny looks at it for
a moment, then hands it back.

                            DANNY (CONT'D)
          Thanks. I'll have your drink up in a sec.

                                MEGAN
        Thank you.
                            (to Art)
        I can't believe they're still carding me.

                                ART
        I can't believe they're *not* carding *me*.

An awkward moment passes.

                                MEGAN
        That was a great class today.

                                ART
        You think so?

                                MEGAN
        Yeah, all the students were talking about
        it afterward. Even Michael.

                                ART
        Michael too?

                                MEGAN
        Yeah. He's been having a hard time.

                              ART
Seems like it.

                             MEGAN
Yeah. His father is such a prick.

                              ART
I should probably know more about you
guys, but it's difficult when—
                         (drops off)
So tell me about Michael's father?

                             MEGAN
His parents divorced when he was a baby,
and about a year ago his father suddenly
shows up out of the blue and starts promising him the world.

                              ART
Making amends?

                             MEGAN
Probably, with strings attached. He's got
a job lined up for him after college.

                              ART
Michael told me. And what does his father
do, anyway?

                             MEGAN
He runs some kind of online company.
Michael says they're trying to land a
contract or something with Bigelow.

A look of realization crosses Art's face.

                              ART
His father is Jack Cutter?

                    MEGAN
Yeah. I think he uses his mother's birth
name.

                     ART
              (shaking his head)
What the fucking Jesus Christ.

                    MEGAN
What's wrong, Art?

                     ART
Oh, nothing that another ten or twelve
pints can't fix.

Alissa enters the bar and joins Art and Megan.

                ART (CONT'D)
Megan, meet Alissa, our Forbes Scholar.
                (to Alissa)
Megan is in my lit class.

                   ALISSA
              (shaking hands)
Nice to meet you.

                    MEGAN
        (awkward, picking up her drink)
Nice to meet you too. Well, I should be
getting back to my friends. Thanks for
the drink and enjoy Thanksgiving!

                     ART
See you in a couple of weeks. With your
final paper!

Megan rejoins her friends, Alissa sitting in her barstool. Art reaches down, picks up his briefcase, and rummages through it.

> ALISSA
> (smiling)
> One of your admirers?

> ART
> (not looking at her)
> Yeah, I guess so.

Art withdraws a thick paper from his briefcase, handing it to Alissa.

> ART
> Here's your intro. I've marked it up and added some comments on the back.

> ALISSA
> Thanks so much!

Art isn't responsive. Alissa places the intro on the bar.

> ALISSA (CONT'D)
> What's wrong, honey?

> ART
> Well, for starters, I just found out that Michael Killian is Jack Cutter's son.

> ALISSA
> I thought everyone knew that.

> ART
> You mean you knew?

                         ALISSA
Yes, of course. Waldorf treats the kid
like he's the heir apparent, and he's not
even an English major. Why are you asking?

                          ART
I figured he was the complaint.

                         ALISSA
Complaint?

                          ART
You do understand that I'm the new guy
here, right? That it might help to know
if I have a made man in my class? Snoop
didn't know who the kid was either—adjuncts
don't always have the kind of insider
knowledge that even grad students have.

                         ALISSA
What's the big deal? He filed a complaint?

                          ART
Never mind.
                    (gulps down the
                    rest of his beer)
So tell me, what's a young woman like you
want with an old man like me?

                         ALISSA
So we're going to have *that* conversation,
are we?

                          ART
We are.

                    ALISSA
For starters, you're not that old, and
I'm not that young.

                     ART
Oh c'mon. My briefcase is half as old as
you.

                    ALISSA
And I've dated men older than you.

                     ART
I'm sure.

                    ALISSA
What, you don't think I'm your equal?

                     ART
I'm not *your* equal.

Danny returns.

                    DANNY
                 (to Alissa)
What can I get you, Alissa?

                    ALISSA
Just a Lite, Danny, thanks.

                    DANNY
Sure thing.
                 (to Art)
Another?

Art nods.

                    ALISSA
What's wrong, Art?

                     ART
Everything.

                    ALISSA
Art—

                     ART
              (cutting her off, and
              beginning to perspire)
I can't do this anymore, Alissa.

Alissa is stopped cold by this.

                    ALISSA
Is it—is it that you don't love me?

Danny returns with the drinks.

                ALISSA (CONT'D)
I've loved you for years. Don't you know
that?

                     ART
You're a brilliant scholar, with all the
promise in the world. I don't even have
a Hail Mary left in me, let alone another
book. I'm history, my goose is cooked,
I'm tits up, the ship has sailed, the
train has left the station, the parade
has passed me by.

                    ALISSA
How many metaphors are you planning to mix?

Art chugs half his beer.

                    ALISSA (CONT'D)
I know you love me. You think I don't
understand you, but I do.

                         ART
                    (looking away)
I can't tell whether it's love or need.
And if it's need, then—
                    (looking back)
then this isn't fair to you.

                       ALISSA
What right have you—

                         ART
Game over. This is over. Go be a winner.
It's easier to win without some loser
dragging behind you.

Art is staring right at Alissa now, who's
frozen in her seat, tears beginning to stream
down her face. Then he looks away. She stands,
clutching her purse. It takes her a moment to
compose herself.

                       ALISSA
So, deep down inside you really are a
coward, is that it Art?

Art stares into his beer and doesn't respond.

                    ALISSA (CONT'D)
                 (grabbing her intro off the
                  bar and wagging it at Art)
Thanks so much. See you in another fucking
life!

Art drops his head as Alissa storms out. Patrick has been sitting at the far end of the bar, and he watches Alissa leave, then turns back to his beer.

INT. HANK'S HOUSE - AFTERNOON

Art is seated at the kitchen table with Hank, Rachel, Abby, and Kayla. A half-devoured turkey sits at the center of the table, and everyone is just finishing up their meals. Art looks tired but is doing his best to be sociable.

                    HANK
    That was some meal, honey. The turkey was
    perfect-o.
      (spooning some stuffing onto his plate)
    And this stuffing is to die for.

                    ART
    Yeah, you really outdid yourself this
    time, Rachel.

                    RACHEL
    The key is to brine the bird. And I hope
    everyone left room for dessert. We have
    pumpkin pie, and Abby's favorite, choco-
    late pecan pie.

                    ABBY
    Yummy!

Art is just about to put his final forkful of stuffing in his mouth, and catches himself.

                    ART
    Good lord, dessert? But where am I going
    to put it?

> RACHEL

Why don't you and Hank take a walk around
the block together, work up an appetite.

> ART

Rachel, I'm not leaving you with the
dishes again.

> RACHEL

Listen Art, I have a very special way of
loading the dishwasher. Takes a PhD in
homemaking. Plus I have my two helpers
here—
> (gesturing to Abby and Kayla)
so please, help my oversized hubby burn
off a few calories before he stuffs his
face with pumpkin pie. You look like you
could use some fresh air yourself. Just
try not to light up a cigarette.

> HANK
> (to Art)

See how great it is being married to
someone who knows you?

Art and Hank leave the kitchen.

EXT. HANK'S NEIGHBORHOOD - AFTERNOON

The two men are walking around the block, autumn
in full swing. Art is smoking, Hank's shirt
has come untucked.

> HANK

How's your break going?

ART

I've got a stack of grading a foot high.

HANK

Tell me about it. Thanksgiving—it's letter
of recommendation season too. I've got
nine to write. So: do you like it here?

ART

What's not to like?

HANK

There's Waldorf, for one.

ART

Everywhere you go there's a Waldorf.

HANK

I suppose so. What about Alissa?

ART

What about her?

HANK

I mean, you two still a thing? She is
going to be graduating soon.

Art measures his words now.

ART

As a matter of fact, we broke up.

HANK

So that means you're going to apply for
the tenure-track job then?

Art is silent.

                    HANK (CONT'D)
Well?

                         ART
Well for starters, Hank, Dunning & Kruger
have gone out of business.

                        HANK
What?

                         ART
Yeah. But let's face it: book or no book,
Waldorf will see to it that I don't even
make it into the interview room.

                        HANK
Not if you play it cool.

                         ART
Play it cool?

                        HANK
Yeah, dude.

Art stops walking and turns to face Hank.

                         ART
Is that the word from Waldorf, Hank?

                        HANK
What do you mean?

                         ART
You know exactly what I mean.

                        HANK
I'm just—

> ART

Hank, you're full of shit and your shirt's untucked.

Hank looks down and starts to tuck in his shirt, flustered.

> ART

I could understand it if you were down and out. But look at yourself, Hank. Great family, job security, nothing really to lose but another five grand a year in exchange for your *fucking tenured soul*.

> HANK

You don't have my responsibilities.

> ART

You're goddamn right I don't. But what's the point of responsibilities if they only make you treat others irresponsibly?
> > (pauses)

You know that Waldorf has me over a barrel, don't you Hank?

> HANK

If it's for your own good, what's the difference?

> ART

The difference is that I get to decide what's good for me, not you or anyone else in this chickenshit profession. Tell me, was it tenure that did this to you or were you always this way?

Art is perspiring now, but forceful.

                        ART
You know all about Waldorf's threat to
sabotage Alissa's career, don't you Hank?

Hank is silent.

                        ART
Of course. And the only way for Waldorf
to be certain Alissa and I had broken it
off would be for you to pry it out of me
somehow. So first you play matchmaker, but
when Waldorf barks, you—

                        HANK
                    (shouting)
You're a bad influence on her!

Art takes a moment to let this sink in.

                        ART
A bad influence. I see. So Waldorf and her
entertainment con—that's a good influence.

                        HANK
You just don't get it. I'm trying to help
you, to help Alissa, to help my family.

                        ART
You mean, the way you helped your friend
Trane?

                        HANK
What do you mean? I voted for her.

                        ART
I'm sure you did. But you knew she didn't
stand a chance.

                          HANK
What are you—

                          ART
You've been conspiring right along with
Waldorf and Cutter, Hank. Your friends
think you're working the inside for their
benefit. But you really have sold out,
haven't you Hank? And you sold Trane down
the river, didn't you?

Hank looks down at his feet.

                     ART (CONT'D)
You knew damn well what the outcome of that
tenure vote would be. Tell me, Hank—did
you canvass the faculty to try to drum
up votes for your friend Trane? Did you
make the case for your friend, or did you
sit silently by and watch Waldorf take
away your friend's bread and butter? So
you cast your vote for her to ease your
conscience, big fucking deal.

                          HANK
Sometimes people—the individual has to be
. . .How do you know that Waldorf doesn't
have the best interests of the department
in mind?

                          ART
Because she doesn't give a shit about
anyone but herself, Hank. Because back
when Waldorf was making her way up through
the ranks—like you, Hank—she decided that
becoming successful justified stepping on

other people's heads. So now she's addicted
to it, and if she isn't stepping on someone's head, she's not doing her job.
                    (loud)
Capisce, Hank?

Hank is dumbfounded.

                 ART (CONT'D)
                  (disgusted)
Aw, fuck it.
          (flicks his cigarette away)
Tell Rachel thanks and give her and the
kids a hug for me.

                     HANK
But what about dessert? And what do I tell—

He catches himself. Art walks off shaking his
head, leaving Hank by himself.

EXT. BSU PARKING LOT - MORNING

Art is just getting out of his pickup, cigarette in hand, when Patrick walks by.

                   PATRICK
Hi, Professor.

                     ART
Hey, Patrick. I keep telling you it's
Art—just Art, Sergeant.

                   PATRICK
          (motioning toward the cigarette)
That stuff'll kill you, y'know.

ART

I've heard. How are things going? When do you graduate?

PATRICK

I've got one more semester.

ART

And then?

PATRICK

Tough to know what to do with an English degree. English and infantry.

ART

I hear you. Finding meaningful work isn't easy. Still, we need people who can ask not just the "how" or "what" questions but the "why" questions.

PATRICK

Yes sir. And I've learned—thanks to your class—that asking questions is some kind of work.

Art smiles.

PATRICK (CONT'D)

Art—I was wondering. Do you think you could write a letter of recommendation for me?

ART

More than happy to. Better to ask someone with tenure, though—a tenured signature carries more clout.

                         PATRICK
Thing is, I just don't know many faculty
all that well. Transferred in from a community college.

                           ART
I'll have it to you by the end of the
week. Check your email.

                         PATRICK
              (reaching to shake Art's hand)
Thanks Art, I really appreciate it. See
you in class.

The two men go their separate ways.

INT. BAILEY HALL - DAY

The day of the union forum. Alissa rounds a
corner to find Hank leaning against a wall,
evidently waiting for her.

                          HANK
Alissa, hi. Thought I might catch you here.

                         ALISSA
                    (standoffish)
Hello, Henry.

                          HANK
Listen, I read over your newest revision.
It's good. Really good. Loved the changes
you made to the intro.

                         ALISSA
Art's doing.

                    HANK
I—I heard you two aren't—

                    ALISSA
None of your business, Henry.

                    HANK
Alissa, I'm—well, I'm sorry.

                    ALISSA
Are we done here, Henry?

Hank looks down at his feet. Alissa starts to
walk away.

                    HANK
Hold on a second. There's something I
think you should know.

                    ALISSA
Is that so?
        (sensing something important)
It's about Waldorf, isn't it Henry?

Hank hesitates.

                ALISSA (CONT'D)
It's always about Waldorf. Tell me what
you know. Did she say something to Art?
Henry?

Hank looks at Alissa and takes a deep breath.

INT. BAILEY HALL LECTURE ROOM - DAY

The union forum. The lecture room is crammed
with people. In uniform and armed, Sam sits in
a chair at the front of the room, off to the

side. Alissa sits near the front with a cadre
of grad students. Hank sits on one side of
Waldorf, Jack Cutter on the other. Martha is
at the podium. Art is nowhere in sight.

> MARTHA
>
> So as I see it, it's imperative that we
> vote *for* a faculty union as soon as our
> bylaws permit, next semester if possible.
> The ground beneath our feet is shifting
> radically, and—

Art walks in late, and everyone takes note as
he stands at the back of the room, leaning on
the wall behind Trane and Snoop and the rest
of the adjunct faculty, including Nancy, Diane,
and Brewster. A look of alarm crosses Alissa's
face.

> MARTHA (CONT'D)
>
> —and it's our job as faculty to decide
> how best to teach our courses. Tenure is
> simply no longer sufficient in itself to
> safeguard academic freedom and to ensure
> that we keep our focus on learning and
> not on some CEO's idea of education.

Applause. Martha returns to her seat. Alissa
stands and begins to walk to the podium. Waldorf
stands, shooting Sam a look, and he rises
and walks reluctantly to the podium to block
Alissa's way.

> WALDORF
>
> Excuse me, Ms. Dust. This is a faculty

forum, and you were invited as a professional courtesy.

                    ALISSA
You mean I can't say a few words on behalf
of the graduate students?

Alissa and Art exchange glances, and Alissa
looks at Hank, who's clearly conflicted.

                   BREWSTER
    Let her speak!

           SNOOP   TRANE
    Let her speak!   Let her speak!

A number of grad students and faculty shout
"Let her speak!"

                   WALDORF
    Parliamentarian?

Hank shrugs, baffled.

                WALDORF (CONT'D)
                  (relenting)
    Very well then.

Waldorf sits, nodding to Sam, who returns to
his seat as Alissa takes the podium.

                    ALISSA
    I know I'm young, I know I don't have
    the kind of experience many of you do.
    But I did want to say that it seems to me
    higher ed is changing, and that some of
    these changes are inevitable. There's no
    point in arguing over whether we'll be

using more online technologies—of course
we will. We already are.

Waldorf looks pleased, some faculty murmur
"hear, hear."

                    ALISSA (CONT'D)
At the same time, I wouldn't want to see
us lose sight of what we're about. We're
all trying to learn together, with our
students, and while learning for learning's sake is something we all believe
in, it's probably the case that what we're
about ultimately is making the world a
better place. We try to do this through
our teaching, and through our research,
our writing. And sometimes—sometimes we
have to take risks.
            (looks directly at Art)
Sometimes we even have to risk what we
love in order to do what's right.

Art is paying close attention. Waldorf takes
note.

                    ALISSA (CONT'D)
And yet we can't do our jobs well if we
have to worry about money all the time.
If we don't have health benefits. If our
financial futures are precarious. And we
can't do our jobs well unless the classroom remains a place where we're not only
free to challenge received wisdom, but
where it's our civic duty to speak truth
to power. So I don't understand why, given
the kinds of changes afoot in higher ed—

                    (looks around
                    at the faculty)
I don't understand why we all *wouldn't*
want to organize.

Alissa takes her seat to applause and some
head-shaking, and sees that Art is nodding his
approval. Waldorf rises and makes her way to
the podium.

                    WALDORF
So nice to witness such an animated
exchange. Despite my initial reluctance,
I must say I'm especially pleased to see
our graduate student cohort so ably represented by Alissa Dust. Let's all give
her a hand.

Polite applause.

                    WALDORF (CONT'D)
I think in her assessment Ms. Dust may
have neglected, among many other things,
the cost to the faculty of conducting
union business, union dues, and so forth.

Waldorf smiles dismissively at Alissa, who
stares right back at her.

                    WALDORF (CONT'D)
But anyway. Colleagues, let me add a few
sobering thoughts to all this talk of
organizing. First, please be aware that
the disruption likely to ensue in the wake
of a collective bargaining agreement will
almost certainly force the administration

to freeze all hiring. As you know, we've been approved for two new positions, and it is crucial to our department profile that we hire on these lines.

Some concerned murmurs.

> WALDORF (CONT'D)
> Secondly, as other departments are also holding forums, let me alert you to the probable repercussions of the English Department electing to go forward with a vote, while other departments choose not to. This will weaken our standing in the campus community.

More concerned murmurs.

> WALDORF (CONT'D)
> And finally, let us not lose sight of the extraordinary opportunity now afforded us by Advanced Learning. Jack Cutter—
>> (nods at Cutter, who smiles)
> has assured me that a collective bargaining arrangement would prove most detrimental to our curricular plans. To put it bluntly: we need to improve our market share if we hope to remain a competitive presence in higher education.

To judge by the looks of concern, Waldorf's remarks have turned the tide.

> WALDORF (CONT'D)
> I do appreciate how appealing the prospect of union representation might be to

those of you romanced by the memories of
the sixties, or seventies. . ..
　　　(stares directly at Alissa)
but, as was earlier suggested, any additional benefits that accrue to *some* of you
will only be deducted from *others* of you.

She surveys the faculty.

> WALDORF (CONT'D)
> Please do keep all of this in mind through-
> out our deliberations.

Some applause. Waldorf returns to her seat,
pleased with herself at regaining the upper
hand. A moment passes.

Art walks to the podium, all eyes on him.

> ART
> 　　　(looking right at Alissa)
> Collective bargaining, unions—
> 　　　(pauses)
> unions won't solve all of our problems.

Waldorf is savoring this. Alissa is not sure
how to react.

> ART (CONT'D)
> Unions won't tell us the difference between
> great teaching and mediocre teaching.
> Unions won't tell us which of our col-
> leagues' books are worth reading and which
> aren't. In fact unions will probably make
> it harder to deal with deadwood faculty
> who can't teach and won't write and just
> take up space.

Art surveys the faculty, a few of whom shift
in their seats.

> ART (CONT'D)
> And unions won't provide us with more
> enthusiastic students. They won't reduce
> tuition and fees, they won't make it
> easier for deserving students from poor
> families to go to college, and they won't
> help us figure out how to use the digital
> world to really enhance learning. Unions
> won't fix higher education for once and
> for all. And they could even make some
> things worse.

Some faculty are concerned, others are surprised.

> ART (CONT'D)
> For that matter, unions won't make us
> good-looking, or rich, or famous, and they
> probably won't help us live longer. Hell,
> they won't even do the dishes. Unions
> won't get us to the promised land.
> (looks at Trane)
> Unions won't solve all of our problems.

Trane wells up. Art is beginning to perspire
a bit. He looks at Waldorf, a victorious
smirk on her face. Then he looks at Hank,
whose expression is one of deep concern,
then at Alissa, who's still uncertain. Art
looks down a moment, thinking, shifts his
footing. Waldorf thinks he's about to step
off the podium, and starts to rise. Then Art
raises his head and begins again.

                    ART (CONT'D)
Y'know, when my brother and I were kids,
we used to like climbing willow trees. I
bet some of you folks liked climbing willow
trees when you were young too, right?

Waldorf sits back down, slowly, a look of alarm
crossing her face. Many of the faculty appear
confused.

                    ART (CONT'D)
                  (Art smiles)
Anyway, so one day, just before supper,
my brother decides to climb way out on
the branch of our favorite tree. He was
always a better climber than I was—I had a
healthy fear of heights, but Richy, Richy
was downright fearless. Still, I scampered
up after him. And the thing is, once we
were way out on that limb, it wasn't easy
to climb back down. I mean, I was lower
on the branch, for one thing, which meant
I'd be slowing us both down. And we could
hear our mother calling out for us. "Art,
Richy, supper-time, supper-time!"

Art has got the faculty's attention.

                    ART (CONT'D)
So you can probably guess what happens
next. My brother, he looks at me and says,
"Let's jump!" And off he goes, sailing off
the limb and landing on the ground. And
the second his feet hit the ground, he
does a forward roll, leaps up, and he's

running home. And that leaves me up there by myself.

Art takes a moment again to look around at the faculty.

>   ART (CONT'D)
>   Now I could have climbed back down—
>   (smiling)
>   gingerly, but here I just saw my brother
>   make the jump, right?— my kid brother by
>   sixteen months, mind you—so something
>   is tugging at me to do the same. Hell,
>   it's maybe only ten feet, but ten feet
>   when you're ten years old can seem like
>   a hundred feet. And so I sit there, the
>   skies darkening, and I can hear my mother
>   calling for me, but I'm frozen in place,
>   paralyzed with fear, and I can't move.

Everyone is paying close attention now.

>   ART (CONT'D)
>   Now my brother, the climber, the jumper,
>   the fearless one?—my brother Richy died
>   in a climbing accident five years ago.

Gasps. Hank drops his head, Alissa turns pale. Everyone—everyone but Waldorf, whose face now registers dismay—is clearly moved.

>   ART (CONT'D)
>   But this isn't about what I've lost. It's
>   about what I *gained* that evening before
>   supper-time, sitting way out there on that
>   limb, against the stars.

(pauses)

You see, I suddenly realized that my
brother had just shown me the way. And
not because he was trying to, but simply
because he was my brother, and we did
things together like climb willow trees.
And when you do things with your brother—
or your sister—you learn from each other,
and maybe, if you're lucky—

(pauses)

if you're lucky—

(pauses)

you end up a little more courageous, a
little less hungry, a little stronger.

Art stops for a moment, letting this sink in.

ART (CONT'D)

And so I jumped. And jumping off, taking
that leap—you can call me a lot of things.
But nobody—

(pauses)

nobody calls me late for supper.

Art smiles, staring right at Waldorf. For a
moment the faculty is dead silent. Tears are
streaming down Alissa's face. Then Hank stands,
slowly, and applauds, and Alissa follows suit.
Then everyone stands, even Sam, and this builds
to a thunderous applause. Art tips his head at
Hank, who smiles. Waldorf realizes she's lost
the battle, if not the war.

INT. THE SUNSPOT - NIGHT

The bar is crowded. Trane and Snoop sit together,

while Alissa sits with Patrick and a few grad students. Art walks in and heads for the bar, Danny placing a pint in front of him without Art saying a word.

Alissa spots him, says a few words to Patrick, and makes her way to the bar. Trane and Snoop take note. She takes a seat next to Art, and they both act as if it's old times.

                    ALISSA
                 (joining Art)
Finished your manuscript. I wasn't expecting a campus novel.

                    ART
                  (smiling)
Neither was I. But we don't control such things. So what's the verdict?

                    ALISSA
Pretty brutal. Have never read anything quite like it.

                    ART
I'll take that as a compliment.

                    ALISSA
It is. Have you found another publisher?

                    ART
Not yet. I really am thinking of going the self-publishing route. Might be time for us writers to take matters into our own hands.

ALISSA

I hear you. Before I forget, do you want
the manuscript back?

ART

Nah, hang onto it. I keep tweaking it.
Snoop and Trane are taking this in from
a distance.

SNOOP

Think those two have a chance?

TRANE

I hope so, I really do.

Alissa is struggling with what to say.

ALISSA

Never did thank you for editing my intro.

ART

Hope I wasn't too critical.

ALISSA

Not at all. In fact Henry has greenlighted
my diss.

ART

And that's all she wrote. Happy to help.
When's the defense?

ALISSA

Next week. The graduate school gave me
special dispensation at Henry's urging.

ART

Good for Hank.

                    ALISSA
                  (hesitant)
    So I guess you're not applying for that
    job opening next fall?

                     ART

    Nope.

                    ALISSA
    You probably don't have much of a shot
    at it now?

                     ART
                  (smiling)
    Never did, really. You were right about
    that. For a while there I was willing to
    entertain the fantasy, but. . .now *that's*
    entertainment.

    They both laugh, but their laughter trails off
    to a bittersweet note.

                    ALISSA
                  (hesitant)
    Art, you shouldn't have let Waldorf—I
    mean, she already hates me.

                     ART
    She might have hated you more. And speak-
    ing of greenlights, that was brave of you
    to stand up there and—

                    ALISSA
    You're the brave one.

                     ART
    Fools rush in.

                    ALISSA
But you shouldn't have let her—

                     ART
Besides, things have turned out for the
best, don't you think?

Alissa doesn't know quite what to think.

                    ALISSA
It was nice of you to write that strong
letter for Patrick.

                     ART
He earned it.

                    ALISSA
              (a little awkward)
Well, maybe we can get together before
the semester wraps.

                     ART
You'll be a doctor then, just about.

                    ALISSA
I almost can't believe it.

                     ART
Believe it. Hey.
              (dead serious)
You are the real deal. Don't let anyone
ever tell you otherwise.

Alissa takes this in.

                    ALISSA
You haven't told me what your plans are

after you leave Bigelow. Do you have
another teaching gig lined up?

> ART

Not this time.

> ALISSA

What are you going to do?

> ART

I'll figure something out. And hell, maybe
I do have another book in me. *Per aspera
ad astra*, right?

> ALISSA

"Rough roads lead to the stars." As long
as the road isn't *too* rough. And you get
yourself in to see a doctor while you
still have health insurance, right?

They gaze at each other a moment. Art touches
Alissa's shoulder.

> ART

Give you a call after classes are over,
OK? I'd like to catch at least one more
drink with the future Dr. Dust.

> ALISSA

I'm buying.

> ART

Damn right you are. Oh and hey—I left an
envelope in your mailbox.

> ALISSA

An envelope?

                              ART

Call it a graduation gift. You know us
writers—always have to put it in writing.
Promise me you won't open it till the
semester is over, OK?

                            ALISSA

Promise.

Art smiles and Alissa stands, touching Art's
shoulder, and they both smile at each other
for a moment. She forces herself to leave, a
look of concern flashing across her face as she
makes her way back to her table.

INT. ART'S CLASSROOM - AFTERNOON

It's the last day of classes. Art has just
collected the final papers and is putting them
in his briefcase, after which he leans against
the desk and faces the students.

                              ART

I'll email you each a response to these
final papers in a week or so, from which
you should be able to deduce your final
grade for the course. Remember: I grade
A, B, or C. No whining.
                          (pauses)
So, as a kind of pre-Christmas gift, I'll
now answer any final questions you have for
me. Any questions at all. And I'll try
to answer them as honestly as I can. OK?

                    HEIDI
Do you mean questions about this class, or—

                     ART
I mean questions about anything, Heidi.
Of course I can't answer a question like,
What will Josh—
                  (he points to a
            CURLY-HAIRED STUDENT)
be getting for a final grade in the course.
I mean, assuming he passes.

Laughter.

                ART (CONT'D)
But in my experience you guys usually
have questions for me that, for whatever
reasons, you haven't asked, and so here's
your opportunity to do so. And if you
don't have a question, that's fine too.

Art waits a moment, and Heidi raises her hand.

                ART (CONT'D)
Go ahead, Heidi.

                    HEIDI
Will you sign your book for me?

                     ART
My book?

                    HEIDI
      (pulling a book from her backpack)
Your novel.

ART
Heidi, how sweet of you, you shouldn't
have!

HEIDI
It only cost me three dollars online.

Everyone laughs.

ART
I'd be happy to sign it, Heidi—right after
class, OK?

Heidi nods and smiles. Megan raises her hand.

MEGAN
Who's your man crush?

ART
Oh, I don't know. Some of the guys I
admired when I was your age are either
getting old or are six feet under.
          (smiles, thinking)
I guess I'd have to say Neil Young. He's
the "old man" now, but he's still out
there earning a living.

Art starts to perspire. He walks over to the
window, which is cracked open, bracing himself
against the frame. Patrick raises his hand.

PATRICK
Do you think there's any hope for us? I
mean, for our species?

Michael takes particular note of this.

ART

There's always hope, Patrick.
          (looking at the class)
As I recall, hope was the last thing out
of Pandora's Box. But—but there's no hope
without some kind of justice.

Art sits in the chair next to the window. It's
a cold, grey, overcast day. He's perspiring
more heavily now, is visibly not well. Megan
takes note. Michael raises his hand.

MICHAEL

What's justice?

ART

That, Michael, is a very good question.
What is justice?
               (pauses, looking
               out the window)
Martin Luther King once said, paraphras-
ing the great reformer Theodore Parker,
that "The arc of the moral universe is
long, but it bends toward justice." But
what is justice?
               (pauses, weak, rambling)
Parker contracted TB, moved to Florence
to be with his friends, which included
Robert and Elizabeth Barrett Browning,
and died there without treatment a year
before the Civil War. He was 49.
               (thinking out loud)
Is that justice? Though maybe, in the final
analysis, justice isn't really about the

fate of the individual. Maybe it can only
be about the collect—

Art stops, gazing out the window. A light snow
has just begun to fall.

                    ART (CONT'D)
    I need a smoke. Can't believe it's almost
    winter. Fuck me.

Several students chuckle as Art falls silent.
A moment passes.

                    MEGAN
    Professor Falcone, are you OK?

Art doesn't answer.

                    MEGAN (CONT'D)
    Art?

No answer.

                    MEGAN (CONT'D)
    Art!

Art slumps, gazing out the window. Patrick jumps
to his feet to pull out his cell and dial 911.
Heidi dashes out the door.

                    HEIDI (O.S.)
    Alissa!

Alissa and Heidi burst back in seconds later,
Alissa rushing to Art's side. Patrick finishes
his call and, with Alissa's and Megan's help,
lifts Art gently out of his chair, placing him
on the classroom floor to conduct CPR. The class

is in shock, some weeping, as Patrick applies chest compressions. Even Michael wells up. Hank and Janet enter, Janet holding her hands to her face, Hank slumping against the wall.

EXT. BSU QUAD - MORNING

The sun is out, the air is crisp and cold, and Alissa and Hank are chatting while walking across the sparsely populated quad, which is lightly glazed with snow. The trees have lost their leaves now. Alissa sports a backpack, while Hank is carrying her small suitcase. They pass an evergreen strewn with Christmas decorations.

                    ALISSA
Place looks deserted. Half my students have already left.

                    HANK
Yeah. But the administration and staff are still here.

                    ALISSA
You'd never know it.

                    HANK
Admins are paid to keep the place running. They deserve our gratitude for that much anyway.

                    ALISSA
And this is when they get ideas, I suppose. While we're gone.

                              HANK
While we're gone. Ideas. Exactly. And
people like Waldorf draw their power from
these hallowed halls.
                        (pauses)
So, what about you two?

                             ALISSA
We're going to talk things out on the way
to my parents', come up with a plan.

An audible disturbance intrudes upon the tranquil
scene. The noise grows louder as they round a
corner, where they find a crowd of students and
faculty gathered in front of their destination,
the Alumni House. Protesters are gathering,
some holding signs that read "Unionized We
Stand" and "Strong Teachers = Strong Students."
Nearly all of the students from Art's class
are participating in the rally. Hank and Alissa
survey the scene.

                        ALISSA (CONT'D)
     And what about you?

                              HANK
     Me?

                             ALISSA
Yeah—what about you, Hank?

Hank gestures toward the rally.

                              HANK
"Poca favilla gran fiamma seconda."

                    ALISSA
Your favorite line from the *Paradiso*?

                     HANK
                   (nodding)
Translation, Dr. Dust?

                    ALISSA
Too easy, Dr. Livingsworth: "A great flame
follows a little spark."

Hank smiles, and he and Alissa share the moment.

                     HANK
Y'know, when you told me about Art's
letter—that he'd decided to self-publish
his novel and was dedicating it "For my
tesoro, Alissa"—I must admit, I was a
little jealous.

                    ALISSA

Jealous?

                     HANK
Yeah. I realized that you've—you've been
my tesoro too. You saved my ass, Alissa.
I'm gonna miss you.

Alissa sobs a bit, and the two hug. They turn
and walk to Art's pickup, which is parked,
running, on the street adjacent. The passenger door pops open as they approach. Then the
driver's door opens—and Art gets out, a little
gaunt but with some color in his cheeks, and
no cigarette. Hank places Alissa's suitcase on
the floor of the pickup and walks around the

vehicle to see Art. Alissa takes off her backpack and climbs into the cab.

                    HANK (CONT'D)
        (resting his hand on Art's shoulder)
    Dude, how you feeling?

                        ART
                (twinkle in his eye)
    Under the circumstances, like one lucky
    motherfucker.

                        HANK
    Same old Art. You're gonna go a little
    easier on yourself, right? Man with a
    stent can't be too careful.

                        ART
    I'm gonna try, Hank. I'm gonna try.

The two men hug. Art gets into the truck and
lowers the window. Hank ducks his head in.

                        HANK
    You two look after each other.

                        ART
    You and Rach too. We'll see you down the
    road a ways.

Art smiles—a sad smile—and Hank nods, both men
recognizing that it might be some time before
they all see one another again. Art and Alissa
drive off together, Hank waving goodbye. Then
Hank picks up a sign and joins the rally just
as the protesters start to march. Megan and

Michael stand on the sidelines, watching. Heidi
approaches them.

                    HEIDI
        Do you guys need a sign?

Megan looks at Michael, who thinks about it.

FADE TO WHITE

PLAN B
Past as Epilogue

It is precisely those artists and writers who are most inclined to think of their art as the manifestation of their personality who are in fact the most in bondage to public taste.

SIMONE WEIL

All told, the words stung.

Samuel Taylor had always been good on his feet. And though having commenced awkwardly owing to the initial reticence most faculty exhibit on such occasions, the Q & A *had* ended on a spectacularly positive note, almost as spectacularly positive as the first sentence of the second paragraph in the email he'd received from the chair three days later, the second sentence of the first paragraph of which letter having indicated that the search committee had not, *regrettably*, decided to pursue his candidacy further.

The search committee did want me to be sure to relay to you that they found your talk indeed memorable. I too thought it a splendid illustration of how fact in the guise of fiction can be more compelling than fiction passing itself off as nonfiction.

At the time, Samuel Taylor had noted in the second sentence of this second paragraph the *passing* swipe at certain practitioners of the nonfiction trade, and to him the collapse of his own work into unadulterated fact, as if his fictive overtures were to be so summarily glossed, smacked of snark. That the chair had felt obliged to offer his personal assessment ostensibly as a sort of consolation prize now struck Samuel Taylor as proof positive that his talk, while indeed memorable, had fast become a distant memory in the minds of all who had witnessed it. All but Kass. In truth he was himself uncertain, then as now, regarding the extracurricular status of the truths he had conjectured, which emerged from some tangle of fact and fiction that—another conjecture—could never be adequately understood via such terms as *fact*, and *fiction*, and *nonfiction*. Yet he was nonetheless committed to some kind of fact, and to some kind of fiction, and to some kind of nonfiction, some recombinant manifestation of which would with any luck articulate some kind of truth, not to say some kind of lyricism. And all the while aspersions would be cast by the aforementioned chair and those of his ilk, and all the while a commercial publishing industry hooked on such confining genre distinctions would snub and resist and handwring and only after prolonged deliberation, if then, permit agented manuscripts bearing such formal divagations some kind of hearing as potential loss leaders.

Hence with Sunday morning coming down on the surprisingly tasty Bavarian cream he'd picked up earlier at Casey's, what had begun on this sunny warm day in July as mere indulgence in the melancholic pleasures of a past failure soon acquired the tragic proportions of some dramatic and embarrassingly public misfire, and he was beset unexpectedly with the fear that he had been a casualty not of circumstance, but of self-sabotage. Before long he located, in a folder on his desktop buried in several other folders, the pertinent file, "Three Chords and the Truth," and began frantically to scour his job talk of six months prior, a twice- or thrice-told tale, for evidence that the fault was in his stars.

*

"First of course there's engineering, that bastard discipline—and not just a discipline, or disciplinary practice, but a messy workaday practice—which, since the last century certainly, has had as much to do with business as it has with technology. The profession emphasizes the technical-scientific underpinnings, while the job ensures commitment if not fealty to the creaky machinations of bureaucracy and, OK, to the profit-driven contours of what we'd come to call late capitalism, and then, in a somewhat facile turn of phrase, postindustrial capitalism— Bell had argued for a growing emphasis on communication as against transportation infrastructure, but given perpetually increasing demand for industrial products and processes, this felt in some sense like a stab at the knowledge-working zeitgeist—and now, with some justification, finance capitalism. Imagine walking into an English department in the not-so-distant past, a licensed Professional Engineer, only to find yourself smack in the middle of Theory with a capital T, which rhymes with P, which stands for—poststructuralism, postmodernism, what have you. He'd spent the summer prior, following his departure from Fortune 500, reading plays. He'd gotten it into his head that perhaps instead of poetry, playwriting—yet another p, that playful Parnassus—was his calling. Poet or playwright or no, he had in any case been attuned, as had the national news outlets, to the passing of Lillian Hellman on the 30th of June, at 79.

"The same may not be said of the death five days prior of Michel Foucault, at 57.

"Let us pause for a moment to savor this epistemological? ontological? foolhardy? transition in all of its alloyed and hyphenate splendor.

"His engineering expertise had been predicated on book learning, but in the manufacturing facilities where he oversaw construction projects or designed modifications to process systems, there was a persistent instrumental dimension that exuded the material aura of man's work. Occasionally the projects he presided over took the form of sheer brawn, but tools and equipment, construction materials, sophisticated hardware: these were things and practices that appealed primarily, or so went the anachronism, to men, an anachronism fortified by the faltering (and ultimately failed) national effort to pass the ERA. His project work was facilitated through blueprints, written specifications, memos, and so forth—the symbolic permutations of a corporate workplace put in the service of applied physics, applied chemistry, applied thermodynamics, the countless applications of applied knowledge. To get the job done, talking the talk preempted walking the walk, and without stopping to consider the discourse *as* discourse. But there was walking entailed too.

"The division of labor was strikingly unambiguous: almost all of his coworkers, whether engineers or draftsmen, had been men, and the vast majority were white. All of his bosses had been men, and all of the clerical workers, women. And the hourly mechanical and electrical technicians and contracted construction crews who fabricated his designs and labored over his instructions, many of them veterans of Vietnam or Korea or even World War II, became the gold standard of manhood against which his modestly pedigreed profile doubtless appeared a mite feminine (an anachronism fortified by…). Throughout most of his engineering tenure—a pre-digital tenure, as this was prior to the Web, smartphones, social networking—he'd lived with his (irregularly employed, or regularly unemployed) father, himself a furniture man, former assembly-line worker, and divorced World War II vet whose trade, and whose spirit along with it, had fallen on hard times. At any rate New York—Syracuse, New York—was killing him.

"So here he was, boxing up his license and degrees and all the technical and aspiringly masculinist expertise these implied to traffic in, la dee da, the life of the mind. In pursuit of which, he would wave goodbye to his father's, and his hometown's, increasingly fractured industrial lifeways, along with a presumably secure and securely heteronormative future. With maternal encouragement and to help defray the costs of school, he'd decided to live with his mother—his guide in all things intellectual—for the first time in something like sixteen years, embarking on an advanced degree or two absolutely intent on honing his expressive talents, such as they were. He would sell his two-year-old Datsun; he would sell his one-year-old Honda Nighthawk; he would leave behind the promise of what the dismally dismal science of the day had informed him was trickle-down wealth, never mind his dependent father (then eligible for Social Security, and with his brother gainfully employed at GE to help him along); he would grow a beard, like any self-respecting bard; and with the help of a lean, strong mover, his father's one-time coworker Carl, he would leave his hometown and relocate 125 miles east to exit 25 of the New York State Thruway—Schenectady, NY, where his mother was employed as the main receptionist at GE CR&D, her desk located in a large atrium right across from Edison's original desk, atop which burned for a virtual eternity one of his original incandescent bulbs. There would be no looking back.

"Looking back, he would wonder why it hadn't at the time occurred to him, or occurred to him in so many words, that he was regendering his life, leaving behind the masculine in a return to the feminine—to the womb of his multilingual mother's erstwhile intellectual influence. Leave it to the Lacanians to work out the Oedipal provocations of his trajectory. In fact *gender* wasn't a part of his working vocabulary prior to this time—at least, not outside of confusing it with sex, like everyone else in his off- and on-the-job world. He was all control valve and vapor pressure and JLG, though he *had* cultivated a healthy suspicion of Big Brother. But he sensed, and could at this point only sense, that to return to school was to ensure that he would never again see his old stomping grounds in the same light, that the old neighborhood with its idyllic confines, where everyday housewives dreamed of a second bathroom and wondered aloud to their assembly-line husbands whether the rumor was true that the three-bedroom house across the street boasted a second bath, and where the husbands wondered how on earth someone could afford a finished basement with a bar and regulation Brunswick billiard table and Wurlitzer jukebox, was not only a thing of the past, but a thing of his past.

"To be sure, his entry into the groves—or is it knowledge factory?—of academe was marked by a progressive, or successive, relinquishing, in essence, of one kind of esoteric knowledge for another, though again, the applied aspects of his engineering work, couched as they were in the rhetorical imperatives of big business, gave it all a down-to-earth burnish. Here he thought he'd learned something about how the world worked, physics underwritten by a tacit metaphysics. He'd never stopped to ask what he learned later, as a grad student, were questions over which doctoral candidates spent long hours mulling, not least because what he knew, or thought he knew, seemed to square so closely with the world as he, and he thought everyone else, had experienced it. He believed there were things one *could* know, in fact, along the lines of water seeking its own level. He believed history worked that way too—that there were historical realities one *could* address with some degree of certainty, such as the conditions under which a single abusive regime might wreak all manner of global havoc, as his mother had experienced as a refugee in France during the war. Moreover, he learned that there were *shoulds* to accompany those *coulds*. He held as indisputable certain social injustices, such as the rich getting richer while the poor—among which one could count his peasant grandparents—got poorer. Some things were true, some things were false, and where there was controversy over these matters, there was always room for reasoned debate. But some things were as good as set in stone, which was particularly the case when it came to the material world. Empirical knowledge, there he was. Epistemological uncertainty and poetic indeterminacy—which would lead eventually to particle entanglement and agential realism and sleepless nights spent wrestling with the demons of coherence, and a new philosophy—here he came. As a former engineer and budding savant he tried, often unsuccessfully, to split the difference. Rather, différance.

"Looking back, it would be easy to see whence the difficulty arose. The material world, for him, was composed of interrelated elements and substances and forces and energies that, or so he had taken on faith, could be proximately described and understood in (what else but?) human terms, much as evolution had given us a place, for once and for all, to hang our hominid hats. Hell, Spencer Tracy thought so, and who was he to disagree with Spencer Tracy? Whatever the nuances of theoretical speculation regarding the subatomic or the cosmic, this would not alter one's experience of the macroscopic analog world, or detract from the beauty of a block and tackle. The knowledge corresponding to such experience, derived from millennia of trial and error, would guide us in our everyday endeavors, with due allowance made for new mechanisms, new explanations. He had been given privileged insight, it seemed, into those creature comforts—or better, necessities—that so many in the industrialized world take for granted. Electricity. Refrigeration. Running water. The inexorable logic of the light switch. The obvious mechanical advantage—and accessibility advantage—of the inclined plane. The reliable efficiency of a pump. Accuracy and precision had been his calling cards, and a working knowledge of process-related hardware his métier, along with a certain interpersonal flair. He'd been a senior project engineer at twenty-six, for Christsakes. He must have known *something*, whatever his illegible (to him) carbon footprint.

"But as a returning student, he was nothing if not game, eager to leave behind the trappings of organization man, to trade in his useful knowledge for what some of his engineering pals would see as useless knowledge, to subject himself to further examinations in his quest for the examined life. *Take my testicular discourse*, he said, or as much as said. And thanks largely to the cutting edge of Continental theory—Theory with a capital T—to which he was predisposed if only out of respect for his mother's birthright, away it went, in trade for the promise of a silver-plated lectern. And it wasn't quite as bad as it sounds, not least because his engineering cred, such as it was, had functioned under the aegis of an industrial-strength vise. He felt no small measure of relief.

"Not surprisingly, as his anti-uppercase-E-Enlightenment enlightenment proceeded—this was not too many years prior to Paul Bové presiding over a general wake—it brought with it a number of revelations. For one, and according to what he was reading in his coursework—corroborated for him by what some of his professors and peers were insinuating to his face and, for all he knew, behind his back—he was a blithering *positivist*. That needed to change, he was certain of it. But first he had to look up the word."

*

That last bit, at least, had garnered a few laughs, and this in a crowd where at least some would likely recognize Samuel Taylor's plight and subsequent re-education as an example of "high-road transfer," while others would be puzzled as to why he'd refrained from using the term *Aufheben*. But how on earth could he have imagined this sort of thing landing him a job teaching *fiction*?

It no longer mattered. The connections, correspondences, correlations, all the presumed causalities and casualties of prior generations had, either because of prejudice or ineptitude, yielded the ruins and fragments upon which his generation had attempted to construct their own livable edifices, which were, as was to be expected, also proving to be sporadically unlivable. But a fragment of a whole is not an infinitesimal dot streaming at you from some corporate beyond. There was sense to be made of all this senselessness. And many of the kids he was teaching, those who could see, had not even set their eyes on the Milky Way, let alone bothered to connect the dots of the Big Dipper. Yes, those constellations were a myth, but they were no less for that a must, the ever ancient light having provided context and an enduring source of wonder for our ever fallible lights.

In which light it now dawned on him that Nora having texted "I owe you" had in all likelihood been her ironic way of saying "I love you," her tough-as-nails intellect landing—he assumed inadvertently but couldn't be certain—upon a word whose haphazard etymology linked owing to owning. In truth they'd owed each other their mutual happiness, and in a sense that only lovers understand, they'd possessed each other. And now he owed it to himself to measure up to such a love.

It was long past time to let the academic enterprise go, he thought, and with it, his enterprisingly academic if unapologetically scabrous and studiously unreconstructed self, a childish thing indeed and, what's worse, a self devoid of that childlike glee suited to a clown with his pants falling down. The requisite fall from grace having been at times ungracefully weathered, it was time to move squarely into that hypothetical future, with its hypothetical past, which would serve the anything-but-hypothetical needs of his present circumstances. Time now for a further foray into . . . well, but even someone as fast on his feet as Samuel Taylor knew he would do well to establish a firmer footing in urgencies of flesh and blood—and capital?—were the aim to entice others to heed his variegated efforts. His second act might be as seemingly inchoate as his first, or as one private reviewer had alleged, "lost"; and Samuel Taylor would himself concede that the thicket of infernal attributes which had marked what he had shamelessly touted as his *campus novel from hell* was a gambit akin to illuminating Cimmerian darkness using only a Roman candle. But he would nonetheless put his best foot forward (the exercise clearly having much to do about feet), once more unto the breach of that splintered structure shielding fact from fiction, or fiction from fact, his quest for refuge from the compromising affiliations of getting and spending—which his financial irresponsibility, not to say turpitude, had all but guaranteed him—henceforth to become the quest for higher fiscal ground upon which one might get and spend in less harried, not to say more ennobling, circumstances, without the constant threat of, not to put too fine a point on it, going broke; upon which one might even envision—it seemed too much to ask for, even as the AARP membership appeals arrived with increasing frequency in the mails—upon which one might even envision a thrifty day free from the toil of workaday labor, free from a job working for others, free from all but the more incidental vestiges of bureaucratic regulation, to which his engineering core had proven itself to be stubbornly amenable even as his romantic yearnings had precipitated all manner of transgressive, not to say gauche, fumbling of the sort one expects from another not to the manner born and thus untutored in the felicities of bienséance; free to rest on one's modest bourgeois laurels, free simply and blessedly to make stuff, even as one searched hither and yon for a place on earth with peace enough to provide for the life that struggles through the mind's noisy recreations, a place from which there would be no exile. Form was in the offing, form was always in the offing, which meant folly would be close at hand. *My*, he thought—*what we owe love*. And here our Hollywood adventure begins . . .

Acknowledgments

An earlier version of "Say," in Episode 6, appeared in the journal *MiPOesias* and later in the collection *Finger Exorcised*, published by BlazeVOX [books]. Grateful acknowledgment is made to both.

An earlier version of Plan B, *Show and Tell*, was published by Argotist Ebooks, to which grateful acknowledgment is made.

Thanks to Voyage Media for assistance in developing Episode 8, *The Adjunct*.

Thanks to Illinois State University for a generous grant that aided in the completion of this project.

And thanks to Comic Life for the great app and to Mike for the photos.

VIA FOLIOS

A refereed book series dedicated to the culture of Italians and Italian Americans.

MICHAEL PARENTI. *Waiting for Yesterday: Pages from a Street Kid's Life*. Vol 90. Memoir. $15

ANNIE LANZILLOTTO. *Schistsong*. Vol 89. Poetry. $15

EMANUEL DI PASQUALE. *Love Lines*. Vol 88. Poetry. $10

CAROSONE & LOGIUDICE. *Our Naked Lives*. Vol 87. Essays. $15

JAMES PERICONI. *Strangers in a Strange Land: A Survey of Italian-Language American Books*.Vol 86. Book History. $24

DANIELA GIOSEFFI. *Escaping La Vita Della Cucina*. Vol 85. Essays. $22

MARIA FAMÀ. *Mystics in the Family*. Vol 84. Poetry. $10

ROSSANA DEL ZIO. *From Bread and Tomatoes to Zuppa di Pesce "Ciambotto"*.Vol. 83. $15

LORENZO DELBOCA. *Polentoni*. Vol 82. Italian Studies. $15

SAMUEL GHELLI. *A Reference Grammar*. Vol 81. Italian Language. $36

ROSS TALARICO. *Sled Run*. Vol 80. Fiction. $15

FRED MISURELLA. *Only Sons*. Vol 79. Fiction. $14

FRANK LENTRICCHIA. *The Portable Lentricchia*. Vol 78. Fiction. $16

RICHARD VETERE. *The Other Colors in a Snow Storm*. Vol 77. Poetry. $10

GARIBALDI LAPOLLA. *Fire in the Flesh*. Vol 76 Fiction & Criticism. $25

GEORGE GUIDA. *The Pope Stories*. Vol 75 Prose. $15

ROBERT VISCUSI. *Ellis Island*. Vol 74. Poetry. $28

ELENA GIANINI BELOTTI. *The Bitter Taste of Strangers Bread*. Vol 73. Fiction. $24

PINO APRILE. *Terroni*. Vol 72. Italian Studies. $20

EMANUEL DI PASQUALE. *Harvest*. Vol 71. Poetry. $10

ROBERT ZWEIG. *Return to Naples*. Vol 70. Memoir. $16

AIROS & CAPPELLI. *Guido*. Vol 69. Italian/American Studies. $12

FRED GARDAPHÉ. *Moustache Pete is Dead! Long Live Moustache Pete!*. Vol 67. Literature/Oral History. $12

PAOLO RUFFILLI. *Dark Room/Camera oscura*. Vol 66. Poetry. $11

HELEN BAROLINI. *Crossing the Alps*. Vol 65. Fiction. $14

COSMO FERRARA. *Profiles of Italian Americans*. Vol 64. Italian Americana. $16

GIL FAGIANI. *Chianti in Connecticut*. Vol 63. Poetry. $10

BASSETTI & D'ACQUINO. *Italic Lessons*. Vol 62. Italian/American Studies. $10

CAVALIERI & PASCARELLI, Eds. *The Poet's Cookbook*. Vol 61. Poetry/Recipes. $12

EMANUEL DI PASQUALE. *Siciliana*. Vol 60. Poetry. $8

NATALIA COSTA, Ed. *Bufalini*. Vol 59. Poetry. $18.

RICHARD VETERE. *Baroque*. Vol 58. Fiction. $18.

LEWIS TURCO. *La Famiglia/The Family*. Vol 57. Memoir. $15

NICK JAMES MILETI. *The Unscrupulous*. Vol 56. Humanities. $20

BASSETTI. ACCOLLA. D'AQUINO. *Italici: An Encounter with Piero Bassetti*. Vol 55. Italian Studies. $8

GIOSE RIMANELLI. *The Three-legged One*. Vol 54. Fiction. $15

CHARLES KLOPP. *Bele Antiche Stòrie*. Vol 53. Criticism. $25

JOSEPH RICAPITO. *Second Wave*. Vol 52. Poetry. $12

GARY MORMINO. *Italians in Florida*. Vol 51. History. $15

GIANFRANCO ANGELUCCI. *Federico F.* Vol 50. Fiction. $15

ANTHONY VALERIO. *The Little Sailor*. Vol 49. Memoir. $9

ROSS TALARICO. *The Reptilian Interludes*. Vol 48. Poetry. $15

RACHEL GUIDO DE VRIES. *Teeny Tiny Tino's Fishing Story*. Vol 47.
Children's Literature. $6

EMANUEL DI PASQUALE. *Writing Anew*. Vol 46. Poetry. $15

MARIA FAMÀ. *Looking For Cover*. Vol 45. Poetry. $12

ANTHONY VALERIO. *Toni Cade Bambara's One Sicilian Night*. Vol 44.
Poetry. $10

EMANUEL CARNEVALI. *Furnished Rooms*. Vol 43. Poetry. $14

BRENT ADKINS. et al., Ed. *Shifting Borders. Negotiating Places*. Vol 42.
Conference. $18

GEORGE GUIDA. *Low Italian*. Vol 41. Poetry. $11

GARDAPHÈ, GIORDANO, TAMBURRI. *Introducing Italian Americana*. Vol
40. Italian/American Studies. $10

DANIELA GIOSEFFI. *Blood Autumn/Autunno di sangue*. Vol 39. Poetry. $15/$25

FRED MISURELLA. *Lies to Live By*. Vol 38. Stories. $15

STEVEN BELLUSCIO. *Constructing a Bibliography*. Vol 37. Italian
Americana. $15

ANTHONY JULIAN TAMBURRI, Ed. *Italian Cultural Studies 2002*. Vol 36.
Essays. $18

BEA TUSIANI. *con amore*. Vol 35. Memoir. $19

FLAVIA BRIZIO-SKOV, Ed. *Reconstructing Societies in the Aftermath of War*.
Vol 34. History. $30

TAMBURRI. et al., Eds. *Italian Cultural Studies 2001*. Vol 33. Essays. $18

ELIZABETH G. MESSINA, Ed. *In Our Own Voices*. Vol 32. Italian/
American Studies. $25

STANISLAO G. PUGLIESE. *Desperate Inscriptions*. Vol 31. History. $12

HOSTERT & TAMBURRI, Eds. *Screening Ethnicity*. Vol 30. Italian/
American Culture. $25

G. PARATI & B. LAWTON, Eds. *Italian Cultural Studies*. Vol 29. Essays. $18

HELEN BAROLINI. *More Italian Hours*. Vol 28. Fiction. $16

FRANCO NASI, Ed. *Intorno alla Via Emilia*. Vol 27. Culture. $16

ARTHUR L. CLEMENTS. *The Book of Madness & Love*. Vol 26. Poetry. $10

JOHN CASEY, et al. *Imagining Humanity*. Vol 25. Interdisciplinary Studies. $18

ROBERT LIMA. *Sardinia/Sardegna*. Vol 24. Poetry. $10

DANIELA GIOSEFFI. *Going On*. Vol 23. Poetry. $10

ROSS TALARICO. *The Journey Home*. Vol 22. Poetry. $12

EMANUEL DI PASQUALE. *The Silver Lake Love Poems*. Vol 21. Poetry. $7

JOSEPH TUSIANI. *Ethnicity*. Vol 20. Poetry. $12

JENNIFER LAGIER. *Second Class Citizen*. Vol 19. Poetry. $8

FELIX STEFANILE. *The Country of Absence*. Vol 18. Poetry. $9

PHILIP CANNISTRARO. *Blackshirts*. Vol 17. History. $12

LUIGI RUSTICHELLI, Ed. *Seminario sul racconto*. Vol 16. Narrative. $10

LEWIS TURCO. *Shaking the Family Tree*. Vol 15. Memoirs. $9

LUIGI RUSTICHELLI, Ed. *Seminario sulla drammaturgia*. Vol 14. Theater/ Essays. $10

FRED GARDAPHÈ. *Moustache Pete is Dead! Long Live Moustache Pete!*. Vol 13. Oral Literature. $10

JONE GAILLARD CORSI. *Il libretto d'autore. 1860–1930*. Vol 12. Criticism. $17

HELEN BAROLINI. *Chiaroscuro: Essays of Identity*. Vol 11. Essays. $15

PICARAZZI & FEINSTEIN, Eds. *An African Harlequin in Milan*. Vol 10. Theater/Essays. $15

JOSEPH RICAPITO. *Florentine Streets & Other Poems*. Vol 9. Poetry. $9

FRED MISURELLA. *Short Time*. Vol 8. Novella. $7

NED CONDINI. *Quartettsatz*. Vol 7. Poetry. $7

ANTHONY JULIAN TAMBURRI, Ed. *Fuori: Essays by Italian/American Lesbiansand Gays*. Vol 6. Essays. $10

ANTONIO GRAMSCI. P. Verdicchio. Trans. & Intro. *The Southern Question*. Vol 5.Social Criticism. $5

DANIELA GIOSEFFI. *Word Wounds & Water Flowers*. Vol 4. Poetry. $8

WILEY FEINSTEIN. *Humility's Deceit: Calvino Reading Ariosto Reading Calvino*. Vol 3. Criticism. $10

PAOLO A. GIORDANO, Ed. *Joseph Tusiani: Poet. Translator. Humanist*. Vol 2. Criticism. $25

ROBERT VISCUSI. *Oration Upon the Most Recent Death of Christopher Columbus*. Vol 1. Poetry.

CPSIA information can be obtained
at www.ICGtesting.com
Printed in the USA
FFHW02n2250270818
48028622-51723FF